SHAMPOO
PLANET

Also by Douglas Coupland

GENERATION X

SHAMPOO PLANET

DOUGLAS COUPLAND

A TOUCHSTONE BOOK
Published by Simon & Schuster
New York   London   Toronto   Sydney   Tokyo   Singapore

First published in the United States of America by Pocket Books,
a division Simon & Schuster Inc, 1992

First published in Great Britain by
Simon & Schuster Ltd in 1993
First published in Great Britain by
Touchstone, in 1993
An imprint of Simon & Schuster Ltd
A Paramount Communications Company

Simon & Schuster Ltd
West Garden Place
Kendal Street
London W2 2AQ

Simon & Schuster of Australia Pty Ltd
Sydney

A CIP catalogue record for this book is
available from the British Library
ISBN 0-671-71843-6

Printed and bound in Great Britain by
Harper*Collins* Manufacturing, Glasgow

PART
ONE

I

My mother, Jasmine, woke up this morning to find the word D-I-V-O-R-C-E written in mirror writing on her forehead with a big black felt pen. Of course she didn't know the word was there as she was awakening. Not until she stepped into the bathroom to brush her teeth and looked in the mirror (a mirror surrounded by a long-suffering wandering-Jew vine and the mirror in front of which I learned to shave several years back) did she see the word, now facing the correct way, at which point she screamed loud enough to wake the dead, which in my house means my sister, Daisy.

I, however, wasn't home when my mother's awakening occurred. At the time I was in a 767 zooming homeward over the Atlantic. But Daisy subsequently told me over the telephone all about the ordeal, and at this moment, while I reflect upon Daisy's news (Jasmine apparently is in no state to talk) I am sitting on the sixteenth floor of a delicious middle-class hotel bordering LAX in Los Angeles, California, overlooking the runway—overlooking jets descending while flocks of birds, immune to the jets' howling, quietly perch to the side of the runway, feeding.

"Something to do with a game of Scrabble, Tyler. The explanation was blurry," Daisy said. "So awful. Such a horrible thing to do. Really base. I feel sick."

"Where did Dan go?" I asked, Dan being Jasmine's now-(I suppose) ex-husband as well as now-ex-stepfather to Daisy, me, and my little brother, Mark.

"No idea. Mom can't even go out in public. The ink won't come out of her skin for days. I had to physically drag her away from the sink. She was turning her forehead into hamburger trying to rub the word off. She's on tranks now."

Well, I think to myself, *fatherless again.* Jasmine sure picks some winners, her predilection for substance enthusiasts paying off once more. And once again—like the time when my biological father, Neil, left Jasmine to go get permanently wasted in Humboldt County—I feel like the front doors to my house have been opened and the parents have announced to us children inside, *Whoops! Sorry, but we just lost you in a poker game. We're afraid you'll have to be clearing out now.*

Daisy feels the same way I do. And now, after our phone call has ended—a call in which Daisy mostly cried and in which I mostly listened—I sit on the side of my bed in my LAX hotel room, a room so quiet I can hear the nice clean furniture, and I think.

I know I should be depressed, but to be honest, depression is hard. Now is an exciting period in my life and I refuse to let fate steal away my excitement. I'm back in the New World now, back in the world of jumbo ruby

Florida grapefruits and understandable telephones, of bottomless coffees, decent malls, and high ambition—back after spending a summer of thrills in the Old World of Europe. And as I sit here I actually feel glad I missed my connecting flight back up to Seattle, glad I was too plugged into my Walkman to hear the connecting-flight announcement (extremely torrid tunage from London beckoned—songs about money written by machines).

I'm *also* glad because had I not been stuck in L.A. overnight, I wouldn't be walking out to the balcony as I am at the moment, looking down over my view below, the Pacific sunset, utterly unused and orange and clean, like shrink-wrapped exotic vegetables. And I wouldn't be holding a dollar bill up to my nose to see what it smells like—a clean and pleasingly anonymous smell like that of my perfect hotel room inside, a room lit by a honeyed whorl of sun. *And* I wouldn't be having the sensation, while standing here on the balcony overseeing the extraterrestrial tangerine grid of Los Angeles, that were I to jump from this balcony I would float in the warm air, above the amber palms and freeways, float off past the legislated memories of Disneyland, float over the warm mountains and deserts and forests of my New World home—float *home*.

But enough of this.

I rotate and walk back into my hotel room, closing the smoked-glass sliding doors behind me, and then fall backward into my cool Fortrel-sheeted bed, when suddenly a new feeling washes over me—a feeling at once destructive, romantic, and grand—like falling into a swimming pool dressed in a tuxedo. I have this feeling no room is ever really quiet; this feeling that even in the quietest, emptiest, and most uneventful of rooms there is always an event of profound importance occurring. This event is Time itself, foaming, raging, and boiling like a river, roaring through this room and through all rooms— Time flowing through the beds, gushing from the minibars and churning from the mirrors, and Time, with its grand, unfightable sweep, taking me along with it.

2

Hair is important.

Which shampoo will I use today? Maybe PsycoPath®, the sports shampoo with salon-grade microprotein packed in a manly black injection-molded plastic motor-oil canister. Afterward? A bracing energizer splash of Monk-On-Fire®, containing placenta, nectarine-pit extract, and B vitamins. And to hold it all together? First-Strike® sculpting mousse manufactured by the *plu*TONium™ hair-care institute of Sherman Oaks, California. It's self-adjusting, with aloe, chamomile, and resins taken from quail eggs. Gloss, hold, *and* confidence. What a deal.

Figuring out your daily hair is like figuring out whether to use legal- or letter-size paper in a copy machine. Your hair is you—your tribe—it's your badge of clean. Hair is your document. What's on top of your head says what's inside your head. Wash every day? Use ComPulsion®, with marigold and beer. Hormone-hair changing texture every five minutes? Use MOODSwing®, the revitalizing power toner from Sweden with walnut leaf for self-damaging hair. It's hot—nuclear—bust the needle on my scorch meter.

3

If you ever have a free moment, you might consider checking out the travel brochures for the town in which you live. You might be amazed. You might not want to live there any more.

Lancaster, if nothing else, is a casual kind of town. Raccoons saunter across our back patios smoking cigarettes. Noisy blue Steller's jays wear earrings and know all the latest dances. The deer watch TV.

It has been six weeks now since I returned here to Lancaster from that hotel room at LAX, and while many aspects of this, my hometown, are radically different from the way they were when I left for Europe at the beginning of the summer, many aspects have remained unchanged.

Lancaster's population is still about 50,000, the population of Paris during the Dark Ages. The town still rests, of course, where it always has and always will, in the dry plains of southeastern Washington State, scientifically and strategically located so as to be as far away as possible from anywhere meaningful or fun, in the center of the arid belt of the sort-of desert that stretches all the way from the Sonora in Mexico right up to the Arctic Ocean.

Some more Lancaster nuggets here: Lancaster is almost entirely rain-free, cold and dry in winter and hot and dry in summer. The pulsing, chocolate-toned conduit of the Columbia River buckles through town like a strip of compressed metal. Trees are a looked-forward-to treat here in Lancaster, too, what few of them there are being entirely imported, punctuating the landscape like domestic help just itching to escape to a better job: dry, scraggy poplars and messy, dandruffy cottonwoods. Lush they are not.

One of the good things about Lancaster (and there are many good things) is that all of the town's buildings are large and there is much space in between all these large buildings. Space is cheap here, as is electricity to heat what buildings there are. So why not build big? And everyone has cars to get around in. Lots of cars.

As in most small towns, nothing much changes in Lancaster. In my eyes, this changelessness is most embodied by the old men and women—trolls and Popeyes and broken people—who drift about the downtown and the small suburbs, amid the barking dogs and chain-link fences, peeking into trash cans, chitchatting with hood ornaments, and staring at the many satellite dishes that now sprout like babies' ears from Lancaster's soil, ears cocked to the heavens, waiting to hear corrupting secrets from far up above. These old drifters seem to me to be Lancaster's last connection to the town's brief past, connected to that past by mere virtue of their being too poor to participate in the willful amnesia that propels the rest of the town's citizens into the sparkly and thrilling future that I desperately want to share.

It was never a mystery to me, growing up in Lancaster, how the town's citizens managed to fill their days. You either worked at the Ridgecrest Mall or you worked at the Plants. On days off you either shopped, drove your car around really fast, shot animals, or blasted about in speedboats painted bright colors.

Oh . . . the Plants. I'd better explain them, because an understanding of the Plants is pivotal to understanding why and what Lancaster is. You see, Lancaster was once the world's largest producer of, how shall I say, *forbidden substances*—unpronounceable superconcentrated broths, dusts, slugs, rods, buttons, and cylinders—substances more wicked than your darkest secret times a billion—substances whisked away by the government, just moments after their birth, like UFO babies, taken away to their new homes deep in the cores of ships, rockets, weapons, and power plants.

The alchemy of these substances' manufacture occurred in the Plant buildings themselves, located a fifteen-minute drive away to the north, a complex of vast, windowless Art Deco-ish boxes my little brother Mark has preserved forever on a drawing pinned to the family refrigerator. When asked to describe the buildings, Mark said they were a strand of parade floats left behind by a race of shrinking-brained, now-dead giants, their original purpose now forever lost. Weird kid.

But hey: my description of the Plants makes them sound so dismal and grim, but they aren't that way at all. Growing up, the Plants even made our lives fun in ways we both knew and didn't know. The 4-H club ran an ever-popular Most Misshapen Potato contest. My high-school basketball team was called the Neutrons (the junior team, the Neutrinos), and the team had a mushroom cloud as our logo and jacket crest. And Lancasteroids, like families enduring a relative with a chronic health problem, are cavalier in their everyday usage of hip high-tech words like *isotope, percolation, iodine,* and *half-life.* Kind of like the lyrics to synthesizer music from Germany. Hot.

The bogeymen of our young dreams were the mythical undead cheese-complexioned Plant workers, their wispy hair popping out of their skulls in tufts and clumps while they chewed sticks of spearmint gum, taking turns to look out the Plants' one porthole window and telling Daisy and me tales of braziered cities, too-hot suns, and all the fish in the world floating belly up in the seas.

Growing up we were also continually shown black-and-white Armed Forces films during hygiene classes, films that attempted to justify to young minds the necessity of the Plants' existence. These films must now surely be oxidizing trendily in canisters lost deep within a Beverly Hills vault, calmly anticipating their perky reemergence into the world of the living as backdrop fodder in hip L.A. nightclubs.

But a discussion of the Plants is all in the past tense now. The Plants closed down at the beginning of the summer, right out of the blue, the day after I left for Europe, and with the Plants went most of the Ridgecrest Mall and the bulk of the town's other commerce, leaving the citizens of Lancaster stumbling about in a trance. Citizens bumble past the plywooded remains of the mall in the stilted, balance-upset walk of old people trying Walkmans for the first time, their eyes blank and deinstitutionalized. These are souls experiencing severe shopping withdrawal and goal withdrawal, their lives now converted into free-time management. I wonder how the people of town will fill their days now. How will they ever escape?

Me? I'll escape. I know that. I have a plan. I have a brother and sister. I have a good car and a wide assortment of excellent hair-care products. I know what I want from life; I have ambition.

4

The sky is a nutritious deep electronic blue today. I'm standing in the middle of a pumpkin field bordering Lancaster, snapping Jasmine's Polaroid portrait as she sits in a chair I've brought along, the spindly wooden legs digging deeply into the rusty soil. The sun has just set, and on the field's perimeter, Mr. Ho Van and his wife, Gwei-Li, the field's owners, are scratching their heads and wondering why they ever permitted two nutbars like us inside. I try to persuade Jasmine to do something more interesting with her face.

"Change your name to Fifi LaRoo, Jasmine. Go to Las Vegas. Throw your motel key on Wayne Newton's stage. Be a love toy."

"Oh, Tyler. Stop it."

"Be wanton. Go nuts. Have a fling."

"Tyler, stop!" Jasmine says stop, but she really doesn't mean it. She's smiling for what must be the first time in weeks, and she's primping her pretty long gray hair, so I know I can push her just a bit further. My relationship with my mother, as with most family relationships, resembles a relationship with an old door, impossible to enter not only unless you have the right key but also unless you know how to jiggle that key and grip the doorknob properly, too.

"You're an attractive woman, Jasmine. A real dish. You should be out dating strange dark men."

Naive credulity that never ceases to amaze me: "You really think so?"

Jasmine was/is a total hippie, even though sometimes she can be too modern for words. Jasmine has the perennially breathy, childlike quality particular to the ex-hippie group, a childlike quality we, her children, understood early on in life. Because of this quality, Daisy and Mark and I have always felt parental toward Jasmine, have always been on "hippie parent alert": inspecting the microwave oven for chunks of hash before friends came over to watch videos (Jasmine rushing in to the slap of sandals: *"Ha ha, how careless of me to leave my, uh, saffron, in the oven"*), or whisking dinner knives blackened from hash hot-knifing from the sight of friends visiting for lunchtime meals, their eyes preoccupied watching the sunlight glint off of Jasmine's unshaven armpit hairs as she leaned over to serve meals of Arizona bee-pollen capsules and fava-bean pilafs. Jasmine gave a Christian name to every tomato that ripened in the garden. *("That's Diane you're eating there.")* Friends rarely came over twice to eat.

Today's photo-taking session comes at Jasmine's request. She wants to have a portrait of herself, "for posterity, for my grandchildren." Since Dan left Jasmine she has been almost entirely morbid, locking herself into an unthinking routine of work, sleep, and closed-door moping, seemingly convinced she is doomed, allowing only the most minor of deviations in routine from her schedule: shopping for dark sunglasses and frequenting the Recovery section of the Sun & Air New Age Bookstore. Today's foray into the unknown, this photo session, comes as a good healing indicator as well as allowing me to indulge in my hobby of photography, my "creative side" as it were.

Jasmine is holding in her lap a jack-o'-lantern bearing a fierce yet smiling face she carved herself and lit on the inside by a small yellow candle flaring like a uranium ingot gone critical. Jasmine's long gray hair is tangled in the fuzziness of her shawl and strands are blowing into her freckled, unmade-up face. Jasmine never wears makeup; Daisy wears gobs.

"Hurry up, my scrumptious little yo-yo," she says to me, "I'm getting chilly here."

"No offense, Jasmine, but could you show a little more feeling for the camera?"

"Honey, feelings normally grow out of me like hair, but for the time being you'll just have to take what few strands you get. Here—let me hold the pumpkin up higher . . ." She hoists the pumpkin up on her shoulder.

"I like that. Keep the pumpkin up there."

Jasmine screws up her face. "Tyler, you know, I should probably be better about these things—your life, I mean. The last weeks have been a drain, but I still think about the lives of my children. What are your plans after you finish school this year. In April?"

"The same as ever. I want to work for Bechtol in Seattle."

"Bechtol? Tyler, I still can't believe that. We used to *firebomb* Bechtol."

"Get modern, Jasmine. Bechtol is a fine company in the growth mode and they offer fast advancement potential and a shockingly good pension."

"You're *twenty*, Tyler."

"You have to think ahead, Jasmine. The world's a much rougher place than when you were young."

"I suppose you're right." Jasmine does a hippie fade-out, her thoughts retreating back to her own life and problems.

Jasmine was an earth mother back in the 1960s. Sometimes we call her this . . . *oh earth mother, dear!* But more often than not we just say *earth to mother . . . earth to mother. . . .*

"Earth to mother. Earth to mother—"

"Yes, my little donut?"

"Make love to the camera, please."

"Oh, sorry." She tries a wan smile. "Do you think the pumpkin face is scary enough?" she asks. "I tried to carve *evil.*"

"Boo," I say.

"I think pumpkins are inherently godlike" (uh-oh . . . hippie talk), "like orange happiness bulbs. It's hard to imagine a pumpkin being truly frightening. Will this be an arty photo, Tyler? I want my grandchildren to think I was cultured. That I was different."

"It'll reek of art. Some emotion *please*, Jasmine."

A clattering charcoal blotch of migrating crows smudges the sky above us as they follow the river south for the winter. Jasmine just won't stop being glum. I ask her if she'd rather get her portrait taken some other time.

"No. No. Now's great. It's just the crows have got me depressed. Something that happened when I was young, growing up in Mount Shasta."

"Please tell the studio audience."

"It was an afternoon. Dad—your grandfather—was trimming the pine next to the house and was bickering with Mom, who was giving him instructions. A pile of branches had fallen to the ground when we noticed a pair of mourning doves frantically darting around them. Mom shouted *stop* and they looked and realized too late they'd chopped down the branch with the doves' nest inside."

"Jesus, what a depressing story, Jasmine."

"Mom ran inside crying. Dad tried to tell her that doves are as dumb as a sack of hammers and will lay again in another week, but even still, Mom says to this day she'd give anything to take back that moment. . . ."

"Are you *through* yet?"

"Don't move to Seattle, Tyler."

"Don't say things like that to me, Jasmine, okay? Time out. I've got a life. Things change."

"I hate crows. They eat the eggs from other birds' nests."

"Jesus *again*, Jasmine. Take a nap. Lighten up, or I'm walking. How am I ever going to get a good photo if you keep talking like that? Think of something cheerful, like frolicking kittens or something."

But, of course, I can understand why Jasmine might want to furnish her interior world so bleakly at the moment. I imagine her situation is not unlike banging your head into the corner of a cupboard door and receiving a pain so sharply intense, so highly concentrated in such a small area, you hit the wound so as to dampen the pain —to spread it outward from the center.

"Try a different pose," I suggest, carrying my tripod in closer, zeroing the focus in on just Jasmine's face and the jack-o'-lantern. "Swivel your head and stare Mr. Pumpkin right in the face, okay?"

"Okay."

"Now pretend you're having a stare-down contest to test who can stare the longest without blinking, okay?"

"Fair enough."

Boring shots. No big deal. "Let's try something different.

Let's pretend Mr. Pumpkin is Kittykat" (our family cat) "and you're gazing into Kittykat's eyes trying to establish a flicker of intelligence—interspecies communication."

"Okay."

Slightly better shots, but not *much* better. I need something more torrid. "How about this: pretend Mr. Pumpkin there is the one person in the world who frightens you the most, who wants to destroy you, okay? Eat you up." I could just kick myself as I say this, but I'm too late. Jasmine's strong features buckle with fright and my finger pushes the shutter button and a portrait of Jasmine is created: a portrait that will be seen by her grandchildren and the one that they will remember her by—a portrait of Jasmine, facing the world as she does at this point in her life, utterly frightened by a monster entirely of her own carving.

5

My memories begin with Ronald Reagan—thoughts and ideas and remembrances like an explosion of white birds released upon the coronation of the king. Of the times before Reagan I remember little: fleeting, ghostly webs of images, the strange, undeniably dreamlike phantasms of a gray era: rocks as pets . . . underwear you ate . . . rings that told you how you felt. I must have been asleep then.

I have more memories. Let me tell you about a commune of hippies, of life as a child in the trees on an island in British Columbia. Let me tell you of sleeping bags that smelled of salmon, of growling gray dogs with ice-blue eyes, of adults lost in the woods for weeks at a time, stumbling back into the commune, their skin scabbed and broken, their hair tangled like bracken, their eyes blinded by the sun, and their speech garbled with talk of Answers.

Let me tell you of clothes caked in mud and then discarded, of a younger Daisy and me naked and whipping each other with seaweed bulbs while Jasmine and Neil sat by staring blearily into a beach fire, our clumsy cedar commune house nestled far away inside the trees.

I remember books strewn about the house's wobbly planked floor. I remember robes made of flags, pots of stew, and candles made of beeswax. I remember adults spending hours staring at the small skittering rainbow refractions cast from a window prism. I remember peace and light and flowers.

But let me also tell you of when the world went wrong, of hairy faces violet with rage and accusation, of sudden disappearances, of lunches that never got made, of sweet peas gone dead on the vine, of once-meek women with pursed lips and bulging forehead veins, of gardens gone unweeded, of lawyers visiting from Vancouver—the mood of collapse, of disintegration—of the daylong scenery-free drive, in the back of a rusting Econoline van, the rear doors opening on Lancaster at night, a town as dry as the island was lush, as barren as the commune was dense.

Let me tell you of the house that became our new home and the new wonders inside: switches, lights, grills; immediacy, shocks, and crispness. I remember jumping up and down on the novel smooth floor and yelling, "Hardness! Hardness!" I remember TV, stereos, and reliability —lights that would never fail.

I was home.

6

I remember the night John Lennon was assassinated, back near the dawn of my consciousness. Jasmine, Daisy, and I were roaming the Food Fair at the recently opened Ridgecrest Mall; we were eating chocolate-chip cookies from a chocolate-chip-cookie boutique, a novelty back then. A buzz of information was visibly passing through the seated Food Fair crowd. Women crying, redneck cowboy pipe welders from the Plants mute and shaking in their down vests. The wave of news passed over our table. The assassination meant nothing to us children, but the then-pregnant Jasmine began to cry, leaving us confused, Daisy knocking over her cherry Slush-Pup as we clicked into the parental mode, becoming crutches to escort Jasmine out to the parking lot. Daisy held my hand and sang the words from *Hair*, lyrics gleaned from having listened to the song often on the recently departed Neil's quadriphonic system.

More than a decade later, Daisy, Mark, and I are well aware of who Lennon is. Daisy in particular is interested: Lennon the popstrel, balladeer of her mother's youth.

Daisy and her boytoy, Murray, can't grill Jasmine enough about that era.

"Did you ever make love in a river, Mom?"

"What made you decide to not shave your armpits, Mrs. Johnson?"

"How many tabs of acid did you do?"

"What was protesting like?"

"Your mother is totally groovy, Daisy."

"I know. She's so mod."

"Tell us about San Francisco again, Mrs. Johnson."

The trio are down in the living room right now, drinking chamomile tea amid the room's macramé, sand candles, incense fumes, and granny knickknacks. Jasmine's taste. They are sitting on the floppy couch—a couch that is minus a cushion, a condition dating from last year's notorious Case of the Vanishing Throw Cushion (case solved: Daisy had pirated the paisleyed foam to fashion a kittening nook in the basement for Kittykat).

I hear earthenware mugs clinking. I hear Murray making ripping sounds as he pulls back the acetate sheets from the sticky-board inside of the family photo album.

Jasmine is earnestly trying to tell Daisy and Murray about her youth: "Sure they were freaks, but we honestly believed the freaks had keys."

Blank, uncomprehending stares.

"Look at it this way. We thought freaks had access to magic secrets. Your father was a freak, Daisy."

"What kind of secrets?" asks Daisy.

Jasmine goes silent a moment: "Secrets of what was on the other side. Of the possibilities of perception."

More blank stares.

"Oh, all right. Look at it *this* way: when I was your age, people only used shampoo to wash their hair, and conditioner wasn't even invented."

Audible gasps of disbelief. I hear Jasmine stand up. "You kids are driving me crazy."

"Your mom's the hippest, Daisy."

"Isn't she great? Mom, do you ever have flashbacks?"

Poor Jasmine. She darts upstairs and into my room to eclipse Daisy and Murray's grilling. "Those kids. They make me feel so *old*, Tyler. I don't need that right now."

"Have a seat," I offer. "Cocktail?"

"Thanks. I think I will."

I reach over from my ultramodern L-shaped foam sectional couch where I have been sitting with my zapper trolling late-nite TV for cool bits and look into my sleek Italian minifridge for a beer for Jasmine.

Jasmine sits perpendicular to me in the classic talk-show-host/sidekick configuration. I spritz open her beer as I hand it to her. "What is the verdict on the new dos?" I ask her, the dos in question being Daisy and Murray's brand-new blond dreadlocks, unveiled at tonight's dinner just after Jasmine and I got in from shooting the photos out in the pumpkin field. They're Jell-O dreads, made by pouring semidissolved Jell-O over cornrowed hair. The gelatin protein dissolves the hair protein; total hair loss is stopped halfway through by pouring pineapple juice on as a stopper.

"Who am I to speak? Your father had hair down to his coccyx. But I think Daiz is going too far with the sixties thing. I mean, doesn't she want to have a *now*? And I am stunned by how she manages to befriend every single male in Lancaster with a Jesus hairdo. I mean, we live in a small town, Tyler. What's happening?"

"They're the McDead, Jasmine. The sixties are a like a theme park to them. They wear the costume, buy their ticket, and they have the experience. Their hair may be long, but it smells great. I should know. Daisy uses most of my shampoo."

Jasmine swigs her beer and picks up my copy of *Young Achiever* magazine. "Your subscription must almost be out by now. You want a renewal for Christmas?"

"Pretty please."

"What's this . . . *Entrepreneur?* Want a subscription to this, too?"

"With nacho sauce on top."

Jasmine flips through a back issue of *Cadillacs and Dinosaurs* comics and idly rolls a 100-sided dice my pal Harmony gave me for Christmas. "Tyler," she says, "I want you to do a favor for me."

I call my room the Modernarium, the only room in the house into which Jasmine's hippie stained-glass decorating sensibility has not been permitted to seep. No seedy spider plants. No depressing sand candles. No gruesome rainbow merchandise. Just extremely tasteful black modular sofa units, a TV and CD sound system built into the man-high "entertainment totem" (black), the incredibly tasteful nonshag carpet (gray), the futon (gray-and-white stripes), the aforementioned sleek Italian minifridge (gray), the computer (off-white—the catalog says "oatmeal"), books and tapes, a clock (black), my collection of globes on the table near the window (nickname: the Globe Farm), and a mirror featuring a bright red, totally desirable Porsche in the middle. The walls are gray. All ornament has been neutralized. It is—yes—*hot.*

I have my own bathroom, too, a small bathroom with a shower and my extensive collection of fine hair-care products, which Jasmine calls my "shampoo museum" and which my girlfriend, Anna-Louise, calls my "landfill starter kit." In spite of their meanness, though, I note that they, like Daisy, have no compunction about borrowing gels, mousses, foams, lotions, salves, conditioners, or rinses from me when their *own* supplies run low.

And yes, I still live at home, but then, who doesn't? And besides, I need to save my money—build equity—hone my abilities, increase my marketworthiness, and all of this activity takes time and freedom from poverty. Poverty. Ick. Like a wolf baying and clawing at my door, strip by strip inching that much closer to me.

Kittykat, orange and white like a Creamsicle, slinks through my ajar door, prowls across the carpet, and jumps onto Jasmine's lap for a quick pleasure-soaked massage.

"Kittykat's driving me crazy, Jasmine. She's up on the roof at night running around endlessly, all thumpety thumpety thumpety. Are there mice up there? Does the moon make cats go crazy?"

Jasmine doesn't reply, as she is playing patty-cake with Kittykat's little white paws. They're both in on a secret. And nothing will change, regardless of what Jasmine says. Kittykat will continue pacing back and forth on the roof and I'll never know the secret.

"Didn't you want to ask me a favor?"

"In a second."

We sit watching the TV, the patty-cake with Kittykat continuing. A vaguely Third World image appears on the screen and I promptly zap it into something else.

"You shouldn't be so afraid of being poor, Tyler," says Jasmine. "You'll only call poverty onto yourself by running away from it."

This is why I watch TV alone: no irritating intrusions. Watching TV with another person is vaguely embarrassing—you feel like you're partially on display—like you're riding in a glass elevator at the mall.

"Mom, go worship your crystals. Poverty blows. I'm not letting poverty happen to me."

"What makes you think money is so hot, anyway, Tyler?"

"If money isn't so great, then why do rich people keep it all to themselves?"

"Maybe being poor for a while would do you good."

I mute the TV to command her full attention. "Earth to mother. Earth to mother. Poor people eat lousy food. They smoke. Their houses never have trees. They have too many kids and they're always surrounded by crying babies. They're suspicious of people with educations. In short, they love everything that keeps them poor. Think poor; be poor. Not me."

"I can't believe a son of mine is so heartless. So uncompassionate. Callow."

"So call me callow." I turn the TV back on but I'm too conscious of the fact that my mother thinks I'm a creep. I can't concentrate, and I don't think she can, either.

I make amends: "Poverty isn't what freaks me out, Mom. What freaks me out is what if the world ever turns bad? There are no safety nets. No wisdom. Just fear. Fear and stigma."

"I want you to go visit Dan for me."

"Huh?"

"Just once. Go see him and see where he is and then tell me about what you see. Your going will remove him from my blood faster. Trust me. You are my eyes and ears now, Tyler. You are my arms. My legs."

I know Jasmine used to worry about me all the time. Troubled teens. But suddenly somewhere a velvet-covered switch was flipped and now I worry about Jasmine all the time. When did this happen?

27

7

"You're beautiful, Tyler."

"No, *you're* beautiful, Anna-Louise."

"Tyler, you are fabulous. Truly fabulous. Stop being so fabulous. Just *stop* it."

"I love you, Anna-Louise. From the bottom of my heart I want you to know how much I love you, Anna-Louise."

We kiss.

Anna-Louise and I are speaking to each other in Telethon-ese. That's how we met last year at Lancaster Community College. She was camped out at a photocopy machine making hundreds of copies and I only needed to make three, so she let me line crash. I told her she was fabulous and she told me I was even more fabulous and, well, it kind of got out of control. Telethon-ese is all about acceleration: "Anna-Louise, the work you do for those kids. It's . . . *beautiful.*"

"Come on, let's hear those phones start to ring."

* * *

Meeting Anna-Louise was like finding a stranger's shopping list on the mall floor and realizing there are other, more interesting diets than your own. It was the first time I ever felt incomplete.

Most people like Anna-Louise because she seems so normal: B+ average, corduroys, a wheat-tint body wave, and the ability to relate to computer geeks. But that's all surface. I think of her more as an alien trapped inside a flesh dummy, just waiting to pop out. Anna-Louise can make coins appear from my ear. At night we go out together and rescue potted houseplants people have left outside their doors and on their balconies. If the two of us are eating eggs and Anna-Louise tastes so much as a fragment of eggshell, she'll vomit, as once happened at the International House of Pancakes over the state line in Idaho. Once, last spring, I secretly followed Anna-Louise when she was strolling downtown, trying to see her as might a stranger, her young legs so tender under her little plaid skirt and the weather so fine, when, under the clear blue sky, she held out her hand as though she had just felt a drop of rain. Imagine.

I imagine I sow cuttings of Anna-Louise's hair, like the fine stems of dried flowers, and watch sunflowers grow from the cuttings. *I* imagine I bury a pocket calculator with liquid crystals spelling her name, then watch the earth shoot forth lightning bolts. "We should open up a seafood house together," Anna-Louise says when she wants to torture me. Now that's love.

School's out and Anna-Louise is melting into the black seat of my Nissan, aka: the Comfortmobile, and fidgeting with a queen of spades playing card on a shoestring necklace, a bauble I made for her last Saturday. She's bathing me in warm sugar-free-gum fumes as we roar away from the front doors of the college.

"God, what an ugly building," she says as Lancaster Community College's main hall recedes into the distance, "designed by a man, no doubt."

She's right. Lancaster Community College is composed of brutal 1970s cement cubes and looks like dead air conditioners linked together by the little mesh catwalks of a hamster's fun-run. The school's facade is graced by what appears to be a Lexan molecule amplified ten trillion times and constructed out of steel dodecahedrons, like public art you'd find back in communist Germany outside the Stasi headquarters.

"A byte bleak," I concede.

"Not by half. If you ever want to film a movie in a bleak, cheer-free future, here's the set."

School.

Anna-Louise is studying commerce, second year. I'm in my second year of hotel/motel management studies, and yes, we're both enrolled at Lancaster Community College: intellectual puppy mill, the Harvard of Benton County.

I think hotel/motels are a career with a future. I like hotels because in a hotel room you have no history, you have only an essence. You feel like you're all potential, waiting to be rewritten, like a crisp, blank sheet of 8½-by-11-inch white bond paper. There is no past.

Once, ten years ago, back when I was ten and Daisy was eight—shortly after John Lennon was assassinated and while Jasmine was in County General pupping Mark—Grandma and Grandpa hauled Daisy and me along with them to a hotel in Hawaii. We landed in Honolulu late at night and I fell into a deep plumeria-scented sleep as we drove down Kalakaua Avenue into Waikiki. The next morning I remember waking up and emerging downstairs into the lobby, there feeling a sense of freedom and liberation that has since been hard to top. A Pacific breeze swept over my marshmallowy mainland skin and I realized the hotel had no doors, a facet of the building I hadn't remembered from the night before. Imagine that—a hotel with no doors. They exist. And ever since then, I've thought of hotels as most ideal places indeed to be.

Across the oat-colored plains Anna-Louise and I sail, snug in my little car, inhaling hot electronic tunes sung by depressed British children. We rush through the sunny air past copses of scarlet trees, fields fencing snorting horses, and the 70mm sky above us is big and blue, like a jigsaw puzzle completed just moments ago.

"Oh, Tyler, did you book a hotel yet?" asks Anna-Louise. The two of us are planning to go up to British Columbia the weekend after next.

"Yes, my little runner-up."

"Is the hotel Marge? It has to be Marge. I want atmosphere." Marge is Anna-Louise's word describing sad, 1950s-ish diner-type places where the waitresses are named Marge.

"Yes, it's Marge."

"What's the name. The Lucky Puppy? The Plucky Ducky?"

"The Aloha."

"It's Marge."

"Tyler?"

"Yeah?"

"You are my trailer park."

"And you, Anna-Louise, are my tornado."

* * *

Nature soon ends as we drive past the failing Ridgecrest Mall, half sheathed in plywood, the parking lot mostly deserted, interior lights in the pyramid-roofed galleria bravely shining. The marquee of the Eightplex Theater where Anna-Louise works bears the temperature and time: 52°, 4:04 P.M. Pacific War Time. (Well, all right, Pacific *Daylight* Time.)

"I wonder," says Anna-Louise, "if the future is going to be like the Ridgecrest Mall."

"How so?"

"You know. Improvised, sort of. Solid cement and steel structures from our own era, but with cardboard and straw for windows. Exxon stations with thatched roofs."

"Goats feeding in the dead fountains of the fashion plaza."

"Exactly. The year 3001. Shit everywhere. Mutants traipsing through the rubble in search of antibiotics. No new products ever being made again. I think there's a flaw in our DNA making humans invariably need to recede into the Dark Ages."

I think her idea over. "You know, Anna-Louise, I wouldn't mind if consumer culture went *poof!* overnight because then we'd all be in the same boat and life wouldn't be so bad, mucking about with chickens and feudalism and the like. But you know what would be absolutely horrible. The *worst?*"

"What?"

"If, as we were all down on earth wearing rags and husbanding pigs inside abandoned Baskin-Robbins franchises, I were to look up in the sky and see a jet—with just one person inside even—I'd go berserk. I'd go crazy. Either *everyone* slides back into the Dark Ages or *no one* does."

"Well, Tyler, unless your study habits pick up, *I'll* be the one up in the jet, and *you'll* be the one down on earth slopping the pigs."

"Don't harass me, Anna-Louise. I've got a lot on my mind."

"Like?"

"Like, I have to go see Dan tonight."

"No way."

"Way. Jasmine asked me to."

"When was the last time she saw him?"

"Not since before the felt-pen incident. It's all lawyers now. Not that either of them has money to haggle over."

"How's she feeling?"

"Twenty percent chance of rain. She's stopped eating TV dinners and she's back onto the lentils again. We're allowed to say his name. She's depressed. She's lonely. She says she's cheered up because she hasn't gained a pound during the whole episode. She's ringless."

"How long now, since he left?"

"Five weeks. Good riddance."

"You haven't seen him yet?"

"Not since I left for Europe, and that was in June."

"Scared?"

"Yes."

The road on which we're now driving runs between the Ridgecrest Mall and the Plants. The only natural scenery along the way is a microvalley between two lame hills just past the Ridgecrest Mall, a microvalley known locally as the Onion Canyon after the crop that used to grow there before an auto-mall rezoning both deleted and reformatted the landscape. The road is wide and gently curving; locally we call it Route 666. After the Onion Canyon there's zero to see until the Plants, a good five or six songs on the tape deck away.

This afternoon Anna-Louise and I are headed to our hangout, Top's Restaurant, more reasonably known as the Toxic Waste Dump. The Dump theoretically is supposed to serve Texicano cuisine, "But let's face it," says Anna-Louise, "it's diner food garnished with jalapeños, but that's okay. It's Marge."

My regular order at the Dump is a Fungus Humungus Burger: hamburger meat Mr. Velasquez purchases from the Mafia (chockablock, no doubt, with aspen sawdust and ground murder victim) garnished to the point of overloading with meaty chewy nuggets of mushrooms, like chunks of freshly flensed whale blubber. Anna-Louise always orders diet colas.

"Tyler," says Anna-Louise as we approach the Dump, "I missed you while you were in Europe, you know."

"I missed you, too."

"Tyler—" A pause. "Did something happen to you over there? I shouldn't have asked. Am I torturing you? It's not fair of me to ask. I'll shut up right now."

"What are you talking about?"

"It's just—" She's loving this. "You seem more distant now than you did before you went away. I think when people are distant, usually it means they have a secret they can't tell you because they don't think you can handle it."

"What?"

"It's nothing. It's all in my mind. Look. There's Skye's Wagoonmobile." She turns to me. "But you'd tell me if you had a secret, wouldn't you? I can deal with anything. You know that."

"I know."

"Good. Let's go inside."

As Anna-Louise heads into the Dump, I double-check to make sure the car doors are locked.

* * *

Imagine you are sitting down in a chair and on a screen before you you are shown a bloody, ripping film of yourself undergoing surgery. The surgery saved your life. It was pivotal in making you *you*. But you don't remember it. Or do you? Do we understand the events that make us who we are? Do we ever understand the factors that made us do the things we do?

When we sleep at night—when we walk across a field and see a tree full of sleeping birds—when we tell small lies to our friends—when we make love—what acts of surgery are happening to our souls—what damage and healing and shock are we going through that we will never be able to fathom? What films are generated that will never be shown?

Fair's fair. Something *did* happen in Europe. What happened was I met someone else—*Stephanie*—there, I've said her name—and for a time I stopped remembering Anna-Louise.

But of course I remember her again, now.

And sure, my relationship with Anna-Louise has changed. Much of the earlier urgency is gone, but that's a relief. Ours was never a beer-commercial kind of love to begin with. I used to get depressed because our relationship wasn't more like a beer commercial. You know: warp-speed cars blaring nuclear tunes while twenty blondes from Planet Beach roast babies on a spit while threatening to get it on at any moment. You settle for what you get.

If Anna-Louise and I make too big a deal about liking each other, it merely reminds us we're not as passionate as we're told we should be. We feel corny. Best not to overthink these issues.

I like Anna-Louise. We feel natural around each other, and I hope this is enough. I get exhausted thinking there must be more.

8

"Tyler! Anna-Louise! Top o' the food chain to you! Here, check these out." Anna-Louise's friend Skye tosses me a pair of designer knock-off sunglasses manufactured in some Southeast Asian archipelago nation—glossy glasses reeking perversely of fresh, uncooked lamb. Skye and a gang of friends—Pony, Harmony, Davidson, Leslie, Mei-Lin, and Gaïa—occupy the Siberia booth at the Dump, out back by the video ghetto. Davidson is snapping away with *my* instant camera and *my* film and the seven are lost in a primping frenzy, like German pesticide magnates having their Polaroid snapped by Andy Warhol. Amid the food are developing snapshots. It's strange seeing my friends behave badly—like seeing the moon in the sky in the middle of the day.

"Uh-uh. Bad fakes," I say, returning the glasses.

"My my. We *have* been to Europe, haven't we?"

"Take a nap, Skye. Whether these glasses are fakes or

36

not has nothing to do with me and Europe. You know that."

No one challenges my authority regarding designer knock-off merchandise. That's how I paid for my trip to Europe, as well as the Comfortmobile and the Modernarium: fakes—watches and T-shirts. I was the on-campus rep for a company out of Provo, Utah, that was the bane of Chanel's existence. And Ralph Lauren and Rolex and Piaget and Hugo Boss. A lucrative little business I had going, too, until, of course, the cops swooped in to terminate the fun.

"Smile." Gaïa takes Polaroids of Anna-Louise and me doing Hollywood smiles while across the Dump a flock of mall rats, skatepunks and skatebetties shriek with laughter at the antidrug logo flashing at the end of a video game. Hot tunes roar from the CD juke. Much idle chat. Mink, my favorite waitress, takes my Fungus Humungus order, then sighs while Anna-Louise orders her one millionth diet cola. Harmony—a Dungeons and Dragons freak and enthusiast for Ye Olde Merrie Englande—orders "a chalice of mead, fair damsel," and Mink sighs, then asks Harmony if he wants a diet or regular cola.

"This summer in Amsterdam," I say, "I met these preppies from Boston at a hostel. They spent the week getting sick smoking hash, eating strawberries, and picking at bites from the mosquitoes in the canals. They had a hangup about making sure everyone else in the hostel pub knew how rich they were. One of these preppies, a guy named Chris, kept going on about the Rolex watch his dad gave him for his birthday, and then he made a crack about Lancaster and the Plants, asking why I wasn't glowing like the watch dial, so I said to him, 'Hey, Chris, let me see your watch,' and he did. The watch was a fake. I told him so."

"How could you tell!" chimes in the mob at the table.

"Easy. Real Rolexes have smooth second-hand sweeps. Fakes go tick tick tick. The difference is obvious once you know. I felt bad I told him, though. I mean, his dad gave him the watch as a present. But then he was being such a creep, and besides, if your dad gave you a fake and tried to fob it off as real, wouldn't you want to know?"

Silence greets my question. I realize not one of my friends at the table has a biological father present and stable in their lives, me included. So I guess the answer is we'd take any crumb our fathers might give us and never ask a question. I note here that the last gift my biological father, Neil, gave me was a Stetson filled with pot from his dope ranch in Humboldt. The box arrived UPS when I was sixteen and Jasmine hovered over me during the unwrapping in anticipation of just such a gift. "Keep the hat," she said, whisking the remainder away in the blink of an eye, and that was *that. C'est la vie.*

"So, Tyler," asks Skye, breaking the silence, sensing communal intimacy, "what we've been hearing about your mother—that Dan wrote D-I-V-O-R-C-E on her forehead. Truth?"

"In mirror writing?" adds Harmony. "I mean, now the subject's come up."

"Yes. He wrote D-I-V-O-R-C-E backwards—except he messed up the *R*, if you must know. Now mind your own business, and Skye, stop being such a tough cookie. It's unappealing."

"Is Jasmine going to take him to the cleaners?"

"Jesus, Skye, stop."

A few minutes later when Skye visits the bathroom Anna-Louise tells me Skye can't stop herself when she falls into her hard-as-nails routine. She says Skye is like a small but valuable object you buy in a store—an object given way more packaging than it needs, just to prevent shop-lifting. "She was born divorced," says Anna-Louise.

"She's too hard," I say.

"She's had a hard life. Her dad's doing twelve to fifteen years."

"Skye looks like a jackpot," adds Davidson. "She looks like TV. She's like a soft-porn Disney version of herself, all shiny and fresh-off-the-shelf."

"I guess she's just hungry for experience," I say, seeing Anna-Louise giving me a glare.

"And that's hard when you live in a small town," says Anna-Louise, "so go easy on the girl."

When I first started going with Anna-Louise, her friends laser-scanned me with actuarial glances and found me a bit dull—marriage material. I think they figure that with types like me they can return later, after they've been for a spin around the block. Thank the Lord Anna-Louise is softer, more forgiving than her friends. Last week Anna-Louise and I had a fight on this very subject. I egged her on more than I should have:

"Don't your friends know that guys can tell within three-billionths of a second when a woman is sizing them up as marriage material? Talk about off-putting. Skye and her buddies think they can go out and have all of the fun in the world and then come home to some schmuck like me and suddenly turn into Carol Brady."

"You'd prefer foot binding? And what are you saying—guys can go out and sow their wild oats and women can't? Where are we—*1971*? You're a pig."

"You're misinterpreting me. I wish Skye and Mei-Lin and Gaïa would slow down. They're terrifying."

"Am *I* terrifying?"

"You're not your friends."

"Maybe I should be. And if you're so worried about being considered boring material suitable only for marriage, then change yourself into Mr. Witty, but don't go talking about *my* friends like *they're* the flawed people. Don't impose your corny preconceptions about womanhood onto *them*."

"*Whoa*. Time out."

"You need work, Tyler. And to think your mother's a hippie. I'm going to have a talk with her. Heaven help the world."

This exchange of last week took place in Anna-Louise's apartment, a bottom-floor suite—one of four suites in a subdivided falling-apart old brick house located in Lancaster's small historical center on Franklin Street.

Anna-Louise is the only person my age I know who lives alone. Independence suits her. Her mother and brother are in Spokane, too far away from the community college to commute. Her new family consists of a pair of semi-bag-lady maiden sisters in mirror-image apartments across the hall and a Popeye who lives directly above her whom we've labeled "The Man with 100 Pets and No TV." We see him only rarely, hauling home dolly-loads of kibble from the bulk pet food mart on Lincoln Avenue.

Another event of last week: Anna-Louise telephoned me long after I'd finished dinner and was sitting down at my PC to reclassify my CD collection using my new RapSheet® music spreadsheet software I mail-ordered from the TuneFreak™ Corporation of Memphis, Tennessee (*"with the push of a button, reclassify your entire CD, tape, or record collection by artist, album title, or date. 25,000-name artist index included. Also try RockSheet®, JazzSheet®, Bach-Sheet®, DeadFreak®, ElviSheet®, and over 50 specialized music spreadsheet options"*). Anna-Louise told me she'd had a strange experience. She'd been swimming near closing time at the community college pool and had been solo in the pool when the power blacked out and she was treading water in the center.

"I twinked," she said. "First I was scared, but then I relaxed and I swam underwater with my eyes open. With no light there were no gravity cues. It was outer space with chlorine."

The experience had made Anna-Louise, well, randy, and I was summoned to her apartment. By midnight, hours later, we were both lying blissfully on her futon, under the down coverlet, her face and body like a recently vacated carnival site, disconcertingly unchanged by the burst of life so recently bubbling on top.

We were eating too-hot microwave popcorn and discussing how we'd change our lives if we won a billion-dollar lottery. Our final decision was to buy ten thousand acres of land outside of Lancaster and bring in irrigation systems—rivers and streams—and we'd build a forest for ourselves, and surround the forest by a quartz wall as high as a drive-in movie screen.

Inside this walled prairie we would then sow millions of seeds and seedlings—future groves and thickets where previously only the emptiness had lain. For the first few years the forest would be only as high as our shoulders, but the green would rapidly outgrow us, fleshing in, giving homes to birds and insects and small animals within rapidly generating nooks and dark spots. And as Anna-Louise and I aged, so would the forest, until finally, one hundred years later, we would both lie together under a willow beside Lake Saint Anna while chirpy quackettes of ducklings sounded from clumps of nearby brown irises and power surges of wind blasted outward from a sentinel wall of poplars. The sun would shine down on our wrinkled old skin and bones and with one gust of wind, our skins would be swept away and we would emerge as two small butterflies, revolving in each other's wonky orbit, flying upward into the air, higher and higher, up above our garden, our tree fort, above the quartz walls we had constructed and whatever the world outside had by then become.

And *that's* why Anna-Louise and I are visiting British Columbia the weekend after next. At the end of our forest fantasy she mentioned she had seen a forest named Glen Anna on a map of southern British Columbia. A billion dollars is a long way away and we figured we needed to see a forest sooner than that.

Anna-Louise stays at the Toxic Waste Dump while I leave to visit Dan. I exit the glass doors (WELCOME: *FEED THE NEED*) into the bracing see-your-breath weather, out into the cold October—into the coming-alive streetlights and the backlit Plexiglas signage seemingly crinkling in the mirage wavelets caused by the cooling earth. A lone car chugs down Route 666 and rush hour from the Plants is only a memory.

Hunting season has started here in Lancaster. Driving down Route 666 to Dan's I observe that every hormone-soaked galoot with no life and a 4 × 4 in this time zone has flocked to the bioregion expressly for the privilege of not shaving, making it with grade-Z hookers, drinking scotch in stale motel rooms, and donning goofy neon-color floppy hats to take potshots at what few remaining fragments of nature have had the mixed blessing of surviving both the Plants and last year's crop of goons. Warlocks hurling animals into their invisible caldrons. I think we're simply going to run out of Nature before we have a chance to destroy it.

9

One afternoon several years ago, at Pimm's Offramp Diner, my stepfather Dan couldn't find a Kleenex and so he sneezed into a dollar bill. Within a month he was bankrupt. To this day he blames that sneeze rather than, say, his business abilities, for his downfall.

Dan is, or rather *was*, a land developer and was "rich as a bitch" (his joke; what a yuckster) back when he married Jasmine, back when I was in junior high.

"A land developer will tell you *anything* to get you into bed," my mother once joked to a friend at a party she and Dan once held, back in the heyday of Nova Scotia salmon, burglar alarms, and certified letters from Switzerland—an era when Jasmine experimented for the first-and-hopefully last time with crepe soap-opera dresses, makeup, and scampi hors d'oeuvres—hobbling about monkey-suit cocktail parties with the fashion-android wives of Dan's contractor buddies, all of whom went Broke City when The Fear came. "Cheat, flatter, beg, lie, promise, steal—and once he gets you there, what happens?"

"What?"

"You're fucked." Cocktail-induced humor.

Dan was a dangerous and intoxicating novelty in Jasmine's orbit a decade ago, she being bored, I guess, after eons of seeing hairfaces. And for a while they were happy in their own manner; they had the animal confidence money affords. I even have a few okay memories of Dan, all revolving around cars, the only place Dan ever seemed relaxed, preferably a fast car.

I remember driving along Route 666 in the V-12 Jaguar, Dan shouting *mush!* as we booted past the Plants, fishtailing into reverse at high speed to see if reverse measures on the odometer. (No.) God, what a car that was. Sheer perfection. Pampered. I remember asking Dan what a certain slot was on the dashboard. "That's where you insert hundred-dollar bills."

I remember a time Dan stuck a pair of adhesive purple nipple tassels onto the front headlights of Jasmine's car, tassels won in a Yakima strip bar and tassels Jasmine adored and let remain where they were glued until they decomposed naturally.

I remember driving under high-tension wires on the highway, Dan shouting cover your jewels, making us cup our hands on our crotches.

I remember Dan being a monster in parking lots, a real undead, stealing blue spots away from the handicapped, parking diagonally across two slots, immune from prosecution because of a handicapped permit obtained black market from a crony at town hall.

I remember one episode where Dan, then on a bodybuilding kick, was driving home with Daisy and me from the gym when suddenly he yanked the car into the Circle-K convenience mart, dashed inside, tore the top off a carton of half-and-half from the dairy case, then guzzled the cream inside. Daisy and I followed him, freaked out, watching viscous white goo slop down his chin, through his chest hairs, staining his tank top, then forming mini-puddles on the floor.

"Steroids," he informed us. "If I don't eat something right away, my stomach'll start to eat itself. Pass me that clump of bananas."

Those were big years, big times.

I am standing in the hallway outside of Dan's door and I can feel cold air pushing out of the keyhole.

Dan's apartment building virtually shimmies with hope-lessness. The building is a nest for people whose common thread in life is that they somewhere, at some time, missed a train. I don't want to touch the elevator buttons, I don't want to smell the sad meals whose fragrances waft down the hallway. I sense ex-fry cooks with tuberculosis. In the alcove downstairs there are stalagmites of unforwarded mail. There is a flat of desiccated, never-planted marigolds beside a window overlooking a tree stump that will never be pulled. There is litter tangled in the uncleared brush posing as a hedge by the road.

I knock on the door. There's no answer but silence doesn't surprise me. Dan's philosophy is that you should never answer a door until the third knock; you should never answer a phone until the sixth ring.

After the third knock the door opens.

"Oh. You."

"Hi, Dan. Don't overgreet me or anything."

"Hi. I guess."

Dan looks at me, his brain focusing me like the projectionist focusing the film on the Eightplex screen. "Well. Come in if you're here."

I follow Dan into his freezing apartment, where bachelor rubble adorns all flat surfaces like litter on the Eightplex floor after multiple matinee screenings of *Bambi:* underwear, Chinese-food cartons, zappers for the entertainment totem, want ads, empty prescription bottles of Rantidine, ashtrays, drink glasses, and magazines mixed in with some of the stuffed birds he took away with him the morning he left Jasmine—geese, ducks, and hawks, offering proof, if proof were needed, that Nature tends to reward terror.

"Drink?"

"No thanks."

Dan's glass, emblazoned with bulldozers, makes a small *crick* sound as he lifts it from his improvised coffee table —a stack of smooth aluminum "drug lord" luggage left over from the 1980s. "Today's squeaky clean youth," he says.

"Possibly," I reply.

Dan sits in his brown velour chair and tilts his glass vertically into his mouth. "Think I'll have another. How was Europe?"

"Okay."

"Don't talk too much."

Dan crosses the room, pours a drink, lights a cigarette, then returns and sits directly across from me and asks me in mock intimacy, salesmanlike, "So. What's this I've been hearing—you're going around telling people I'm the devil?"

"Well, Dan. Do you have evidence to prove you're not?"

"What the hell are you talking about?"

"Homesick, are you?"

"Jesus, you're weird."

"Statements like that got you to where you are."

Dan stops and smiles: "Haven't changed a bit, have you?"

"Why'd you leave Jasmine, Dan? And why did you leave her the way you did? It was a shitty thing to do."

"I don't want to discuss this. My lawyer says not to." Dan extinguishes his cigarette. "And for that matter, to what do I owe the pleasure of today's visit?"

"Just being friendly."

"Spy mission? What are you going to tell her? Going to give me a good report card?"

I'm silent.

"Okay. I'll lay off. But don't blame *me*. You think you know me, but you don't. What did you do to your hair?"

"It's modern," I say, absentmindedly pawing my gelled spikes.

"Shallow little fuck, aren't you? But fashion is fashion. I had long hair once."

Dan has trouble with aggressively moist hair. But I refuse to rise to his bait. Always keep your mouth shut with a drunk. You can never win with piss tanks. The most you can hope for is to break even. The tactic of choice? Preemptive boringness. Being one-dimensional is the most satisfying method of coping with out-of-control people—with *any* situation that's out of control. Keep your face like a screen-saver software program. Don't let people know the ideas you love, the games you've played, the places you've visited in your mind. Keep your treasure to yourself.

Dan is irked. "You're young. Phone me in ten years. You'll know the limits of your talent by then; just watch doors slam shut all around you. You won't be so cocky then."

Dan sips his cocktail. On the coffee table is Dan's collection of salt-and-peppers, coffee whiteners, mustards, and stir stix stolen from fast-food restaurants. God, I hope my life never becomes as compromised as his, scrambling for pathetic fragments of power, trying to fill the vacuum remaining after my hopes implode. But then again, phone me in ten years and we'll talk then. Scary.

Dan talks a bit more about the family, my school, and his work prospects.

"Tell Jasmine I'm moving out of this dump, if you want to. Into a luxury condo."

"Hmmm?"

"Ronnie's letting me live in an Onion Slopes unit he can't unload. Figures he'll never sell it. Can't tell you what my rent is." Ronnie is Dan's ex-partner.

"No. Of course not."

"Big-screen TV in a pit, blackout curtains, xenon laser alarms, raised-podium Jacuzzi in front of a picture window overlooking Onion Canyon."

"Gosh."

"So *I'm* set. Going to be comfortable again, like the old days. On my own. Life's great." I think the most admirable trait in people who are otherwise short of admirable traits is at least they lack self pity.

"Dan, I have to go now." His attitude is making me queasy. He makes abandoning my mother sound like a spending spree at Kmart after winning big at the horse races.

Dan checks his watch and says he's expecting a call at the pay phone at the corner. The Space Age phone he received free with a tank of gas last year has (surprise surprise) stopped working. He comes down the stairs with me. "You get what you pay for," he shouts, dashing past me on his way to the ringing Bell booth at the corner. "All the next stuff I'm going to buy is going to be high quality"—he picks up the receiver and shouts to me before speaking—"European."

* * *

So.

Maybe Anna-Louise is right—maybe you never *can* know what transpires between two people in and out of love—I'll never figure out Dan and Jasmine. Best not to waste energy guessing.

On the other side of the street is The Man with 100 Pets and No TV, wheeling newspapers to the recycling depot. Social conscience. Panic washes over me and I wonder if the divorce will affect my credit rating on the six bank cards I signed up for from the campus card recruiters last year. ("Just look at these holograms, Mr. Johnson. Imagine *these* holograms in *your* wallet.") Nah.

I enter the Comfortmobile, punch in a hot tape in the hope some random tunage will scramble my mood, but no. I eject the tape, breathe, slam the door, ignite my beast, and float away, like a silver bird atop an alligator floating down the Amazon River.

10

Half the man's age plus seven."

"Huh?"

Jasmine replies that this is the Chinese formula for a successful marriage.

Jasmine was doing housework in the nude when I came in the front door. For modesty's sake she wrapped a hallway throw rug around her waist, then shanghaied a red turtleneck sweater from the laundry bin plus a pair of Daisy's ankle socky-wockies. She is unaware of how ridiculous she looks as she sits in the Modernarium with me. Once again we're sitting in the classic talk-show-host/sidekick configuration.

"Think of all the couples you know, Tyler. I was 31 and Dan was 35 and look what happened there. Dan should have married a 25-year-old. Grandpa married Grandma when he was 24 and she was 20 and they're going to go diamond soon."

Jasmine looks so young. She must have made a good hippie. She must have been a real knockout at twenty.

"Don't be glum," she adds, realizing Anna-Louise and I

are the same age, 20, hence doomed. "It's only a superstition."

Like a true talk-show guest, Jasmine sips her Red Zinger tea and changes the subject. "Anyway—glad to hear Dan has become the sort of guy who gets phone calls at pay phones. Thanks for making the mission. I won't make you go again."

"That's a relief."

"I think he's filtering out of my system now. I'm distancing. Remember how we lived in this house for years and never realized we had spiders nesting in the corners of the ceilings until we saw their webs in the Christmas snapshots? Same thing. Distance. I'm progressing with life. The women's group is a big help. Maybe I'll get a haircut. I *have* been a stick to have around the house the past six weeks."

"Haircut?" My interest is perked.

"At least I don't have to worry about loneliness now you kids are older. I can have real conversations with you. You kids were sweet, but when Neil left—Lego and dollies—I thought I'd go nuts. *Hey* . . . remember when you were eleven and you asked for a document shredder for your birthday?"

"Go on, Jasmine."

"Loneliness. I thought I was going to be permanently warped by loneliness, like a record being scraped by a screwdriver. That's the most frightening aspect of loneliness, Tyler. You think you're being damaged while loneliness is happening to you, and the worry amplifies the pain. And divorced women are box-office poison, too. Friends drop you. They just *do*. Married women won't have single women around their houses. It's a couple's world. That's why I like my women's group. We can talk. Oh— and my elbow eczema's clearing up."

"Your body always chooses its weakest point to express itself," I say, parroting hippie gibberish. Jasmine really nailed us when we were young. This stuff's all stuck inside me and surfaces at the most awkward times.

"You are your mother's child, Tyler. And by the way, you received a phone call this afternoon."

"A phone call?"

"From Paris. A Mademoiselle Stephanie. Ooh la la."

"Did she leave a number?"

"She said she'd phone back."

Daisy pops her head in the Modernarium's door, her yellow dreadlocks comical, fuzzy, and faintly unsanitary seeming. "Hallo meester lady kee-lair. You have speeked with Meese France?"

"Hi Daisy."

Daisy barges in, Kittykat lodged in her arms, managing to look restful against the jolt of electric fuchsia 1960s go-go dress from Goodwill. "So. Who's this Miss France? Spill. Tell all."

Jasmine and Daisy both bob their heads forward, in expectation of rich dirt.

"A friend" is all I say. They turn to each other, then aim my way in unison.

"You can do better than that, Ty," Daisy chastises.

"Sorry, kids, but I'm out of quarters." I turn off my eyes and enter the one-dimensional mode. Further probing on their part will be useless.

"We can wait. We'll find out, Ty. We always do," perseveres Daisy. "By the way, Jasmine. Guess what? You've become the cult Halloween costume for this year."

"No way."

"Way. Everyone at school is planning to go dressed as Jasmine Johnson and write stuff on their foreheads."

"Out!" Suddenly I want to be alone. Jasmine and Daisy

have become frivolous. Flippant. I don't like flippancy. Not in my room. Flippant people ask stupid questions and expect answers. Secrets divulged under flippant circumstances aren't valued. People don't value other people's secrets, *period*. That's why I keep my secrets to myself.

Daisy, Jasmine, still yakking—their talk like a maxed-out credit card, drained of potential—gaggle out the door with Kittykat. In the new silence I walk over to my Globe Farm and spin the planets. I think about Jasmine and Dan. I think about how I think I know a person then *poof!* I discover I only knew a cartoon version. Suddenly there's this fleshy, demanding, noisy creature in front of me, unknowable and just as lost as I am, and equally unable to remember that every soul in the world is hurting, not just themselves.

I look for the furthest spot on earth away from Lancaster—Lancaster's *antipode*—the middle of the Indian Ocean. The antipode of Paris is Christchurch, New Zealand. The antipode of Honolulu is in Africa—Harare, Zimbabwe.

I think of how people can betray me simply by not caring enough to hide the fact of how little they care.

I think of how the person who needs the other person the least in a relationship is the stronger member.

I spin my planets round. Why did Stephanie call? I thought she was out of my life.

Downstairs I hear Jasmine cooking and Daisy singing and teaching Mark how to freedom dance, putting his feet on top of hers.

I remember being a baby. I remember birds singing on the edge of my crib. A hippie picnic? I remember the first time I saw the sky.

11

I am walking across a turnip field, a baseball cap guarding my eyes from the sun. Underfoot are root vegetables—cool, nutritious, and silent—awaiting either Thanksgiving or scavenging by ravenous radioactive mutants.

I am thinking about the future.

I am optimistic about the future.

The future to me is like the Bechtol headquarters in Seattle, a shiny black needle, a tall thin machine—a building that can deliver a promise—a vaccine.

Jasmine, incidentally, never firebombed Bechtol headquarters the way she claims. Other hippies did; Jasmine merely identified with them. Back in Jasmine's days, Bechtol only made boring military radar systems. Nowadays, while they no doubt still manufacture death rays and other megatech items, they also make untold millions of people happy in their chain of spiffy luxury hotels spanning the globe, hotels in which I want to be employed and hotels which are part of Bechtol's brilliant corporate diversification strategy.

Bechtol, for that matter, is involved not only in hotels these days, but in genetic research, poultry ranching, fish farming, chromium mining, ready-to-wear sportswear, and a myriad of other exciting and profitable ventures. This diversification was spearheaded by Mr. Frank E. Miller, CEO of Bechtol, a man whose biography, *Life at the Top*, I have reread many times and heartily recommend to all of my friends.

As a prospective employee of Bechtol, I plan to make myself so desirable they will have no choice but to hire me. I see myself playing catch with Frank at a Bechtol corporate picnic, or better still, advising Frank against a bum merger over a London prayer breakfast—or elegantly explaining my precious metals marketing strategies with Frank over cocktails in his Twinair 9000 corporate jet en route to inspect a neutrino-powered smart-bomb facility in Alabama. Frank will listen. He'll steer me into a good slot—be a pal.

I like to think of the future when I walk through the crops, through fields of onions and sunflowers and hops, all alone like today, looking over the hills and imagining radio waves beaming in from real cities like Portland and Seattle and Vancouver pulsing through my body.

One might think these prairie walks would be silent, but no, the wind almost always whistles past with urgent, undecodable messages. While walking in winds like these, I like to imagine that there are young people like me walking through fields like this all around the world—in Japan, in Australia, in Nigeria and Antarctica—and we are all sending each other messages of hope and concern. Being global.

I think of myself being global. I see myself participating in global activities: sitting in jets, talking to machines, eating small geometric foods, and voting over the phone. I like these ideas. I know there are millions of people like me in basements and fashion plazas and schools and street corners and cafés everywhere, all of us thinking alike, and all of us sending each other messages of solidarity and love as we stand in our quiet moments, out in the wind.

We discuss the future a lot, my friends and me. My best friend, Harmony, says that in the future, torture will once again become the recreational sport of the rich. He thinks the future will be like rap music and computer codes, filled with X's, Q's, and Z's: "Letters liberated by the computer keyboard."

Skye thinks that in the future there will be a boredom tax, that every time you rent a video or need a bikini wax you'll have to pay a surcharge for the luxury of boredom.

Anna-Louise is a more day-to-day thinker, and prefers not to "treat the future as casually as you guys." She thinks of the future more in terms of where her friends will go in life and what sort of children she might have.

Myself, yes, I see the future as being like the Bechtol headquarters, but I also see another vision as I hopscotch diagonally across a recently plowed potato field, back to the Comfortmobile, careful not to upset the rows of dirt. I see this vignette in my head—a dry drunk—this guy who's been off the bottle for years—but he still goes through life with his every waking moment being trailed by a small cartoon thought balloon containing a bottle of vodka. I see this guy and he's sitting in the River Garden restaurant having Chinese dinner all by himself, and afterward he receives a fortune cookie with his check, which he opens up. When he reads the fortune inside, the cartoon bottle of vodka that has been haunting him floats away and he is free. The fortune says: WHAT YOU THINK WON'T HAPPEN WON'T.

Jasmine and Dan met on Independence Day seven years ago.

Mom's friend Rainbow was dating Dan at the time, and the couple showed up for a barbecue at our old house. Rainbow quickly became wasted on hash in the gardening shed, moving into the living room where she sat with baby Mark reading tarot cards all night. The chemistry between Jasmine and Dan, meanwhile, was immediate. We kids, of course, were too young to recognize chemistry for what it was—we merely noticed how hard it became to get Jasmine's attention. ("Jasmine, where is the ketchup?" "It's in the kitchen, dear. Could you fetch it yourself? Now tell me about that rezoning downtown, Dan. . . ." "I tell you, Jasmine, this neighborhood is begging for gentrification." "You really think so?")

I remember there were fireworks that night exploding across the town in Uranium Park. We sat on the balcony overlooking the backyard, trying, but unable to see the fireworks behind a wall of trees, hearing only the noises they made—dull squeals and thuds that sometimes made the walls pulse faintly.

And as I watched Jasmine and Dan, those sounds of the fireworks on the edge of town reminded me of sounds I had heard before—sounds I had heard on TV—in a documentary about WW II. I had seen a documentary in which certain cities of Europe, much to the confusion of their citizens, were being invaded by the Nazis with tanks and artillery shells and bombs. These were citizens who, never having bothered to awaken to the technological and psychic changes in their world, hadn't bothered to defend themselves, hadn't bothered to build walls or plan counterattacks or build weapons—asleep inside their collective dream, thinking for all the world that the unthinkable would never happen. Thinking they were safe.

12

Action time: Jasmine's parents called early this morning saying they had "exciting news that will change our lives."

Jasmine charges through the hallway shouting, "I will repeat the phrase, *'change our lives,'* for all of you in the studio audience. We could each of us do with a few life changes at the moment. Now up up *up*."

Daisy lies like a lump on her futon as Jasmine passes the message on and moans, "I can't believe you're dragging us up like this. What could be so majorly important we should lose a REM cycle?"

"Mom and Dad didn't say, honey, but the news sounded important and they want to meet all of us for brunch. Now Scotch-tape together your dreadlocks or whatever it is you do with them. Mark! Tyler! Up and at 'em."

"Where's *there?*" I mumble, stumbling toiletward down the hallway, squinting and semiconfused, like all Johnson children an ungracious early riser.

"The River Garden."

"The Chinese place?"

"That's right."

"For *break*fast?"

"For *brunch*. Dim sum. You know, where they wheel around the little carts and you pick and choose what you want? And I hear dim sum's quite la-di-da, so dress nicely and help Mark coordinate. You inherited the taste gene in the family. I'd probably just commit another fashion crime."

Several bathtub rotations later we crabbily assemble in Jasmine's Chrysler, a mammoth secret-service-white number with a blackout windshield. Kind of white-trash. Jasmine yells at Mark to stop picking at the gummed circles remaining on the headlights from the nipple tassels Dan stuck there years ago. "Mark, hop *in*," she yells, while Daisy and I do up our seat belts in preparation for a bout of Jasmine's heavy-footed driving.

We lunge out of the driveway and charge through Lancaster's dry flat streets, our neck muscles rigid with stress. "Earth to mother," calls Daisy from the back. "I thought ex-hippies were supposed to be gentle cuddly drivers."

"I'm only driving the way Dan taught me to, sweetie pie."

I bring up the subject of Grandma and Grandpa's secret: "Maybe they'll ask us to share in their loot," I suggest, but Jasmine nixes this suggestion.

"Hardly, Tyler, as you should well know from your tuition episode."

The *tuition episode* was just over a year ago, before the first year of college began and before I began making money peddling fake watches. Jasmine had to burst into tears and paint a doomed portrait of me manning a french-fry computer at Happy Burger until the year 2030 in order to cajole Grandpa to cough up a bit of dough for tuition, a fraction of his and Grandma's estate, which includes their house, a time-share condo in Maui, stocks-o-rama, and, of course, a monster of a mobile home named Betty.

Ten minutes later we lunge to a halt outside the River Garden, a white stucco box next to the Columbia River with a corrugated tin roof and big Chinese letters tacked onto the facade. Outside the main door is parked Grandpa's Lincoln Continental, nickname: The Building—possibly the largest passenger vehicle ever built.

Jasmine's dad is an engineer, and like most all of Lancaster's population, he moved to town after the Second World War, bringing Grandma, Jasmine, and Jasmine's two brothers along with him from their old hometown of Mount Shasta in northern California.

I wish I liked Grandpa more than I actually do. I mean, he could help me if he wanted to but he . . . I'll just shut up here. But I *will* say that after he retired a few years ago, it became increasingly apparent that all he was concerned with was monitoring his investments, crowing over their success, and conspicuously not sharing his winnings with his family, as though keeping us in the economic Dark Ages was behavior to be proud of. And I find there is a vaguely and consistently wasteful aura about the way both Grandpa and Grandma live their lives, like streetlights left on during the day, the way they like to have three of everything. But I guess Grandpa's simply growing old: aging with nothing to show for it except a heap of consumer durables. Or, as my friend Harmony would say, "He's become a pod person: functioning but without a soul." Maybe this theory would explain the aura of strained, undiscussable pseudo-cheer near my grandparents, like partying in a house in which the mother has recently died.

The last time—and only time—Grandma and Grandpa spent any real time with us was when they stayed at our house five years ago. This was after they returned from Brazil to discover that their freezer-room door had been left open for their entire holiday—three months' worth of prepared-in-advance meals as well as several entire animal carcasses had rotted, creating an almost visible plume of vomitty decay smell to rise over their Onion Slopes house as they opened their bank of Plexiglas skylights to aerate the structure.

Four weeks of reconstruction, fumigation, and cinnamon-scented smell-masker made the house inhabitable again. (Daisy suggested Grandma and Grandpa simply use one of those room deodorizers that function by anesthetizing your nose so you can't smell the smell. "Kind of like Dan's personality," I added, triggering Jasmine to escort me to a weekend-long childing seminar, The Son Within.)

I mention this story to show that my relationship with Grandpa has never been allowed enforced geographic intimacy, like with people who live in huts or caves. A distance between us has been maintained for so long now that were I to attempt emotional or any other type of closeness, Grandpa would probably say, *"Tyler, how corny. Don't bother"*—but Grandpa wouldn't know those words —his generation doesn't think that way. But he'd still feel the sentiment.

As for Grandma, she listens to Grandpa. If you ever look in the obituaries in the paper and see all those women named Edna and Mavis and Ethel, she's of that generation. Like, about two hundred years old. They weren't trained, like Anna-Louise is, to think for themselves. Once, in an almost unheard-of burst of insight, Grandma (Doris) told me she was frightened by how heavily influenced she is by the most recent things she encounters: TV shows, magazines, conversations. . . . "The new things just seem to erase the old things the way new scenery erases old scenery when you're driving down the highway. And light a cigarette for me, okay, baby? At least when I'm in heaven I won't be addicted to these things anymore." Puff puff.

Grandpa takes aspirin to fix his heart—two a day, and he keeps buckets of them on hand. Whenever I visit him he gives me stress headaches, so I swallow some of these aspirin. Mark observes that the pills he uses to fix his heart, I use to fix my head, "so maybe that's why you don't like each other."

Regardless, I still think Grandpa's just cheap and doesn't care about us kids. I mean, don't living organisms have a built-in mechanism ensuring the desire to protect their young from the foulness of themselves—the way rabbits won't poop underground? Don't we humans secrete enzymes that make older humans want to help younger humans?

"Hi kids! Over here!" yodels Grandma, waving a ring that even from the front door of the restaurant looks to have been purchased from a TV shopping channel 1-900 number. Up close we see the full effect: Grandma in her ginger wig snarfing low-tar menthol cigarettes, Grandpa in his hairpiece drumming a cup of decaf coffee with his chopsticks, his body now grown so tubby he can lift his right leg over his left only by yanking upward on his plaid trouser cuff. Soothing and identity-free tunes wash over us from car-stereo speakers staple-gunned to the ceiling panels.

"Hello, babies. Give me a kiss-kiss," says Grandma, and we dutifully line up for the ritual air kiss, kissing the sky above each of Grandma's ears, making a *mwah!* sound as we do so.

"Daisy, what have you done to your hair!" asks Grandma, recoiling from Daisy's blond dreads.

"She hasn't gone and joined a cult, has she, Jaz?" demands Grandpa, who immediately turns to Daisy and repeats himself, "You haven't gone and joined a cult, have you, young lady?" (no time allotted for an answer) "Family members all sit down. Sit down. Let's all have a big big meal."

We sit around a circular table and I leave a spot vacant for Anna-Louise, who will be arriving shortly, bringing Murray with her.

"Let's eat right away, shall we?" says Grandpa. "I'm starved. Your Grandmother and I just love Chinese *kweezeen*. Thought maybe we'd toddle off to China this year."

"Excellent bargains there, I hear," adds Grandma.

"Round-trip tickets for free with our frequent-flyer points," says Grandpa.

"And they have such excellent low salt/low cholesterol meals on the planes these days."

Mentally I'm seeing in my head that New Year's cartoon, the cartoon of the bearded old man holding a torch who represents the old year, except in the cartoon *I'm* seeing, the elder year is refusing to hand over the torch to the baby year.

Daisy mentions torture and political prisoners in China, to which Grandma says *yes yes* and then switches to bargains to be had in Hong Kong.

The dim sum food is wheeled by and portions are placed on the Formica table, Grandpa saying, "Gobble up, kids —our treat": soiled boiled diapers with sprinklings of battery corrosion; unloved soggy weather balloons marinaded in a tepid floor-sweeping broth; bony shrivelled hens' claws garnished with medicine-cabinet leftovers. A sullen hostess wheels by golden cubic chunks of what appear to be sponges, quivering and twitching like puppies recently removed from their mother.

"I can't eat," says Daisy. None of us can. This food is too weird. Fortunately, though, Daisy finds chrysanthemum blossoms steeping in the tea and makes do with several glasses. Mark and I eat a big bowl of fortune cookies and Mark joins the fortunes together to make a necklace. Jasmine halfheartedly picks a diaper, while Grandma and Grandpa devour all food in sight.

"Your loss you don't want to eat this delicious meal," remarks Grandpa. "Kind of reminds me of back in the good old days, back when more was more."

13

Anna-Louise and Murray arrive to break the dietary gloom, and both quickly remove their jackets, overheating after making the transition into the toasty restaurant from Anna-Louise's freezing rusty Volkswagen Rabbit (the Bondo Bunny). There are hellos all around. Anna-Louise says hi to Grandma: "Hi, Mrs. Johnson. *Quelle shake?*"

"Pardon me, dear?" My grandparents love Anna-Louise.

"That's French for 'what's shaking.' Tyler taught me. He's bilingual from Europe."

"I see." This small bon mot washes right by her. As Anna-Louise sits down beside me she asks what the big news is.

"Now that you're here we can tell everybody, dear."

Murray, meanwhile, has been conspicuously ungreeted by my grandparents during all of the helloing, being only gruntingly acknowledged. Today he is even more outrageously dressed than usual, his hair dreadlocked and muddy-seeming, his eyes covered in teeny little black rectangular glasses, and underneath his fringed buckskin jacket is a ripped T-shirt with a psychedelic fluorescent Mandelbrot pattern. Even predreadlock, Grandpa found Murray unbearable and couldn't have envisaged his granddaughter selecting a more unpalatable mate.

I think the problem between Murray and Grandpa is that Murray assumes, with great error yet great enthusiasm, that since Grandpa was instrumental in the construction of the Plants, then Grandpa is also equally interested in discussing the closing down of the Plants and the postclosing cleanup, which is slated to last hundreds of years and gobble up all tax dollars for the next six generations. Murray keeps painfully raising the topic: "Heard the latest about the Plants, Mr. Johnson?"

"No, Murray. You tell me."

"Turns out the ground there is so toxic (ooh, pass me some of those yummy dumplings . . .) and the threat of the toxins leaching into the Columbia River so great, that they're thinking of using special chemicals to turn the earth around the Plants into glass."

"Glass?" asks Mark.

"Yeah. A solid block of glass for hundreds of cubic miles. The process is called vitrification."

"Cool!"

Murray then begins to itemize various items buried beneath the Plant soils over the years: dead beagles used in radiation experiments, dump trucks, jumpsuits, windows. . . .

"So I guess you're all wondering what the good news today is," says Grandpa, pointedly changing the subject. Grandpa, like most of the fun-loving gang who built the Plants, just wants to die or have his brain turn to oatmeal before it becomes too apparent exactly what a nightmare he and his buddies have saddled their descendants with.

"The good news—the news that is going to change all of our lives—is what I have here in this box," he says, whisking up onto the tabletop a cardboard box I hadn't seen on the floor. "Inside this box," he announces, "is *the future*."

The future? My mind is ablaze with the possibilities of what may be contained in the box—never again will I have to trouble wondering to myself what the future might be. What could be in the box . . . a gray goose? a machine? clouds? gold coins? a glimmering pastel monster? All of us around the table are breathless.

"What I have in this box will make us rich," Grandpa continues. "But before I reveal the contents, I want you to think of power and opportunities and work." Grandpa goes off on a spiel, sounding to me impressively like Mr. Frank E. Miller of the Bechtol Corporation. After a few minutes of such inspirational foreplay, Grandpa removes the box top with all the brio of a snooty waiter, revealing a small raised velvet platform displaying what appears to be a dozen assorted varieties of tinned cat food.

Jasmine looks crushed; Grandma is beaming. The anticlimax is palpable.

Anna-Louise leans over and whispers in my ear. "This is so surreal," she says. "I think I'm turning into a melting clock."

14

I don't understand, Grandpa. You keep saying we're supposed to go out and find sales reps to work under us. When do we actually sell the cat food itself?" Frank E. Miller would be proud of me.

"It's not *cat food*, Tyler. How many times do I have to tell you. It's the KittyWhip Kat Food System. *System*. You don't just sell cat food, you sell the *system*."

"I see, but who actually sells the cans of food, what, *door to door?* I don't understand—where's the wealth being generated?"

Grandpa sighs. "Tyler, *you* of all people with your sales experience with the watches should understand how building a network of sales reps works. Five reps sell for you, five reps in turn each sell for those reps, and so on and so on. And you receive a cut of all of their sales."

"A pyramid?"

"A *chain*."

"But when do sales reps actually sell the cans of . . ."

I am cut off: "Daisy! What do you think of the product? Impressive, eh?"

Daisy makes appreciative noises. "I think the little mouse-shaped croutons are cute."

"I like the KittyPump, Grandpa" says Mark. "Can I try again?"

"Of course, son. Go right ahead."

Mark upsets a small cup of lukewarm Chinese tea as he presses down a thin chromed lever on a small espresso machinelike device, causing a wobbly fluted brown pillar of meat by-products to emerge from a smiling plastic cat's mouth on the front of the machine. This sepia pillar contorts, sundaelike, into a glass dish featuring a colorful KittyWhip® logo on the bottom.

Grandma takes this dreadful sundae, sprinkles mouse croutons on top, then waggles it underneath all of our noses. "Isn't it just adorable?" she asks. "Say hello to your first million. Looks so good you'd almost want to eat it yourself. Why—*why I think I just might!*"

The restaurant's owners look on in horror, as do we all. "Grandma!" we shout, "Don't do it!"

"Now, Doris," titters Grandpa.

Doris tinkles with laughter. The two have their sales banter down pat, like a duo of carnival hucksters. Anna-Louise, Murray, Jasmine, Daisy, and I, meanwhile, are gagging, cat food being possibly the most revolting substance in the universe, in this entire space/time continuum.

Work and money; money and work—strange but true. Fifty years of this stuff ahead of me—it's a wonder I don't just hurl myself off the bridge in the center of town right away. How did we let the world arrive at this state? I mean, is this *it?* And where, exactly, is the relief from this creepy cycle supposed to be? Has nobody thought of this? Am I mad?

Maybe I should be more like those older kids down at the Free Clinic, the clinic down the street from Anna-Louise's apartment on Franklin Street. Sometimes I'll watch those kids, most of them in their late twenties, because I'm not quite able to discount the fact that in some way, what they're doing with their lives is not entirely wrong. I'm talking about the hopeless druggies, lunching on methadone and orange juice, Diazepam and placebos, Dilaudids and Tuinals, surprisingly mild-mannered with their ecstatic eyes, shuffling through the streets and talking to the trees, inspecting pay phones for quarters, giving themselves Mohawk hairdos and losing interest in the procedure halfway through.

I watch these kids.

They don't seem entirely unhappy. A few times I've even circled the Free Clinic on foot, trying to catch a closer glimpse of these kids and their lives as they pop in and out of the clinic's Sputnik-era, gone-to-seed building—Lancaster's future trolls and Popeyes loitering out back having hushed paranoid conversations. And once I even went to have a look where they hang out in a big way, out in the delivery bay behind the now-closed Donut Hut, the delivery bay grotto out back with a floor spongy with pigeon shit, chewing gum, cigarette ashes, and throat oysters—dank and sunless. I went to visit this place once when all of the druggies were away, having their druggy lives downtown doing their druggy things: yelling at parked cars and having conversations with amber lights. I visited this place and I was confused: confused and attracted. Who do these people think they are? How can they not care about the future or hot running water or clean sheets or cable TV? These people. And on the walls down at the delivery bay, do you know what they had written? Written in letters several hands high, letters built of IV needles attached to the cement with soiled bandages and wads of chewing gum? They had written the words WE LIKE IT.

15

To help pay for her apartment, Anna-Louise works part time at the Eightplex theater at the Ridgecrest Mall. She's been there for years now, and says the best part of her job is about eleven-thirty when the late show ends and she sweeps the theater to collect the goodies dropped from people's pockets: coins, birth-control pills, photos, tranquilizers, keys, candies, appointment books: "A condensed version of life. Chinos are the worst. The people who bang the doors at midnight looking for keys are guys with chinos. Bad pocket design. Not marsupial enough."

Jasmine keyboard-inputs documents out at the Plants, an occupation out of keeping with her overall hippie-ishness. "I'm allowed to keep a spider fern in my cubicle," she says, "so I don't mind." Jasmine likes the freedom and empowerment a job gives her (and grudgingly, the money, which we need more than ever). So I guess the Plant job is okay after all. Jasmine inputs documents nobody will ever read into a system that doesn't care, like Russia in the 1940s.

Anna-Louise and I once faxed Jasmine a lipstick kiss on a sheet of white bond paper, and she was reprimanded by her boss for frivolity. "Is that lick-the-boot, or what?" said Anna-Louise, disgusted.

I, actually, am informally barred from Jasmine's office because of an incident that occurred there two years ago. I was accompanying Jasmine, who was doing an inventory check for the Department of Energy, on a Saturday afternoon. I spent the first half hour gathering shredded documents to stuff a bean-bag chair for Mark. Afterward I whittled away an hour hopping from desk to desk, playing with the radiation dosimeters and offering running commentary on which coworkers I suspected were on the brink of snapping, as evidenced by the pathetically few fragments of ego Plant management allowed people to keep on their cubicle desktops.

"Ooh . . . a fragment of gneiss. What a funster. And what's *this?* A motivational jigsaw puzzle? Managerial ambition burns here. Check out the Daniel P. Feingold *Think to Win* paperback—not that hot. I read it. And what's behind the framed snapshot of loving tykes . . . aha! *Valium.* Notify the goon squad."

Of course, two other Plant employees were in the cafeteria drinking liquid death from the coffee brewer and heard my entire spiel. So much for on-the-spot psychoanalysis.

But at least Jasmine is employed, her now half-time job being one of a handful of Plant job classifications remaining unaxed. So cash is flowing in. But Mark was upset because he wanted a social worker, like everyone else in his class at school.

* * *

Everybody does work of some sort.

Skye used to do retail at the Saint Yuppie boutique at the Ridgecrest Mall, back before the store filed Chapter Eleven, then suffered a mysterious fire like so many other Ridgecrest Mall businesses. Now Skye telepimps for a telemarketing company. She calls people at dinnertime and asks them if they've done things like purchase latex paint or groom their pets recently. She has to work because she owes roughly nine thousand dollars on all the credit cards she signed up for in high school.

Harmony consults on computer-system installations and he already makes more money than everybody I know combined. He's rich. I tell him he should date Skye, but he's petrified.

Mark wants to work in a kissing booth.

Me, after the fake Rolex and Chanel business was busted, I never applied for another job—though I may need to soon. Job fantasies? I'd like to work at a photo-developing store where I could see people's snapshots come out of the developer machine. You know, poor people engaged in sad random pornography and Persian cats with blood red eyes hissing from atop warm Trinitrons. Or maybe work on a cruise ship publishing the on-ship newspaper. MRS. SIMMONS IS 70 TODAY, or RENT COSTUMES EARLY FOR THE BALL! But you just wait. Ambition lurks. Bechtol will scoop me up. I'll escape.

Dan, like half the population of Lancaster, is on welfare. In Lancaster, all new ideas on how to make money are welcome. Even KittyWhip® offers new hope for the dead.

Last fall, as part of my introductory course in hotel/motel management, Front Office Procedures 105, I tried to involve a few of my friends in a front-desk simulation exercise encouraged by the Lancaster Community College

Hospitality Industry Education Department for students planning to reach top management. This was a noncredit simulation exercise on top of a course load that already included computerized reservations systems, front desk theory, and PBX department & hotel security. All theory and no simulation makes for an unmotivated, unprepared employee. The results of my simulation experiment?

Skye: "What's Biloxi? Isn't Biloxi a drug?"

Mei-Lin: "Uh—what's a valise?"

Harmony: "Fair sir, mightn't thee, perchance, explain to me these kilometer things?"

Bon voyage.

Skye, Mei-Lin, and Harmony are the future of front-desk service. Travelers are doomed. My friends couldn't find their own city on a map. They barely know what year they're living in.

"Those Eastern states are all so tiny," moped Gaïa after it was conclusively proved that she could not locate Boston, Massachusetts, on a map. "Couldn't they all just merge? And wouldn't merging make better business sense?"

"Fair's fair," added Anna-Louise. "I mean, if we're supposed to learn all of the new information people are inventing, we have to throw old information out to make way for the new stuff." I guess history and geography are what's being thrown away. But then what is geography to Harmony or Pony or Davidson, who speak to people all over the planet every day all at once on their computer nets and modems? Or what is history to Mei-Lin or Gaïa, who receive seventy-five channels on their families' dish-TV systems? Anna-Louise is right: fair's fair. And my friends are better prepared mentally than anybody else for the future that is actually going to arrive. Nature always prepares her babies for what they'll need. Me and my friends are throwing-out consultants. Wish us all luck; we send you résumés and kisses.

"Mother!" shrieks Daisy. "You can't be serious. KittyWhip is a joke." We're driving back home with Murray; Anna-Louise left to work the matinee shift.

"Now, cookie, don't be too hard on the idea. Who are we to judge? Maybe there's a nugget of business sense to your grandfather's idea and we're just not seeing it. And think about it—Kittykat must be so bored eating the same pet food day in day out."

"Jasmine, Kittykat is a *cat*. Cats have no concept of variety. Their brain is the size of a pea. They forget their owners half the time when they come back from vacations. And you think they want *salad bars*?"

"Well, you never know. We could at least give the idea a try."

But I can tell from the glint in her eye that Jasmine's caught KittyWhip® fever—like a plague sweeping a medieval walled town—you never know who'll be the next to go. Daisy can see the glint, too, and the two of us make *oh-no* faces. As well, I feel bad because maybe our financial situation is much worse than I had suspected. Callow youth.

Halfheartedly I propose to Jasmine that her father simply share with her a fraction of his fortune rather than making her degrade herself being a KittyWhip® pyramid-scheme rep, but my enthusiasm peters out. We all know Grandpa believes in fierce individualism: no free lunches blah blah blah. He's probably just mean, and besides, today's Mark's birthday and we all want to be in nice moods.

"Stop here," says Daisy. "I want to pop out and buy soy milk."

16

My, my.

It's been a busy week here in Lancaster. Jasmine got a haircut and Grandma and Grandpa went bankrupt.

I'm commandeering the Comfortmobile north, up to the Canadian border, as I scoop out the news bites for my trusty crime-fighting companion Anna-Louise, hunched at my side, fiendishly scanning the FM dial with the SEEK button in pursuit of hiphop stations from the coast, which wonk in and out of reception clarity.

"Dyed red and megashort," I say, "like starfish legs suckered down on her crown. So extreme she looks like she's making a political statement."

"A pixie cut. Retro."

"She says short red hair makes her feel glitter-rock. Bisexual. It looks good, too. Makes her look even younger—like a starlet at Cannes."

"So eating lentils must work."

"I guess. Oh, and she's using makeup now, too. Daisy's pissed because suddenly Jasmine's borrowing extensively from the cosmetics museum. Daisy's whining because Jasmine doesn't have the same season skin tone."

Dormant volcanoes offering the threat of hot sticky lava stand guard to the west, while moisture in the air allows our skins to relax. Forests on either side of the road are a novelty to us prairieites, seemingly full of forgotten secrets, like a place we lived long ago before our memory truly began.

"Speaking of haircuts," I ask, "did you remember to bring the scissors?"

"Right here." Anna-Louise pats her nylon fanny pack, then rattles through the box of CD's, abandoning the FM dial. She's going to try a most superior new haircut on me when we arrive at the Aloha Motel up in Canada.

As for Grandma and Grandpa's bankruptcy, Tuesday night they rang the front doorbell, Grandma in tears, Grandpa ashen faced.

"Dad . . . Mom. Sit down," said Jasmine. "Have some lentil melt. Legumes are calming."

"Beans? I don't know, cupcake," said Grandpa.

"How can you think of your gut at a time like *this?*" shrieked Grandma."

Grandpa, smelling already the spooky, cat-pee bouquet of cilantro, balked at free food: "Maybe later, Jaz. Howzabout a scotch?"

Turns out they lost all their savings and (stupid stupid) their equity in the now-collapsed Roger W. Friedman Cashex 2000 Mutual Fund of Arlington, Virginia.

"Oh, Grandpa. Not your *equity*," I moaned.

"Third mortgages," Grandma desultorily informed the floor.

"*Roger*," hisses Grandpa, "lives in Brunei with a harem of thirteen-year-olds. Can't even touch the bastard."

"Sort of a shame, don't you think?" asks Anna-Louise as we see signs telling us the Canadian border is only half a song away.

"Hardly. Serves them both right for being such cheap weasels with their loot before they lost it all. Imagine making your daughter sell cat-food dispensers while you traipse off to Beijing in Executive Class. Maybe they'll become nice people now. And I won't suffer watching them sell KittyWhip for real." Callow youth. But think about it: Grandma and Grandpa own and run everything—too much money and too much free time. Young people are doomed.

I will mention at this point, though, an incident that happened at the dinner table the night Grandma and Grandpa came over. Just before he left, Grandpa started coughing—real tubercular lungbusters—and we could only sit politely waiting for the coughing bout to end. When we thought he was finished, we were standing up, leaving the table and heading for the door, when suddenly Grandpa made one final last 1,000 kiloton looger, right into the sandalwood candelabra Jasmine bought at the Snohomish craft fair, extinguishing all three candles. We then proceeded to the front door and said our good-byes to him and Grandma. Then, while Jasmine, Grandma, and Grandpa were walking down to the soon-to-be repossessed Lincoln Continental, Daisy, Mark, and I walked back to the dining room table and looked at the candelabra in silence. While Daisy and Mark stood by the candles, I fetched a box of decorative matches from the fireplace, returned to the table, and relit the candles. Once these candles were all burning fully, the three of us moved in on them, and without speaking, we blew them out together, just as Jasmine was walking back in the door.

"What are you kids doing?" she asked us, but we never replied, and she walked into the kitchen. The moment was not one that could be talked about. The moment was entirely ours. As brothers and sister we knew instinctively that if we were going to stand in darkness, best we stand in a darkness we had made ourselves.

17

A strange new country. Just what I needed. Canada: wet licorice-whip roads, strange radio, new foods, and lowered biopressure.

And car cramps, too—several hours' worth. Anna-Louise and I exit the Comfortmobile amid a dense forest a half hour from Glen Anna. We're yawning and gorging on oxygen, like astronauts returning to earth, stretching, jumping up and down, and scratching our scalps while drinking in the trout-gray sky.

"Catch?" I ask.

"Fab." I toss Anna-Louise her baseball glove, and on the gravel roadside we toss the baseball back and forth, an activity with a rhythm that, once established, allows us to almost close our eyes, as though a science-fiction force is guiding our muscles.

Playing catch like this is like dancing, with one dancer taking the lead, in this case Anna-Louise in her red down vest, hiking boots, and corduroys making our game vector off the road, into the forest. With each catch Anna-Louise moves deeper into the trees and I follow, silent, feeling seduced by a genetic secret, like a teenager learning to masturbate, not knowing what I'm doing, but continuing regardless, deeper into the forest, the ball miraculously managing to avoid the staid, butlerlike hemlocks and firs between us, the brush and undergrowth muffling all sound save for the beating of blood in my ears and the slap of the ball in our gloves.

This slapping sound moves closer with each successive volley, closer and closer as Anna-Louise and I move in on each other over the quiet, oh-so-quiet cool dry moss. Closer and closer. Until we meet.

Later, as we leave the forest and hear the crunch of road gravel under our boots, we feel drops of rain on our cheeks, an event that means much to people like us, who live in another, more arid part of the world.

"Do you realize, Tyler," says Anna-Louise, "the entire time we were in the forest it rained steadily and not once did we approach a state of moistness? There was a storm and we didn't even know."

Hopping into the Comfortmobile, Anna-Louise and I sweep the hemlock needles off our bodies, needles that cover us everywhere.

18

Rain is falling in sheets. Anna-Louise is decoding a road map that tells us Glen Anna is mere minutes away, at a road fork just over the hill.

Our recent forest adventure has mellowed us considerably. Slowing us down, too, is the appearance ahead of us of a logging truck, stacked with jumbo Douglas fir logs, the ends of which are spray-painted with red numbers and which are almost piercing our windshield.

"Male handwriting," notes Anna-Louise. "Like on Jasmine's forehead."

I wonder what these numbers and letters mean. Alphanumeric codes, no doubt, to assist a value-adding computer in Yokohama in converting the logs into chopsticks or paper towels.

"My mother told me," Anna-Louise adds, "that tourists helicoptering in to view the ruins from the Mount Saint Helen's eruption flew over clear-cuts and said, 'Oh my God, this is more horrible than any scenario I could have imagined.' "

I mention to Anna-Louise that there's a clear-cutting site I've read about on Vancouver Island so dreadful, so horrifying and violated, it became known as the Black Hole, and even the loggers were sickened by what they had done and the area was closed off to all visitors.

"Ooh! This is my favorite song," announces Anna-Louise, as a psychedelic-revival dance mix bursts forth from the Comfortmobile's speakers. "Pump it up. This girl's just gotta dance."

The logging truck turns out of sight and out of mind, onto a gravel access road. The Comfortmobile throbs like a rave party as we zoom through the Canadian wetness, up the steep hill, our motion liberated. Anna-Louise is freedom dancing as much as is possible within the plush, matte-black confines of the car.

"You have the camera? We're almost there," says Anna-Louise.

"Never without," I answer, pushing down the throttle as we crest the hill, filled with expectation of the vista to come.

There is nothing here. There is no Glen Anna.

Or rather, there *was* a Glen Anna. We just missed it. The forest is gone and there are no words I can say. There are no magic spells I can cast to bring back the trees.

Anna-Louise and I are sitting on a stump, a stump as large as a giant's dinner table, in a prairie of gray mud and stumps. There is nothing on any horizon. There are no birds or animals because there is nothing for the birds and animals. The loss is absolute and Anna-Louise and I are soaking wet, still too numb to cover our heads.

We sit on the stump and Anna-Louise pulls out a small

pink plastic comb and starts to comb my limp, wet hair, the hair she was going to cut tonight. She has removed the scissors from her nylon fanny sack and thrown them away. They lie splayed open across generations of bleeding orange tree rings on the stump on which we sit, and Anna-Louise and I are weeping because all the trees are gone.

Don't talk to me.

19

This is my world: my world, filled with my family and music and school and friends and hopes and worries. Sometimes my world moves too fast and sometimes it's frame-frozen. But my world is mine; it is my chalk circle.

I'm lying on my bed, looking at my ceiling. The only light I see comes from my globe farm across the room, my cluster of orange-and-blue planets generating light and warmth.

This morning before I went to school I was feeding a squawking, pushy blue dance company of Steller's jays from my second-floor window. Cheezie Nuggies: tasty bite-size treats made from petroleum by-products and cheerfully packaged to enhance the pleasure of late-nite TV viewing. The jays were going cuckoo over the Cheezie Nuggies, most definitely savoring the zesty cheddary richness, scurrying back to their nests to regurgitate from their crops their loads of dull little seeds and romping expectantly back to my windowsill for a fresh new load of Nuggies. That was when Jasmine came from behind and cuffed me on the ear.

"Hey, Mom, what was that for?"

"What do you think you're doing, young man? Feeding these poor jays these . . . these . . . *Cheezie Nuggies*. They're about as nutritious as barbecue lighter fluid. Shame on you."

She cuffed me on the ear again, smiling.

"What *is* this, Jasmine—Kent State? The birds have a long winter ahead. They need their calories. I'm saving them untold hours of running around foraging for grubs or whatever it is they eat."

"Birds have no concept of leisure time, Tyler. Listen, you're kind, sure, to feed the jays Cheezie Nuggies, but the birds have to fly south, and if you keep feeding them they'll never be motivated enough to leave. We'll find them lying out in the front yard, dead from technical malnutrition, even though their little bird tummies are full. Now leave the birds be."

The jays' tempers turned testy. One bird hopped onto the windowsill, not one breath away from my face, and screeched ferociously. Pretty birds; unfortunate voices.

"Oh, all right, Jasmine. G'wan. *Shoo!*" The jay darted away and I shut the window.

"Did you and Anna-Louise have a good trip to Canada?"

"No."

"I'm sorry to hear. But we'll have to discuss it at dinner tonight. I'm late for work. What time did you arrive home last night?"

"One-thirty."

Jasmine pecked me on the forehead. "Skip your first class. Oh, and I have a surprise. Guess who's coming to visit Lancaster?"

"Who?"

"Miss France. Your pal Stephanie, nudge-nudge."

"Oh?" I said, my voice cracking.

"That's right. I wrote the times and dates on the blackboard She's bringing her friend, Monique. They're renting a car in Seattle and driving around for a while. She sounded sweet."

"Um. Right."

"And no doubt Anna-Louise will enjoy seeing her, too. Don't you think?" Torture time. "I have to run now, dimples. See you at dinner. Turn off the coffee maker when you go." She winked and left the room.

Now it is night.

So Stephanie is coming to Lancaster. Dear God. I'd intended to keep her buried inside me like uranium ore. I'd intended to keep her an unsolved mystery, like a DC-10 once discovered crashed in the Mexican desert with no wings. Lancaster and Europe used two independent planets, and now these planets are bent on collision. *Quelle* mess.

Above me, Kittykat is batting on the roof with her paws, insistently, gently. What does she want?

PART
TWO

PART
TWO

20

Okay. I'll talk about Europe.

Europe: landing in Amsterdam's Schiphol Airport I could already tell I was in a different world. The Dutch women all looked like stewardesses and the Dutch men all looked like game-show hosts. The pleasingly modern steel corridors through which I wheeled my luggage en route to the trains to downtown smelled contradictorily like the manure spores of the manicured Legolike farms bordering the runway. Waiting for my connecting train to downtown, I fingered a winged name tag I had begged from the airline stewardess as a souvenir for Anna-Louise (HELLO, MY NAME IS: . . . *Oh, Miss?*). I was even then beginning to understand that when you arrive on the doorstep of Europe, you are given a pair of wings—not for using to fly up into the sky, but rather with which to fly backward in time.

* * *

My first six Euroweeks before I met Stephanie are a blur of impressions—experiences rather than relationships. Black bicycles; perfect little berries; omnipresent MTV; intelligent credit cards; ugly denim outfits; hot young Italian kids, *paninari*, on Vespa motorcycles wearing the most scorching outfits—so hip they should be arrested.

The one true friend I made during this period was Kiwi, a New Zealander I met on my first night in Amsterdam at Bob's Youth Hostel on the Nieuwezijds Voorburgwal. Kiwi was a brash, theory-filled, semishaven cocktail enthusiast from Dunedin on the South Island. He was the exception to the rule of youthful summer Eurofriendships, friendships based on "mutual assured disposability," (Kiwi's term) the myriad of relationships experienced between Susans and Petras and Volkers and Clives and Mitsuos and Julios and Daves who meet in Europe's cramped train compartments and squalid youth hostels, which seem to always smell vaguely of sperm and café au lait.

Like most Eurailers, Kiwi and I would travel for a while, drive each other nuts, split up, convert currencies, and then recombine a week or so later in another city with new tales of new firsts. I remember Kiwi shouting out to me, his face beaming from a second-class window pulling into the Geneva *Bahnhof:* "Had me first three-way in Barcelona!"

More Euronuggets, more experiences: the exciting nebulous whiff of potential explosive death while rereading the same *International Herald Tribune* for the 99th time in a Milan train station; affluence (so much affluence!); the eerie chocolate-box melancholy of cities unbombed during World War II—Zurich and Nancy; nuclear power stations silhouetting the horizons; quartets of swarthy, walrus-mustached factory workers sardined into tiny sewing-machine cars, each worker smoking eleven cigarettes at once, each screaming at each other and whizzing pointlessly through the carbon-choked, depressing-as-hell Czechoslovakian suburbs while their ignored womenfolk stand on the side of the road like dime-store cigar Indians. All alien; all charming, but, as I wrote in a postcard to Anna-Louise:

Europe lacks the possibility of metamorphosis (how egghead!). Europe is like a beautiful baby with superdistinctive features who, while beautiful, is also kind of depressing because you know exactly what the child will look like at twenty, at forty, at ninety-nine. No mystery.

Further squished into that same postcard:

I think I'm overdosing on history here. I'm never sure if wearing hip clothing in a church is a "sin." One too many volleys of fireworks set to Rolling Stones music in Monaco. One too many son et lumière shows. All too many domes and refineries and people praying to gods I'll never even know about, let alone understand. Feeling cramped is fun for the first few days but then you become sick of the sensation, but they never uncramp here. Ick. What I want is to be back home and on the coast in a big glass house on the edge of the planet, on the Olympic Peninsula, say, and just look out over the water and nothing nothing else.

I showed this card to Kiwi before mailing it. He agreed with me, feeling like he wanted to be in a glass house on the southern tip of New Zealand's South Island, with nothing in between himself and Antarctica.

"Antarctica?" I asked. "Did you know Antarctica is really two continents, not one, joined together by an ice bridge?"

"Really? Sort of like divorced parents."

"Exactly."

A question: why did I go to Europe in the first place? Well, it's a miracle I even arrived there considering the stupefying wall of indifference I encountered when presenting the idea to family and friends. ("Europe? I don't get it," said Harmony. "We have a perfectly good Europe here at EPCOT in Florida. It's not good enough or something?")

But I had my reasons. I remember peddling my fake watches and wondering what sort of land would make the real watches. And I wanted to see what sort of world my ancestors found so intolerable they needed to leave. And I'd heard reports Europe was the total place for partying.

In general I remember thinking how modern and snappy Europe appeared in photos: lively tinkling geometric buildings sprouting like crystals from the tedious stone drabness below. Europe seemed like a place where the future was advancing more rapidly than in Lancaster, and I love the future, so that was *that*. Funward ho.

But after three weeks of Eurailing, Europe's patina of modernity was dulling considerably. Europe tries to be so modern, but the effort always sort of, well . . . *flops*. Germany, to the country's credit, is higher-tech than the inside of a CD player, but their platform toilets are like a torture device straight out of the Inquisition. France has never heard of Sunday shopping. And in Belgium I saw a nuclear cooling tower with *moss* growing on its convex northern slope. Modern?

* * *

In scanning snapshots of my European trip, I have noticed a trend not apparent to me while I was over there. The trend is of corporate logos having quietly inserted themselves into my memories. U.S. pizza franchises glow behind smiling duets of big-boned Australian teachers named Liz. Cowboy cigarettes and courier vans backdrop trios of travel-worn Ontario sophomores. Camera companies and computer makers' logos endorse T-shirted Cornell University Eurailers. Most surrealistic of all are "cola totems"—cylindrical poster pillories papered to resemble cans of cola, embedded in the drowsy, druggy poodle-shat canalscape of Amsterdam, where millions of IV needles lie encaked in the olive-green gorp beneath the water's surface and where at night tall thin cookie-tin houses separated by narrow lanes seemingly dissolve into the black sky. Strange how I never even noticed these logos while I was actually there, but now I'm home there's no way to excise them from my hard-copy memories.

21

Finally, six weeks before my scheduled return, I was rattling south in a train headed from Denmark to Paris, fleshing out my passport with yet one more stamp (Belgium: red triangle) and rolling my eyes at yet another ungenerous railroad ham sandwich and tinned fizzy orange drink bearing opening instructions in fourteen languages. Kiwi and I were "talking hostel" with a couple from Texas, and the four of us were all in dire need of haircuts, baths, PABA lotion, and multivitamins.

I then read a letter from Daisy, mailed to me care of American Express in Copenhagen. The stamps on the envelope were upside down and enclosed was a nose ring from Murray (*wear nose rings* now!) and Mark's refrigerator drawing of the Plants, which pierced my heart and made me feel inexpressibly tired and lonely and homesick. In an enclosed letter Daisy pleaded with me to swipe a flower from Jim Morrison's grave in Paris and at the bottom of the letter, after a goodly amount of civic gossip, she had written the PS:

Mark has a summer cold and he licked the stamps on this envelope with his nostrils. I hope this doesn't make you sick. D.

The sky outside the train drizzled and glowered colorlessly over the choppy Nord Zee, and the four of us in the compartment lost our will to talk and sat pooped and quiet as we passed ineffectually through the world.

Then slightly further on I noticed a sight still remaining in my mind as representing the low point of my trip. I saw a cold misty pale yellow field of endive rising above the train tracks to the east, at the top of which was a 17th or 18th century redbrick house, isolated and surrounded by not even a shrub, let alone a tree.

Now, while a house in a field is no big deal, what I found peculiar was what had been altered on this particular house. For reasons I can't imagine, all of the doors and windows of the house had been replaced with exhaust louvers, and the house, via these orifices, was breathing a faint steam that drifted downward onto the fields. But from where was this breath coming? In my mind's eye I saw a nuclear power plant outside of Antwerp. Connected to this plant's bowels underneath the earth was a long black tube that ran for miles and miles underneath houses and roads and schools and coffee shops and forests, in the end coughing its dry warm airs through this house's gilled louvers and over the Belgian countryside—over vegetables, over milk cows, and over the graves of dead Europeans of old. I had never seen a landscape in which human beings seemed so irrelevant.

Kiwi asked if I felt I had a flu coming on, and I said no.

Mark's giants had abandoned their parade floats in Europe, too. Right then I knew I wanted to return home, but as fate would operate, before I was able to create new plans, I arrived in Paris.

22

It was mid-July, and the boulevards of Paris were flush with both tourists and Parisians visibly wincing with anticipation for their August holidays, like a man who has to pee badly. The sun shone hot and tanning salonlike over the city's shortbread-yellow buildings, its Gypsies, its smug Euroyuppies, its exhaust fumes, and its decaying ambulance vibratos. Algerians and Arabs were everywhere, as were an inexhaustible supply of American and Canadian tourists in mix-'n'-match traveltime garb invariably tinged with some sort of function: Polo shirts the color of after-dinner mints featuring built-in passport holders; shoes telling the time; women in glossy helmet perms no doubt concealing mace sprayers; men in Kendoll haircuts concealing self-improvement cassettes to be listened to on Walkmans while strolling through the Louvre.

Kiwi and I sat sipping cups of strong coffee in a fenced-in sunny sidewalk café along "*avenue Aimez-Moi*" deep in the Left Bank. Kiwi was cranky as we inspected life's parade passing us by because his passport had been nicked earlier on Avenue Foch and he had to go to the New Zealand embassy to "grovel for a refill."

A glazier's truck meanwhile stopped for a red light on the street in front of us, its mirrored sides casually multiplying the city, and the two of us couldn't help but be spontaneously and severely confronted with a full-length vision of ourselves: tanned and shabby, our bodies fat-free and muscular from six weeks of urban Eurohiking, our bodies ready to burst from within the frayed seams of our overworn garments washed irregularly in bidets spanning the continent.

We were shocked by our appearances; they galvanized Kiwi into action. "Hey, mate. Enjoy-ay-voo at the graveyard," he said, hopping the fence. "I'm off. Meet tonight outside the Quebec Delegation. Nine o'clock." I then watched Kiwi gallumph down the sidewalk, his four-food-group-enhanced body far bigger, more wholesome, and more innocent than the Europeans as a group, as New Worlders so often are.

I then drank my painfully sweet espresso coffee, felt my teeth dissolve, licked my lips, checked my watch, strapped on my knapsack, paid my bill, checked the sun, and then descended into the earth itself in a *métro* entrance, enveloped in its faintly fishy-fecal odor and its chants of beggars and the roars of technology, and then rode, with a faint headache, toward the Père-Lachaise cemetery in pursuit of Daisy's flower.

Once, when I was much younger, I had a friend named Colby who died of misfiring proteins, of cancer, and his body was buried in a cemetery next to an oat field outside of Lancaster. In summer I still go to Colby's grave, he being the only person I ever knew who actually died, and I try to imagine the sensation of being dead—not breathing, turning off my mind—nonexisting. But this imagining never works. Life always wins. I emerge from these bouts triumphant and overflowing with energy, gulping the wind, reaching for birds, feeling so vital I can hardly breathe.

I was unsure if a European cemetery would elicit from me the same reaction as I entered the enormous Père-Lachaise graveyard in the northeast of Paris, entering through its stone gates demarcating another galaxy altogether, a galaxy of rambling widows in black, terse crones, legless nonagenarians, trees trimmed like topiaried show dogs, a steaming midsummer sky building toward a maybe-storm. Dead flowers lay strewn upon elegantly hewn tombs. Traffic noise had disappeared, and boxing me in all around were squared hedges bearing flowers I had never seen before. I felt listless. Pebbles I kicked with my desert-booted toes jumped in slow motion and emitted no sound as I strolled deeper, deeper into the graveyard, all sounds either muffled or gone, as though I were walking into that British Columbian forest with Anna-Louise, Paris already being filtered out of my brain, being replaced by the gas that composes so much of the air but does so little, argon.

I found myself at the tomb of Oscar Wilde, and with no other people nearby, I stripped myself of my shirt and leaned against the stone, suntanning, bagging what diminishing rays there were to be had from the clouded sun. I sniffled with hay fever; I turned my head around and licked the dusty stone. I surprise even myself on occasion.

A drop of rain fell on my taut neck. I felt lost in a room where the river of Time is not allowed to flow, but I was awakened by a crone hobbling by, screeching at the hedges, still mourning, no doubt, for family members lost in a distant and pointless European war.

Kitty-corner across the graveyard I headed in pursuit of the flower from Jim Morrison's grave, needing no map, following instead the kids I saw: bedraggled or chic, sleek and ragtag alike, mostly from the New World, often stoned and quiet, and clashing strangely with the cemetery's ancient Old World mood, outrageously out of place amid its overcarved frumpery, and looking like cartoon ostriches clad in tutus and scrambling quacking through a rainy-day funeral.

"Kind of puts the *fun* back in *fun*eral, doesn't it?" said Mike, a guy my age from Urbana, Illinois, who was burying a joint in the soil next to Morrison's tombstone. Nearby, a trio of Coloradans were painting Canadian flags on the back of their backpacks both as antiterrorism talismans and as their free ticket into the Saint-Jean-Baptiste celebrations to be held that night at the Quebec Delegation building. "It'll be Babe City, just you wait and see," said Mike's friend Daniel, helping a girl named Chyna (Denver) apply a maple leaf resembling a spade from a deck of playing cards more than any maple leaf I'd ever seen. Surrounding me on all sides kids were smoking hash and joints and carving, felt-penning, and spray-painting their names and hometowns and "messages to Jimmy" all over the neighboring stones.

I asked Chyna why she had come to visit the grave as she handed me an unsolicited but much appreciated beer and she said, "Because knowing my idols are dead makes death a lot less scary place."

We clinked bottles and I said "*skaal*," and I told her about Denmark, where I'd just been, where clinking glasses and saying "*skaal*" means you're allowed to switch from using the formal form of *you* over to the casual form. The transition means you can officially consider each other to be friends. "Because of this rule, a lot of Danish humor revolves around avoiding clinking glasses with other people that first time."

"Huh?"

"Never mind. Where are you three headed next?" I asked, referring to Chyna's friends Stacy and Allison.

"Greece—"

"She's taking the sex cure!" shouted Allison, at which Chyna blushed.

"Greece is supposed to be, like PartyWorld," Chyna said, "We're taking the ferry from Italy. You know. The Adriatic thing."

A group of us shortly left the cemetery, beers in hand and me with a daisy for Daisy in my backpack. There were Chyna and Stacy and Allison; Mike and Daniel, as well as two carpentry apprentices from Bergen, New Jersey. The eight of us felt conspicuously young and aggressively alive, feeling, yes, the same way I feel when I leave Colby's grave.

We had the absolution of youth, which bubbled over our brief but ultraintense travelers' friendships—brief friendships allowing us complete license to reinvent ourselves and our personal histories sans reprisal or exposure, to flex our sex wings and imbibe forbidden substances in graveyards.

Our browned exposed limbs popping out of our khakis and T-shirts and our puppy-dog naïveté were our true passports from the New World that afternoon as we entered the real world—our passports and our armor as we entered the jaded, elegant hysteria of Paris.

23

It was that night I met Stephanie.

The noise and the camaraderie and the endless free beer of the Quebec party quickly gave rise to claustrophobia on my part, and I felt the need to remove myself from people and clutter. I ditched Kiwi and the evening's gift sampler of semidisposable Europals and randomly strolled into a district known as the Port Dauphine, the neighborhood naughty Parisians head to when in pursuit of *les jeux clandestins*.

All in all I felt I was at the end of an epoch bigger than just my holiday in Europe. The next day I was planning to change my ticket and jet home, having made my decision on the train from Denmark. Maybe the air of Paris was making me feel like this. Maybe I was just intoxicated by too much pilsner and too much *métro* air; by sweet almond cookies and reflexive recoils from ambulant street trash. Maybe I simply missed Anna-Louise dreadfully, felt isolated and small-townish and couldn't help but notice couples in love around all corners. Again, too many experiences but no relationships, as my travelogue all too deeply reveals.

Life seemed to be hopelessly waltzing by me then as I downed shooters of licorice-sweet 51 liqueur, my emptied glasses lined across the gray-veined marble tabletop of yet another outdoor café in which I chose to rest. And I must say I felt just the littlest bit dozy as I swam through the sultry night air toward a black convertible beetle car, which caught my eyes as its sodium-yellow headlights flashed while it was pulling into a nearby slot. And I must admit, too, I was feeling maybe a bit dreamy as I jumped the bistro's low glass fence and ambled toward that car, toward the lovely carmine-red lips inside, which caught my eyes in particular, lips visible through the windshield, the wipers of which, for an unknown reason, were flipping back and forth.

I saw these lips smile and poke out the window saying " 'allo" to me but I was then also momentarily transfixed by the glinting bistro lights reflected on the onyx skin of Stephanie's car. Yes, as I squinted and looked at those gleaming reflected lights, they looked like—they looked just like the stars.

I think there is a Paris inside us all.

Apparently I passed out almost immediately, but not before I said hello and gallantly kissed Stephanie's lips. Then my knees buckled and I fell to the cobblestones and the bistro proprietor, an inflamed old ogress, assumed Stephanie to be my best friend and made her pay for all my shooters, which Stephanie then did, even though she'd never seen me before in her life and such payments were quite out of keeping with her character, as I learned later on.

Stephanie and her friend Monique, who was sitting in the passenger seat, then loaded me into the car's rear seat, my head lolling over the edge like a waggy dog's, and they drove around Paris all night with me as show-and-tell. At one point, I was told later, I was almost sold into slavery to a clique of Bois de Boulogne transvestites in return for a carton of Marlboros, and an avenue Sebastapol matron walking her dachshund nearly purchased herself a houseboy for a song.

Anyway, I awoke the next morning with gerbils nesting in my brain, but otherwise with no serious damage, cool and comfortable underneath a cotton-and-down comforter in Stephanie's sixth-floor mansard-roofed apartment.

Stephanie and Monique were squeezing oranges in a kitchen that resembled a high-school chem lab accessorized with *Elle* magazine clippings, a collection of bottled vinegars, and derelict coffee cups rimmed with a broad spectrum of colorful lipstick traces.

"Good morning, Mr. America," she shouted to me across the sunny clothes-strewn apartment. "Come over and have *petit déjeuner*. You must be very very hungry."

24

Stephanie.

While Anna-Louise would be content to stay home crocheting Bible covers for the poor, Stephanie is selfish almost to the point of being autistic, dragging me out until dawn, forcing me to escort her to out-of-the-way cocktail hells, never offering to pay for her drinks, all to abandon me at the last minute and catch the dawn's first RER train to Neuilly and her parents in a spur-of-the-moment homesick impulse.

How selfish *is* Stephanie? In bed I ask her to scratch my favorite place, just behind my ears, but she won't scratch even once because then scratching would become just one more task she would have to execute on a routine basis. "How boring," (pronounced "barring": Stephanie never pronounces her vowels right). How attractive.

* * *

I never left Stephanie's apartment after that first morning. Kiwi brought over my backpack from the hostel and he himself became a part of our Flintstonian summer ménage, pairing with Monique, participating in our summer rituals, smug that he and I were natives now, not tourists, and like myself waking up in the morning with a throat sore from having practiced French in his sleep. We would bask on the rooftop of Stephanie's rue Mallet-Stevens apartment block (parentally funded), shiny with sunscreen, Stephanie and Monique's sunglassed faces like time-lapse photos of zinnias following the sun. Evenings we would pay too much for lemonades and watch the sun set over Paris from the rooftop of the Pompidou, afterward descending to the Eurotrash-clogged piazza below to taunt the mimes and watch the digital clock that counts down the seconds to the year 2000.

Stephanie is a rich girl from a mighty bourgeois family. She's a dilettante student at the Sorbonne, blowing off her courses in chemistry (of all subjects), spending her almost incalculable free time steeped in food and clothes, concocting untasty little offerings in "the lab," and waging fashion wars against her peers, justifying the efforts as self-defense. "How you appear is *av*-erything in Paris, Tyler. *Tout*." On the windowsills above Stephanie's kitchen sink is her bottled vinegar collection—elaborately crocked solutions stuffed with sprigs of tarragon, gnarls of rosemary, and fusillades of peppercorns—small, delicious, self-contained but dead ecosystems. Back in Lancaster, Anna-Louise keeps a terrarium.

Are comparisons fair?

Stephanie has short black hair, opposite to Anna-Louise's long wheat-colored hair. Cannibals might pass over Stephanie's willfully undernourished frame, but they'd have Anna-Louise in the pot in a second. Anna-Louise bakes me pies occasionally; Stephanie makes me wait at our café, L'Express, for up to an hour, laughing at my weary crankiness when she sashays in, saying, "Girls are like a restaurant, Tyler, with *tay*-rrible service. Girls will make you wait and wait and wait and wait and wait and wait and wait and just when you think you will scream and leave the restaurant, suddenly a *merveilleux* meal arrives, more fantastic than anything you had hoped for."

One early morning after riding back from cocktail hell on the first subway of the day, Stephanie and I were exiting the subway stop nearest to her apartment, a stop curiously named Jasmin (pronounced *Zhazzmá*). After this we walked home up a steep hill, the butter light of dawn coloring all transactions with innocence, when we saw another young couple, similar to ourselves: he in a bomber jacket and chinos, she in a simple blue dress and gold jewelry.

"If you wave to them," said Stephanie, "and they return your wave, then they are in love . . . because they can be *jay*-nerous with their love."

"If they don't wave back?" I asked.

"Then they do not have any *jay*-nerosity and their lives will be full of pain."

I waved and then I laughed as the couple smiled and bowed in return. But now that I recall the moment, I don't seem to remember *Stephanie* doing any waving. Hmmm. These French girls. They're so street smart. So sophisticated. I once asked Stephanie if she was insulted when I, a complete stranger, came up to her and kissed her that first night in the Port Dauphine.

"But no," she replied. "Why should I be? We are animals.

Our first instinct when we see an object of beauty is to eat it."

Gosh.

To give the impression all was roses would be misleading. We argued frequently, and more than just minor squabbles over possession of the Walkman headphones on long subway rides (one headphone each became the law as we sat shoulder to shoulder, the Dead cranked to eleven on the volume switch).

Like so many Europeans I met, Stephanie enjoyed arguing for the sake of arguing. She was continually egging me on, goading a response, accusing me, Dan-like, of being boring when I wouldn't react to her platitudes about politics, finance, and religion. Preemptive boringness again became the rule. I suspect my nonreplies to her goadings were the main reason she deigned to spend so much time in my company—I imagine I was a radical switch from her French friends.

Not that I know *how* Stephanie interacted with her French peers. Kiwi and I were kept meticulously away from her and Monique's pals. And not that Kiwi or I minded. We were fed up with low-ambition Euroteens. Those teens. All the ones I talked to wanted to be civil servants. So wearying.

"What sucks the ambition out of the kids here, Stephanie?" I once asked on the roof of the Pompidou. She changed the subject.

My time with Stephanie was not a story. I never went from A to B, or anywhere else. Rather, Stephanie offered the promise of pleasures to come. She was an enchanting, utterly foreign, unreachable goal, like being down in the *métro* and seeing the lights of the next station visible down a dark, electrified tunnel.

I'm rambling.

There was one incident in August I remember as being odd. Paris was closed for the holidays, so Kiwi and I went to investigate a mall we'd heard about in a suburb. Versailles? The mall ended up being shut (primitive!), and subwaying back into Paris, a sensation of rootlessness took hold of me—an overwhelming feeling of being untethered, like I'd experienced in the train headed to Paris from Denmark. I told Kiwi I felt homeless, like a snail without a shell. Not five minutes later we met Stephanie and Monique at a restaurant, both downing a tray of hot, garlicky snails.

From there we went window-shopping: *lécher la vitrine* —licking the windows—cruising for TinTin merchandise and Mylar skull stickers on the Left Bank, checking out AirBus fares over crap drinks in yet another café, wishing we had Vespa scooters and the freedom Vespas bring. Walking by us while we sat in the café was an old dog with three legs being led around on a rope by a grizzled Popeye. On the dog's fourth leg, the right rear stump, was attached a hoofed prosthesis—a horse's fetlock. It was a true interspecies moment. Instead of becoming depressed, we laughed.

Monique rarely punctuated my consciousness. She was like a stylist trimming your hair in a town you're only passing through, spoken to in a friendly yet ephemeral manner via a mirror's reflection, in this case, Stephanie.

My lack of attention to Monique surprises me, since Monique is one of nature's sex-oozers. She was fun to hang around with because there was invariably a perpetual buzz of hormones and crime surrounding her, like pubescent girls in a stable or teenage boys in a tree fort. Monique would emerge from department stores wearing the skimpiest of dresses, yet remove several Soviet boxcars' worth of shoplifted merchandise from within the folds. Monique toyed with waiters and gendarmes and made bank clerks nervously fidget with their tie knots. Kiwi once nearly fainted from lust when he casually asked Monique about a certain dust she was brushing from her I've-been-to-New-York scarf and she replied, "Pill dust from my birth-control dispenser."

Summer fast-forwarded all too soon. Yet in spite of this speed, Lancaster and my family managed to become abstract ghosts, hard to picture in my mind, shed skins. Letters and phone calls had ceased two months previously. Jasmine, Daisy, or Anna-Louise couldn't have reached me even if they'd wanted. And like a snot, I'd only let them know of my return date and time by phoning in the middle of the day, Lancaster time, when there was a high probability of getting the phone-answering machine (nickname: Cindy), which indeed was the case.

Kiwi and I were well past the disposable-friendship stage, but the last week in Paris was spacey for all four of us as we cooled down toward each other in our attempts to play down the pain of imminent fragmentation. Our social lives took place in public rather than in private: neutral territory.

Over dinner one night I drunkenly inveigled Stephanie and Monique to come visit me in the States, the suggestion of which caused them both make mock-aghast faces, as though I'd invited them to a dungeon to gnaw on body parts. Later on, when Stephanie and Monique were dancing on the floor together (Europe), a drunk Kiwi told me, "You've got to be careful asking the Euros over for visits, mate. Because they'll come. And they'll stay forever, wanting royal treatment and not a penny for groceries, just you wait and see."

"Kiwi, piss off. You're being paranoid."

"Drop me a postcard when they plop onto your doorstep. I'll be waiting for it."

"Kiwi, why would *any*one want to visit Lancaster? Get a life."

The next day, Kiwi and I headed out to Orly Airport separately, he six hours before me. As Stephanie and I whizzed through town in a taxi on the way there, Kiwi was already somewhere over the Indian Ocean.

Stephanie, beside me in the rear seat holding her mother's evil lapdog, Clarice, looked more, well, *upholstered* than she did merely dressed, wearing a dense black velvet miniskirt with brocaded and beaded fabric, her hair lacquered, her face buffed, her eyes blackout-lensed, her hands sheathed in black lace and her thin legs sausaged into black stockings of a complex floral motif generated by a South Korean textile computer.

"Maybe you should have casters on your shoes instead of feet," I joked.

"Quoi?" When Stephanie wasn't really with me completely, she lapsed into French.

"Little wheels."

"I do not understand. You are a goof. Please be quiet."

"Nothing, then."

Stephanie (never "Steph") was in the selfish/autistic mode, anxious about weaseling a new car out of her dragon grandmother in Fontainebleau, the day's postairport destination. My departure had dropped a considerable number of rungs of significance in her world. More pressing was an Austin Mini Cooper with CD player.

I reached for the small canister of violet candies to which Stephanie was addicted and she slapped my hand, resuming her remote, tight-lipped expression, scanning the drab cement worker housing through which we were passing. I thought that if Stephanie were a room, she would be a suite at the Hotel George V, gilt, ornate, silk tufted, and chandeliered—like so much European beauty, a product of unbending rules and brutal discipline. I thought that if Anna-Louise were a room she would be that glass house on the Olympic Peninsula, overlooking the Pacific, the ceiling so high as to be invisible.

Yes. Anna-Louise. I wanted to go home and I didn't.

There was no explosion of emotion when we arrived at the Orly Airport send-off curb, Stephanie unable to dump me fast enough so as to continue in the cab off to Grandmother's. Amid the diesel fumes, bullhorns, and flaring tempers of the curbside, I felt a stab of insult as my backpack was ignominiously hurled onto the cement by the brute cabdriver barking in Turkish at Clarice, who was erupting like a car alarm in the backseat. Stephanie was tapping her toes waiting for me to depart into the terminal. I grabbed her by her upper arms, removed her sunglasses, urgently needing to make a human connection.

"Oh, Tyler. I suppose you want to be *real* here."

"I would appreciate that, yes."

She pecked me on both cheeks, like a field marshal. "You are so space age."

"You mean New Age. My mother is a hippie."

"Yes. I like you, Tyler. You are a nice boy."

Nice?

"Nice?" I strapped on my back pack. "Is that the only reason you like me. Because I'm *nice?*"

"There are other reasons. Yes."

"Like?"

"This is not the place to speak of such things. This is an airport."

I needed something personal at that moment—something to take away with me besides a French James Dean movie poster folded inside my backpack. "Just tell me one more thing you like about me, Stephanie. Just one more thing, and then I promise you can go."

She looked irritated and shifted her weight from foot to foot. The cab driver was swearing at Clarice. "Okay. I like you because you *brosh*ed your teeth and drank grapefruit juice before we went out to drink wine. I like you because when I think of you as a *yong* boy you are walking over big fields and there are no *skelle*tons in the dirt on which you walk."

"Poetry!"

She smiled, turned around, then hopped into the cab. Once in, she picked up Clarice, opened the window, then popped her head out, like the very first time I ever saw her. "I like you because you have never been in love before. And when you do have love, I know you will survive such pain when it ends. You will always recover. You are the New World."

Stephanie then shouted *mush!* to the driver, a habit of Dan's learned from my stories, which she made her own. She abandoned me there on the curb while around me, in all directions, jets rocketed out into the sky, the unknown.

I had the hallucinatory feeling of consciously doing an act for the last time, in this case, leaving Europe.

She was gone and I honestly thought that was that.

25

Needless to say, Stephanie and Anna-Louise get along like two cats in a sack.

The two met last night after Stephanie and Monique wheeled into town in a gangster-blue Buick rented at Sea-Tac Airport in Seattle, a car that would do Grandpa proud, rating a stone's throw per gallon of gas; with a dashboard touting a casino of digital, NASA-like options.

Jasmine, Anna-Louise, Daisy, Mark, and I had been eating dinner and discussing Jasmine's KittyWhip® sales strategy ("Go global, Mom!") when Mark dropped a bowl of Daisy's RastaPasta®—red, yellow, and green pasta spirals with secret sauce. Daisy said, "God, Mark, you want us to make you wear a helmet as you go through life? How can you just spaz out like that all the time?" when Mark pointed out through the dining room to the front window.

"La Car" had berthed up to the curb several hours earlier than we had anticipated and Stephanie and Monique were emerging from the velvetized interior clad in shiny, brand new country & western outfits. Both wore cowboy hats, ironed cigarette-leg jeans, and tan suede cowboy boots, with a suede bomber jacket on Monique and Stephanie in a glossy black vinyl Jeremiah Johnson fringe jacket with a toy pistol in a holster around her snap-me-in-two waist.

The five of us plus Kittykat moved toward the front window and then watched as Stephanie and Monique did postcar-ride stretchies. "It's the invasion of the Ford models," said Daisy, at which point Monique threw an invisible lasso around Stephanie, who jumped and crouched low, firing imaginary six-shots and mouthing *bang bang* at us behind our window. She then cocked her cowboy hat back, blew away a whiff of ghost smoke, and winked.

"Cool!" shouted Mark.

"I don't see," said Anna-Louise, "why Europeans always need to iron their jeans. Why do they do that? It's so lame."

We waved back cretinously, like we were on medication. Like *they* were aliens.

"I discovered the most excellent way of irritating Miss France," says Anna-Louise tonight as we sit in her ramshackle wood kitchen, rehashing last night's events. "Talk like Elmer Fudd. Mark and I discovered it by accident. Substitute *w*'s for *r*'s—'*I'm wee-wee pweezed to meet you, Miss Fwance.*' She knows you're making fun of her, but she doesn't know how. It makes her squirm. It's great."

"You're being awfully big about entertaining a visitor from a foreign land, Anna-Louise. So much for fostering intercultural harmony."

"Oh, don't you go sanctimonious on *me*, Tyler Johnson. I wore my nicest dress over for dinner last night to meet these Eurotramps, and you know what she asked me? She asked me what I wear when I want to dress up. What a cow. You were off in the kitchen nuking the nachos, *which*, you no doubt noticed, the Misses France did not deign to touch all night."

Hmmm. I must give Anna-Louise the impression I'm unequivocally on her side in these matters.

"Not only that, but she looks like she *knows* she's thin."

As far as I know, Stephanie and Monique are drifting through town "discovering the Wild West" while maxing out *Papa*'s Crédit Lyonnais bankcard. When I tried to phone Stephanie in France before her arrival, maddeningly, all I could reach was her answering machine. As far as Anna-Louise knows, Stephanie and Monique are merely friends of Kiwi, known only casually by me.

While Anna-Louise delivers her verdict on *les babes*, she is kneading the dough that will form the crust of a blueberry pie, patting the dough outward from the center. I, meanwhile, am toasting my hands over her stove's blue gas flame. My hands are frozen because earlier I accidentally locked myself into the frosty little vestibule boot room that separates the front door of Anna-Louise's apartment building from the main structure. I'd lost my key to the inside door and spent a good hour feeling sorry for myself while chattering my teeth, fantasizing I was an astronaut cut off from the mother ship, locked in a decompression chamber, like in the movie *2001*. Anna-Louise was at the community-college swimming pool, and no other tenants—neither The Man with 100 Pets and No TV nor the mirror-image bag-lady sisters—would answer their buzzers.

In the end I was rescued by the old man. He was passing through the vestibule with his kibble cart loaded with beer. In gratitude I helped him up the stairs, and when he opened the door to his apartment at least half a dozen silent, quivering little animal heads poked out, then quickly withdrew, like tendrils. I attempted to poke my own head in to see the old man's zoo, particularly to see the carp pond Anna-Louise told me the man had built on his floor, but I was gruffly thanked (*"Fuggoff!"*), then had the door slammed in my face. I then heard Anna-Louise return downstairs. (*"Are you sure that guy has a carp pond up there?" "I'm sure. I saw it once really briefly when I brought him up a parcel."*)

Anna-Louise pounds the dough.

"Mark is in love," I say. "He wouldn't leave Monique's side all night."

"Mark's just a kid," Anna-Louise snaps. "What does Daisy think of them?"

"Daisy thinks they're politically incorrect. They own furs and think protest is futile. Daisy sees all those hot Paris student riots on CNN and can't imagine what sort of fun-free youngsters wouldn't be storming the Champs-Elysées armed with with bombs, flamethrowers, pamphlets, and Lexan shields." I pick a piece of dough. "But then Daisy also sees the two as a rich dietary source of fashion hints."

I think Anna-Louise is feeling raw over the fashion episode; Stephanie and Monique's wardrobe has left her feeling like a hillbilly. "I see. And what about Jasmine. Does Jasmine like them?"

"Like? Jasmine likes *everybody*. And she was really impressed by—we were *all* impressed—by how much they knew about Lancaster, too. After you went home, we were told facts even *we* didn't know: where to procure an abortion, the region's agricultural output, the name of our congressman, the cheapest place to eat a Mexican dinner, which isotopes the Plants used to make. . . . In Europe they publish these travel guides."

"Why? They're moving here or something?" She thuds down hard on the dough.

"Nah. Only for a few days, tops. Like I told you. Discovering the Wild West."

"Don't they have lives? Don't they have school? I don't get it."

"Stephanie and Monique don't need lives. They're rich. Or their parents are. And I'm not sure about school. I think rich people have separate schools in Europe. Or maybe they've quit school. Beats me."

"So they're not staying at your house? What's the matter—not palatial enough?" She stops kneading. "Sorry. Out of line."

I'm careful not to register offense. I can't risk the consequences. "They're crashing at The Old Decoy bed & breakfast over on Van Fleet Boulevard. Near the mall."

"Hmm. And where are they tonight?"

"The Cowboy Bar."

"The Cowboy Bar? I hope they brought the Armory with them. That's the worst bar in the worst part of Route 666. It's a total scum magnet."

"The Armory" is Stephanie and Monique's collection of antiassault gear purchased in Seattle the day before driving to Lancaster: two purses full to overflowing with mace, spiked Tijuana knuckle extenders, body alarms, and taser zap toys. "The guidebook says the Cowboy Bar has a bull-riding machine. They want to see it."

"Why aren't you there to protect them?"

"They wanted to go alone. 'More authentic.' "

"Hmmm."

* * *

122

I, as can be seen, am tangled in a web of lies, semitruths, and deceit. No, I haven't told Jasmine or Daisy about my relationship to S. That way they don't have to lie to Anna-Louise.

Stephanie, meanwhile, has not been informed about Anna-Louise, though she guessed what was up in three nanoseconds. And now Stephanie is a camouflaged mobile-launched missile roving through Lancaster, footsying me under the dinner table, winking my way, monopolizing Mark's attention away from Anna-Louise, whom she subtly patronizes, making her feel provincial and poor.

Altogether, yesterday's scene was all too much for me. It was mind-blowing seeing Anna-Louise and Stephanie together in the same room—like being in a time-space warp or a tesseract. If two planets the size of earth were placed next to each other, say, only a mile apart, their respective gravities would cancel each other out in between. Were you to stand in that betweenness, you would drift in free float.

As of today I feel like I was sitting in a calm, quiet room when suddenly a Tomahawk cruise missile roared in through one window and out through another, all in a ten-thousandth of a second. Sure, my room is quiet now, but I can never see it as totally safe ever again.

Also: when I woke up this morning, my pillow was over on the floor below my globe farm; I suppose I tossed it in my sleep. But I don't remember what I dreamed.

26

Back in Anna-Louise's kitchen: "Earth to Tyler," calls Anna, lobbing a hunk of pie dough at me, which sticks to my hair.

"What?" I pluck the dough.

"You okay?" she asks. "You're spaced."

I blurt, "I'm bombing out at school." My, my, *that* sure slipped out as a surprise.

"Oh, *hardly*, Tyler,"

"No. Really. I am. This year's not like last year. I'm not working. All I do now is sleep, drink coffee, and go for car rides. Venn diagrams and ledgers are like the dark side of the moon to me." The dam is broken.

"But you look happy enough at school. I see you there every day. And you're in the cafeteria often enough."

"That's me in my recreational mode. That's not real. I tell you, I'm trashing my career potential, Anna, and you know what? I just don't care."

"Of *course* you care, Tyler. Bechtol?"

"Ciao, Bechtol." I shoot my temple with my index finger while Anna-Louise flattens her dough into a pie tin.

"It's only one semester. You can recover. You'll apply for GPA amnesty."

"My GPA's shredded. I might as well apply for night-school courses on operating a french-fry computer."

Anna-Louise trims away excess pale yellow dough like a Beverly Hills cosmetic surgeon coolly hacking away at a pop star. "I'll help you, Tyler. I've got good grades now. I can cram on your course material—I have the time."

Anna-Louise elaborates a plan of action for me that is exhausting even to listen to. After a few minutes, weary, I accept her offer, if only to preclude more sensible details of hellish study schedules, nightmare reading rotas, and dreary tutorials—sensible suggestions made sensibly over a sensible blueberry pie.

But at least I've deflected her suspicions. Anna-Louise will think all of my strange behavior of late owes entirely to an educational crisis as opposed to a crisis of the heart—if that is indeed what my problem is.

God. I feel like such a total cad, a real shit. I know full well I'd much rather simply be wearing nothing but my socks and lying across Stephanie's smooth white legs being fed little green grapes, like a carp being fed in a pond by a geisha's hand, all the while having Stephanie rub my stomach and sing out-of-key mistranslated rock and roll songs into my eyes. What a pig.

"Well, where *have* you been going, then," asks Anna-Louise, "if you haven't been slaving away studying hotel/motel management?"

"The fields," I reply. "The Toxic Waste Dump. The badlands beyond the Plants. Jogging through the old abandoned orchards. I need to gather my thoughts; collect my space.

"We'll start your tutorials tomorrow," says Anna-Louise as she escorts me to the decompression chamber, wiping her greasy hands off on a dish towel.

"On a Saturday?" I ask. Guilt. "Okay. Fine."

"I finish matinee shift at the Eightplex just before four. I have to go to the mall afterward. Can I meet you there?"

"Sure."

"Saint Yuppie. Four o'clock."

We kiss. Her hands, still mucked with domestic substances, preclude intimacy.

Driving home I pass Dan's soon-to-be-vacated apartment. Why am I becoming this human being I am? I wasn't like this before I visited Europe. Is Dan what I am slated to become? Him? Scary. Don't *I* have any say in the matter?

I feel I am forgetting how I felt when I was younger. I have to remind myself that forgetting something behind you is not quite the same as throwing it away.

The night is cold and the stars are twinkling and I wonder what is protecting our world from outer space. I wonder what permits us to keep our air, what keeps our oxygen and nitrogen and argon from being exhaled away forever into heaven. Our world seems so small—so cold against the everythingness. I look at the bare trees and feel myself losing my ability to imagine warmer places, tropical climates. Perhaps underneath this cold crust of rock there lies hidden a different world, one where pink flowers rot and stink and exude perfume all at once—a world where heat is so generous and pervasive that the cycles of life and death become confused and overlap, depositing fruits and leaves and carcasses on the ground with such speed that the soil cannot remain solid, instead forever flexing languidly like the muscle of a sleeping athlete.

My world is moving too fast once again. I think of the fact that my reserves of money will be gone soon and rev my car through the suburbs of Lancaster, but my noise is no competition for the cold, the indifference of the dark sky and the icy, faraway stars.

Once home, I enter the front door, but the temperature in the house is low. Jasmine is out at her women's group; Daisy is out collating her surf-thrash-music fanzine, *Goo*, at Mei-Lin's; Mark is in a sleeping bag watching TV, where a documentary tells how scientists have discovered a new planet. The announcer's voice speaks, saying the universe is unforgiving and cold, and I don't want to believe this.

The screen door slams behind me and I am out in the backyard and I can feel myself becoming messed up, my eyes misting, and I jump up and down, making little baby jumps, then pull my basketball jacket around me tighter, trying to shake the fear.

I see Jasmine's compost box out back near the raspberry vines—her device for generating soil—with its fermenting gluey layers of rotting bouquets, half-eaten meals, and bird gifts from Kittykat. I walk over and kneel down before the compost, sweeping away the top layer of grass clippings, the season's last, and sigh as I stick my hands deep into the hot, living breathing pulp—up to my elbows, staining my jacket—all to feel the heat generated by the planet—by Earth.

27

The birds are wearing little wigs today.

The crows are sipping cocktails and I saw barn swallows drag-racing down Uranium Avenue this morning when I went to pick up my *Wall Street Journal* at Tubs's Newsstand Such tweets and squawks—you'd think it was spring!

Something's up.

Jasmine's newly found haircut-enhanced zest for life is undergoing a momentary lapse.

"G'wan! Giddup, Jasmine! You've got a hot date. Brunch ahoy! Unlimited access to scrambled eggs! Up! I don't have the energy to boot you around the house like a lazy dog."

Jasmine makes a dispirited bleating noise from under a shroud of paisley bed sheets weighed down at the edges with a jumble of half-read self-help books. I open her bedroom window a smidgen, allowing in a fang of cold clear air and the yellow rustle of cottonwood leaves shimmying off the tree and down the street, into the unknown.

"Close the window, Tyler. God. It's so *cold!* Pass me my glasses." A hand reaches out from under the sheets and grabs the granny glasses I offer. The shroud talks: "You just wait, young man. Around thirty you'll start losing interest in meeting new people. Just mark my words. The thought of creating a new history with a new person will seem *so* exhausting you simply won't want to be bothered. You'll become too lazy to invent new memories. You'll rather hang around people you don't like simply because you already know them. No surprises."

Jasmine lowers the paisley shroud of sheeting and sees me throw her a blue dress from her cupboard. "Here. Wear that," I say. "You look good in it and"—I shuffle through her desktop—"use a dab of this." I hand her a bottle of Hell® perfume.

"But I was going to wear my Inca dress."

"Jasmine, the Inca dress is so *before*."

"Before?"

"As in before-and-after photos." I lift up the lower edge of her bed sheets and dangle a pair of blue heels from her toes. "Wear these. They show your legs off."

Jasmine sways her feet back and forth like windshield wipers. "So does Anna-Louise know about you and Stephanie?"

She's guessed. "God forbid."

"Anna-Louise is a bright girl, Tyler, and she's going to figure out soon enough what's happening. Not that the intrigue isn't obvious. Nor that it's my business. I'll shut up. But be careful. You're messing with a person who cares for you."

Jasmine spritzes her granny glasses with cleaning solution, then wipes them with a Kleenex. "I am going to give you a piece of advice, Tyler—advice I wish I'd been told in guidance class back in high school, in between the don't-do-acid and don't-drink-and-drive films. I wish our counselors had told us, 'When you grow older a dreadful, horrible sensation will come over you. It's called loneliness, and you think you know what it is now, but you *don't*. Here is a list of the symptoms, and don't worry—loneliness is the most universal sensation on the planet. Just remember one fact—loneliness *will* pass. You *will* survive and you *will* be a better human for it."

"*I'll* never be lonely, Jasmine."

"I can see *that* was a waste of breath, kiddo. Well, try not to completely forget what I just told you."

Jasmine's bedroom is the opposite side of the earth from my Modernarium. Bead vines dangle from the door; mini-vases of kitty litter support charred incense sticks; ethnic cushions and throw pillows are strewn casually in all corners. There is a rattan throne and photos of us kids pinned to the walls with jeweled brooches. Crystals hang like plump spiders in front of the windows, refracting all views of Mrs. Dufresne's next-door Disney statuary with rainbow CD winks.

We call Jasmine's room "The Harem," a sexy place about which even Dan never complained, even though his own possessions, his laptop PC and briefcase, for example, looked crazy in the environment, invasive and overcomplex, like Stealth bombers in SmurfWorld.

"Is today's lucky bachelor a hairface?" I ask.

"Fortunately," answers Jasmine. "His name's Marv. He's in software and he visits our office once a week. So he's employed."

"Where you guys having lunch?"

"Daley's Rib House over near the auto mall. Can we end the inquisition now?"

Jasmine sits on her low stool, brushing her short orange hair—the hair I'm having trouble adjusting to. I look out the window and see a sizzle of leaves eddying in the satellite dish. She starts to talk: "He'd been to the office maybe a thousand times, and he never looked at me until I renovated my hairdo. So I guess he likes modern girls. What do you think—should I wear shoulder pads?" She crosses her arms and touches her shoulders.

"No. Just be you."

"Thanks." She sighs, does a wrinkle-and-freckle check, the way Anna-Louise does, too, right out of the starting gate in the morning. I have this feeling watching Jasmine—that as you grow older, it becomes harder to feel 100 percent happy; you learn all the things that can go wrong; you become superstitious about tempting fate, about bringing disaster upon your life by accidentally feeling too good one day.

28

Ding ding. Shampoo time. Which brands of hair-care excitement will I try today? I think I'll begin with *Undead!*™, the zombie-grade preshampoo toner and revitalizer, part of my shampoo museum's Medieval and Sci-fi section.

After this? Hmmm . . . a drop of DandruffDungeon® purifying lotion for flaky scalps, followed by a lusty scrub with SlimeWarrior® (for ladies, SlimeDamsel®), the shampoo of conquerors with patented ten-minute algae-plasma slime formula, manufactured by Camelot™ of Paramus Park Mall, New Jersey—one of Earth's four great mall fortresses along with the Sherman Oaks Galleria, the West Edmonton Mall, and the Ala Moana Shopping Center of Honolulu, Hawaii.

Now for conditioner. Tough call—this cold dry weather is hell on hair. Perhaps HotLava® oil treatment? Or maybe the damage is major enough to merit They-Feed-at-Night™, the eight-hour while-U-sleep split-end reconstruction system.

No. In the end I'll condition with Hairhenge®, containing follicle-maintenance secrets devised by the ancient druids, discovered by scientists digging for runes wherever it was druids lived.

And to hold the production together, Mist of Naralon® magic styling spritz containing the revolutionary holding formula SpellCaster®, made by HairQuest™ of Big Sur, California.

Jasmine gave me a bottle of Mist of Naralon® after she spent a weekend seminar in Big Sur years ago, but I haven't used it much—it's not advertised enough and is hence suspect. Always better to buy well-advertised products—preferably those products endorsed by a celebrity like Bert Rockney, my favorite actor—steroidal death toy and star of the blockbuster Hollywood motion picture *HawkWarrior*, which I've seen five times and heartily recommend. You can always maximize your escape dollar with Bert.

Regardless: clean hair; clean body; clean mind; clean life. You could become famous at any moment and your whole personal history could be unearthed. And *then* what would they find? Turn on the shower.

29

Out my bedroom door, I march down the hallway, down the stairs, past Mark taking his daily hit of emotional crack, inhaling color cartoons in his Star Trek pajamas, jittery from too many bowls of presweetened breakfast cereal. I toddle into the kitchen for a bowl of Meuslix with Daisy, who's wearing a random selection of undergarments and sweatshirts, cruising the morning paper for her horoscope, and commencing the day's rally of phone calls.

I'm having trouble adjusting to Daisy's dreadlocks on top of Jasmine's glitter-rock supershort cut-and-dye job. Maybe people with weird haircuts are like structures that become interesting only after being wrecked—Florida ranch houses half-fallen into sinkholes; bankrupt malls; civilizations after a nuclear war. I feel a warm tragic glow knowing I may be of interest to the world only once I have been destroyed. Youthful vanity. Tip of the day: never become destroyed.

In between phone calls Daisy and I squeeze in a conversation. Daisy has her own telephone plus her own phone number to handle the volume of calls she receives. Murray says she has her own area code.

"Do anything hot last night?" I ask.

"Nada. Watched Godzilla videos in slow motion. Fought some crime." Fighting crime is Daisy and Murray's expression for getting it on. "You? Your basketball jacket's a mess. Were you helping a cow give birth?"

"Long story."

"You didn't par-*tay* with the French units?"

"Not invited."

"In any case, they're certainly able to defend themselves. But, boy—the Cowboy Bar must be the uncoolest place in town. On Earth. Oh *look*"—Daisy beams at her horoscope "—today is going to be a day of self-empowerment for me. Goody."

The doorbell rings ("Greensleeves") and Mark scampers to answer. Stephanie and Monique assault him with tickles, grab his arms and legs and swing him like a hammock.

"'Allo, 'allo, 'allo." They beckon to me and Daisy as we enter the hall, the duo fully made up and dressed to kill. "Ready for our *treep* to the mall?" Mark is unloaded, then Stephanie reaches into her purse-cum-munitions dump and extracts a wad of her father's charge cards. "We were at the Cowboy Bar last night, and guess what—Monique met a *millionaire*."

"In *Lan*caster?" asks Daisy.

Monique rubs her fingers together. "I am so lucky."

As I reach for my blazer, Daisy answers the ringing phone. Her face freezes. "It's Dan," she says. "Can you call Mom?"

Over in the living room I see Mark opening the window. He crawls out.

30

I believe that what you do with flowers reveals what you do with your love. Bear with the corniness and hear my examples.

Dan, love god that he is, thinks flowers are a fine idea. "A hundred bucks' worth of annuals circling a house can boost the property's retail price twenty percent. Learned *that* in California. People think flowers have good vibes— it's like an instinct—clients can't help wanting to pay more."

Jasmine thinks flowers are a notion from her past—the wispy daisy chains of the Berkeley years she keeps pressed in the encyclopedia under *M* for memory. When the world is too much for her, she gets fetal in her wicker throne and traces the daisy chains' delicate circles, smiling to herself, humming lost songs. Encouragingly, Jasmine leaves around the house a spoor of jelly jars filled with roadside flowers—hollyhocks, black-eyed Susans, foxgloves—

standing in their yellow broth reservoirs like emergency batteries.

Daisy shocks with her flowers: electric marigold dresses, forget-me-not mists in her hair, and flower salads for her hairgod, Murray *("Just eat them, Tyler. Pretend we're in New York")*.

Mark is addicted to jumbo flowers—WORLD'S LARGEST types—wasting winter days poring over seed catalogs, losing sleep while he awaits the arrival in the mail of Deep Dish Pizza Sunflower seeds and Ninja Japanese Spider Chrysanthemums with Petals Longer than Your Body.

Stephanie likes her flowers in the form of perfume, printed fabrics, and evil little violet candies. It's hard to imagine her in a garden—perhaps in a topiary maze with a Venus flytrap in the center.

Anna-Louise plants flowering trees and likes her flowers wild. In her mother's backyard in Pasco she is trying to build a decaying British garden: lordly thistles guard fallen crabapples; wood furniture weathered to the point of uselessness sits speckled with exquisite bird poops. Anna-Louise scythes her grass because "mowing is anal retentive." Her brother Johann's perennially dismembered 1969 GTO, however, somewhat spoils Anna-Louise's effect of premeditated ruin.

What do *I* do with flowers? Small acts. Last week I bought a box of 250 crocus bulbs and planted them in the dirt outside of Anna-Louise's bedroom window, arranged so that after blooming in April they will spell the words LOVE ME.

Another anecdote springs to mind. Last week at the Toxic Waste Dump, Harmony asked me what I thought would be the coolest way to die. Before I reflexively blurted out a stock response like "naked in a car crash with the tunage cranked to eleven" I paused and thought of a person like me, growing up in a flower-free part of the world and driving to the ocean in a little blue sports car won on a game show, down south to California, and admiring an acid-yellow field of zinnias. Suddenly, *whoosh!* along comes a blast of Pacific wind, rousing the zinnias into a pollen fervor and blasting me with yellowness, shake-and-baking me with a substance I had no idea I was allergic to, and within moments, I go into anaphylactic shock and am dead.

"I don't know, Harmony. Naked in a car crash, I guess. With the tunage cranked up to eleven."

31

Woozle Pups are the best. No waste."

"Excuse me?" replies Stephanie, who, like Monique, is gnawing Woozle Pup hot dogs and glorping down chocolaty-rich tubs of Mall Melts at the Ridgecrest Mall's still-open Woozle Pup stand.

"No waste. Cows go in one end of the Woozle Pup hotdog factory and out the other end emerge trailer loads of hot dogs. No garbage cans or anything."

Stephanie and Monique, being European, are unfazed by tales of viscera: "Not even little leather coats?"

"No."

Stephanie orders one more dog. Woozle Pups, in spite of their history, are nonetheless disbelief-suspendingly tasty.

"Daisy worked at Woozle Pup once," I say. "But she was fired after, like, ten minutes. I came to visit and there was a big angry crowd all wanting service and Daisy was just sitting there by the phone drawing spiderweb borders on her poetry book. She's a vegetarian now."

"*Oui.*"

This is the Ridgecrest Mall. Or rather, this was once the Ridgecrest Mall, in its heyday the malliest of malls, a glistening floating charmed world of escalators and glass elevators, its countless walls surfaced in mirrors and painted in soothing color schemes. There was an ice rink at the Ridgecrest Mall once, plus a sculpture garden and two fountains, and all of it was lulled by impulse-purchasing music. There were phone marts, poster stores, a Food Fair, shoe shops, greeting-card emporiums, toy huts, and a Fashion Plaza, and all were pleasingly heated and free of litter.

The Ridgecrest Mall was where my friends and I, all of us hyper from sugar and too many video games, feeling fizzy and unreal—like products that can't exist without advertising—shunted about in our packs: skatepunks, deathcookies, jocks, pseuds, Euros, and geeks, all of us feeling like the man who was hypnotized onstage by the circus magician and who could never wake up from his trance.

But I was younger back in the days when I was a serious mall rat. I'm almost too old for malljamming now, and to be honest, there's not much of the mall left to malljam *in.* Today around us I see wounded shoe stores, dead pizzerias, plywooded phone marts, and decayed and locked-up sports stores. The tropical plants in the galleria are wizened and Dr. Seusslike. The Saint Yuppie boutique, where I'll be meeting Anna-Louise at four o'clock is, like most Ridgecrest boutiques, plywooded. As well, like many other Ridgecrest stores, Saint Yuppie has had a fire, possibly an arson, and carbon fingers probe outward from the four-by-eight-foot plywood sheets; the electric power is off in that particular wing of the mall. Unloved and dark at the wing's end is one of the mall's two anchors, a FoodLand.

Disheartened young people roam bravely, trying to maintain the semiforgotten tingling feeling of plenty, but to little avail in this postshopping world of frozen escalators and nothing for sale. Black outfits, I note, are back in style once more.

A few stores still thrive, commercial success being in direct proportion to the unnecessariness of the product being provided by that store. Kooky Video is packed. The LuvMart™ is a hot ticket. Shampoo Planet™ is exciting and jammed. The Land of Software™ is expanding into the defunct bookstore next door. The games arcade is as stuffed as ever, the floor strewn with Woozle Pup wrappers and crunched clear plastic bento boxes and chopsticks from The Great Teriyaki Experience!™, detritus from the mall's two remaining outposts of nutrition. Fashion-runway dance mixes of the latest U.K. singles blare over the sound system. You want to be here. The arcade's lure is irresistible, like the lure of wanting to make long-distance phone calls on your parents' bill.

I love the mall. I always have. The health of your mall is important. At the mall people are interested only in staying as modern as possible, continually forgetting the past while envisaging a shinier more fabulous future. Just think of all the wonderful products to buy . . . do these products sparkle? Can you see your face reflected in these products? Are they made of a wonder material like Lucite or Kevlar that exists nowhere in the known universe save for Earth? We are so lucky to be living in the times we do.

In the old days, before malls and before history, if you wanted to see, say, an apple, you had to wait until August. In between there wasn't even one picture of an apple you could look at. Nowadays you can have apples all year round, and that's great.

I think Stephanie and Monique feel the same way about malls as I do, even though they seem bummed out by the unavailability of stuff to buy here at the Ridgecrest today. But this underabundance is good, because maybe they'll become bored and leave town sooner and decomplicate my life.

"Oh, who am I kidding?" I say. "Today is a total drag for the two of you. You can't think this is a normal mall. It's just a total waste. If you'd been here a year ago you could have had six shoe stores to choose from in the Fashion Plaza alone."

"No, no. We like the Ridgecrest Mall. We are enjoying ourselves. Right, Monique?"

"Oh, oui. *Vay*-ry amusing. *Vay*-ry futuristic."

A ragged cluster of skatebrats wails down an echoey service corridor and collides into a burnt wall in front of us, kicking the wall and the window beside it with their little black boots, whooping and shaking ski-gloved fists patterned with antishoplifting magnetic stickers Krazy-Glued onto the fingers. The brats then scream and fly down a dead escalator on their boards, toward the thawed and forgotten ice rink, the surface of which is peppered with cigarette butts and cola cups tossed down from the upper shopping galleria levels. The whole scenario reminds me of the adage that World War Three will be fought with nuclear weapons and World War Four will be fought with sticks and stones. But when was World War Three? I think it must have been an invisible war and now we're into World War Four. There *must* be an explanation for what has happened to the mall.

"Tyler! French babes!" We turn around and see Daisy and Murray clutching armloads of boldly laser-printed antifur, antileghold-trap stickers proclaiming the words CHEW YOUR FOOT OFF. "Come on and help Daisy and me foster interspecies peace!"

I ask Murray if he thinks Lancaster is the right place to protest furs as we instinctively navigate toward The Great Teriyaki Experience!™

"Well, actually, to be honest we haven't found a single fur yet, but we're going to keep looking. When we *do* find a fur, we're going to plaster it with these stickers. We gave a handful to the skatebrats. They wanted to help, too."

As Murray speaks, already I see the whooping brats over across the galleria plastering CHEW YOUR FOOT OFF stickers on blackened shop windows, plywood hoardings, and the forgotten modern sculptures in the sculpture garden.

"Murray, this is Stephanie and this is Monique."

"'Allo."

"'Allo."

"Hi. Daisy talks about you French Babes a lot. You want a sticker?"

The French Babes (new nickname christened) politely decline. We chat for a few minutes over diet colas and cucumber maki rolls. Monique is off soon to have a date with the millionaire she met last night. His name is Kirk. Stephanie wants to go off on a drive by herself in La Car. Daisy and Murray are off to the supermarket downtown to hunt for fur coats and to shop for "skin food" (whatever *that* is). I, as mentioned, am off to meet Anna-Louise at four.

"Daisy and I have decided to declare ourselves independent nations unto ourselves," says Murray, just to make conversation. "Complete freedom and autonomy."

"We're going to become our own countries. We'll declare ourselves Nuclear Free Zones."

The French Babes, with the bureaucratic instincts of

their ancestry alerted, leap into action: "But what about government?" they ask.

"Government?" asks Daisy. "I'll just have mood swings."

The Babes are suddenly deadly serious. "How can all of you be so frivolous about your freedom?" Stephanie asks. "How can you be so cavalier about democracy?"

"Hey, Princess Stephanie," cuts in Murray. "I've always noticed how the word *democracy* is tossed around usually just about the same time somebody is planning to abuse your personal rights."

"I've heard there was a mall in Washington, D.C.," adds Daisy, "but it turns out it wasn't the shopping kind."

Stephanie and Monique roll their eyes heavenward, make curt good-byes, and then rapidly split.

"Well, aren't *they* la-di-da," peeves Daisy.

"The Babes have some pretty lofty 'tude, Tyler," adds Murray.

"They're from France," I say, springing to their defense, but I note Daisy and Murray buttoning on their coats. "You leaving, too?" I ask.

"Skin care and interspecies peace beckon," says Daisy. She pecks me on the cheek and asks me to say hi to Anna-Louise.

"Later, my man," says Murray, and shortly the two are gone, leaving me with much too much time to kill here in the black mall.

32

Scientists sound so smug the way they discuss people who go to malls as though they were ants in an ant farm. Obviously these scientists have never hung out at a mall before—otherwise they'd know what a blast malls are, and they wouldn't spend so much time analyzing them.

Malls are the best. But maybe not the Ridgecrest Mall, and maybe not today. In fact, I'm going to have to face the fact that the Ridgecrest Mall is pretty much just a husk of its former self. We had plenty, and we blew it. I guess human beings just weren't cut out for plenty. Well, *most* human beings. *I* sure am, but where did plenty go?

I'm loafing beside the vandalized sculpture garden ball-point-penning L-O-V-E and H-A-T-E on my knuckles when my friend Harmony taps me on the shoulder and asks, "Deign wouldst thou cometh with myself and my fellow geeks, Sir Pony and Sir Davidson, to the The Land of Software?"

What else is there to do? I tag along, careful to avoid being whacked by the trio's purchases of consumer loot, heaps and heaps, all stuffed into brightly colored plastic bags.

Where from such loot? Harmony, Pony, and Davidson are rich from computer hacking and today they have bought a Jimi Hendrix CD boxed set, computer-knit polyester sweaters, electronic executive desk toys, and candy.

"Hey—where'd you find open stores?" I ask.

"There's always *some*thing open, Tyler," says Davidson. I guess these guys are used to having lots-o-loot. The store name on their bags? SO MUCH STUFF: SO LITTLE TIME®.

Within minutes of being in The Land of Software™ I'm swooning with boredom while the geeks are swarming like bees around the latest gizmo from the futuretowns of the Silicon Valley in California—Santa Clara, Sunnyvale, Walnut Creek, Menlo Park. . . .

"Ty! Checketh out hither hardware," shouts Harmony. "It's *virtual!*"

I am by now completely convinced that my downfall in life is going to be my inability to achieve computer nirvana like a true hacker or hackette. I think this lacking is the most unmodern facet of my personality—the career equivalent of having six fingers, or a vestigial tail. I mean, I enjoy computer games as much as the next guy but . . . well . . .

Lethargically I check out the swarm's focus—an on-screen simulation of 3-D reality in which I can participate using a pair of CyberGluvs®.

"Sire, give the gloves a try," says Harmony, and so I don them, and I have to admit what I see is remarkable. On the monitor is a color simulation of a simple jigsaw puzzle of a bikini blonde, which I can assemble in simulated three-dimensional cyberspace by manipulating my gloved hands up in the air, touching nothing, as though speaking sign language. A pair of simulated hands on the screen assembles the puzzle blonde. I tell Harmony using the CyberGluv® is like clicking the sky with a mouse.

"Exactly," says Harmony, and the computer geeks, ever helpful, all nod monkishly in assent.

I give the gloves over to Pony, who, like a good hacker, is already pumping up several levels higher in puzzle complexity. As he begins, though, a hush comes over the small crowd. I raise my head up to the source of the hush and out in the mall through The Land of Software™'s windows, bent over a box near the Dr. Seuss plants, I see the stick figure of Eddie, Lancaster's official person with AIDS.

When we were growing up, before Jasmine married Dan and we moved into the new house, Eddie Woodman lived next door to us with his dad and his two sisters. We liked the Woodman kids but we never saw too much of them, as they were older. But on Halloween, Eddie, Debbie, and Joann as a rule tended to go whole hog costumewise, with Eddie having the best costumes of all. One Halloween Eddie dressed as "Kitty: Yukon Barfly with a Heart of Perfume" and dumped bowl-loads of candy into our sacks and pulled quarters out from his garter belt to plug into our UNICEF boxes. He was great. The girls adored him; Jasmine did, too. Eddie was no end of help with ideas of what to do with the herbs Jasmine cultivated in her side garden, our family being at least ten years ahead of all others in Benton County in using cilantro "as a focus rather than a garnish."

Then, about five years ago, Eddie left for Seattle, and

Debbie and Joann wouldn't discuss his departure. They were miserable for months afterward, as was Jasmine, who alluded to a confrontation Eddie had had with Mr. Woodman.

And then—and then, well, Eddie suddenly reappeared a few months ago, the new gaunt, deflated, slow-motion version of Eddie, back in Lancaster to the old house to be taken care of by Joann, Mr. Woodman having died of a stroke three years previously and Debbie now being married to a board-surfing god and living in Hood River, Oregon, next to The Gorge. No gossip is sacred in a small town.

So now Eddie is standing in the black mall, and all of us inside The Land of Software™ are painfully aware of Eddie's presence even though we wordlessly pretend to go on as though nothing is happening.

Last week Skye said, "Not thinking about sex these days is like not thinking about what goes into hot dogs." I guess seeing Eddie is, in a way, like seeing the inside of a hot-dog factory. The general concensus seems to be that it's best to think of modern sex as a uniform, abstracted snack—and not to dwell too heavily on its manufacture.

"Bingo!" Pony claps his hands and the Level-Seven bikini blonde rests assembled on the screen. The Cyber-Gluvs® are passed to another geek while outside, Eddie picks up his box and shuffles slowly down the long corridor to the parking lot. I quietly evaporate from the swarm and follow him down the hall. "Eddie—" I call.

He stops, turns around and tries to remember me. "Oh. Tyler Johnson. Hi." His skin is sallow, strangely elephant-wrinkled, like the skin on latex paint when the lid has been lost.

"Hi, Eddie. You headed to the parking lot? Here. Let me help you carry the box."

Eddie stares at the box, remembers he's holding it, pauses, then hands the box over to me. "Thanks."

The box is surprisingly heavy. "Hey, what's in here?"

"A humidifier," Eddie replies.

"Oh."

We walk.

"How's Debbie?" I ask.

"Good. Two kids. Still living in Hood River with BoardGod."

"And Joann?"

"Still on the prowl. You should give her a call sometime. She *likes* veal."

"Eddie! That's so rude!"

We come to smoked-glass doors, which I hold open with the box while Eddie leaves the building and begins his slow march across the chilly parking lot, where his yellow Nissan sits in a lonely cowlike cluster of other cars. Eddie asks me a bit about my family (not that he wouldn't have heard all vital dirt via the Lancaster grapevine already) and he opens the trunk for me and I place his box inside. When he closes the trunk lid the two of us stand there silent, pained, and awkward, myself intensely aware that there is an unidentifiable and crucial task being left undone.

As Eddie slides into the car, I have the hallucinatory sensation of consciously experiencing an activity for the last time, the way I felt leaving Europe, in this case seeing Eddie Woodman alive. I imagine that this feeling is a signature of youth's passing. I hope that's what this feeling is.

"Thanks, Tyler," he says as he guns the motor. "Say hi to Jasmine for me. We'll see you later."

"Right, Eddie," I say. "Bye."

Eddie purrs away while I throw a feeble wave and return

to the mall, opening the smoked doors, feeling the sweet hot rush of mall air in my face, like a sack of warm Halloween candy, a buzz of guilt in my head.

I see Anna-Louise standing down the way outside the carbon-fronted Saint Yuppie. She doesn't see me approach and is standing there with her arms across her chest. I sidle up beside her, slightly from behind, and reaching around her small, warm body, I give her the hug I guess I should have given Eddie.

33

Imagine the person you love saying to you, *"Ten minutes from now you are going to be poked with a sharp stick. The pain will be excruciating and there isn't a single thing you can do to prevent it."* Well then—the next ten minutes would be next to unendurable, would they not? Maybe it's good we can't see the future.

"Anna-Louise, what you do for those kids is fantastic."

"Don't talk to me like a telethon, Tyler. Not today."

"Okay. Fine." Anna-Louise has been a total ice goddess since we left the mall to skim through Lancaster inside the Comfortmobile's matte-black luxury.

Out east I see power lines down in the middle of a harvested barley field. Oddly, the cables on either side of a transmission tower have been severed and drape from the triangulated outstretched aluminum arms like a mother weeping for her kidnapped child, holding forth samples of her missing child's pajamas to the CNN cameras.

Anna-Louise looks terrible. "Anna-Louise, you look terrible. Did you only sleep two hours last night?" Her socks are two different colors, her sweater is pilled, and she has toothpaste residue caked on the corners of her mouth. In her lap she's clutching her Eightplex uniform inside a scrunched-up white plastic grocery bag.

"I don't care."

"I see."

"I suppose Miss France looks ravishing today?"

I am tactfully mute, emphasizing by default that Stephanie might, in fact, outdo Anna-Louise in a point-by-point grooming comparison. "Everyone has bad hair days."

Anna-Louise says, "I had Ding-Dongs and gin for lunch today."

"You went to work drunk?"

Anna-Louise's posture is rigid. She pops in the never-used cigarette lighter on the dash, reaches into the white plastic bag, pulls out a cigarette, and, much to my surprise, lights it.

"Anna-Louise, what are you doing? Smoking is for poor people."

"*What?*"

"It's true. You never see rich people smoking. *Truly* rich people. Ever. Just like the way rich people never have fluorescent lighting in their houses. Bulbs only. Or candles."

"How would you know any of that, Tyler?"

Dare I bring up the wisdom of Frank E. Miller as expressed in his epic biography, *Life at the Top?* "It's obviously true. Smoke, and you might as well move into a trailer park immediately. And wear a sandwich board over your neck saying I HAVE NO AMBITION."

"So maybe I just like smoking."

"It's your career."

Anna-Louise defiantly smokes. The car reeks of a bar and I open my window a crack, causing all of the smoke's blue streaks to whiz past my face, giving Anna-Louise a small measure of satisfaction. "I sure am looking forward to some power studying today," I say.

A terse inhale is my reply.

"Say. Is that a *New Yorker* in your bag there? You should hold it outside the bag—strangers will know you're upmarket."

"I pray in a closet, thank you, *Dan*."

"Anna, why are you freaking out on me?" I ask. "What's with the attitude? Something I've done?"

A snort in reply. I'm reminded of the standard gag where a wife wakes up one morning and slugs her husband for a crime he committed in her dream—the punch line being that in our hearts we know the husband is probably guilty of some equivalent crime in real life.

"Tyler, what do I know about you?"

"Huh?"

"Oh shut up. I don't think I even *really* know you at all. I mean, I know you to a certain level, but then I go no deeper. There's a point at which all knowledge stops—after which you won't allow me to travel further. I'm insulted."

Hmmm. I wonder if people who accuse you of not revealing enough about yourself are the people not actually doing the divulging. "You're being paranoid, Anna-Louise."

"Spare me, Tyler. Just spare me."

Downtown Lancaster is, owing to the downed wires, without electricity. Traffic burps and lolls at the signal-free intersections, and the semigridlock amplifies the Comfortmobile's short-tempered mood.

"This morning before work I went over to your house,"

153

says Anna-Louise, her voice gone flat, her face disinter-estedly looking at the post office and my regular laundro-mat (shirts starched and pressed, only 99¢ apiece), "and already you'd left for the mall. I was on my way home from aerobics class and was dropping off a scarf I'd knitted you like a fishwife doormat. Your mother and I had coffee. When I was leaving to go home and change, a postcard came through the door. From New Zealand."

"Oh."

There goes my credit rating. Blood pounds in my ears and my forehead fills with buzz. I can't concentrate. I feel like I'm inside a film where you see a normal everyday scene, like a couple having breakfast, when suddenly one of the couple breathes bubbles and you realize the whole scene has been taking place underwater.

"Did you honestly think I wouldn't find out, Tyler? I mean, how stupid do you think I am?"

Time collapses.

We're outside Anna-Louise's building on Franklin Street. I'm unable to talk and staring at the center of the steering wheel.

"Anna-Louise, it was only a summer fling. I don't know why she's here . . ."

"You don't think I don't know it was only a fling? You couldn't just tell me—be up front about it? I mean, I would have understood. Instead you give me this weird 'friends of Kiwi' horseshit."

Anna-Louise opens the door, rotates her torso, putting her legs out the door, scrunching out her cigarette.

"You are weak, Tyler. Weak weak weak. And you know, I'd heard guys were stupid, but I never believed it of *you*. Now I guess I do." She exits. "I'll be going now. Thanks for the ride. Sorry—*merci beaucoup*."

She gazelles up the path, enters the decompression

chamber, and it is all over so suddenly, like holding a Halloween sparkler when you're young, believing the spar- kler will flare forever, feeling disbelief when that fine white light so abruptly stops.

I turn off the engine, roll down my window, lean back, and drink in the view. Down Franklin Street, a druggie kid from the Free Clinic is circling a pay phone like a dog circling a dog it doesn't know. The druggie kid turns, catches my eye, then flashes me a V.

I think of a crashing 747, of a thousand oxygen masks descending from the ceiling.

I flash him back a V.

34

I motor aimlessly for a few hours in the off chance I might see Stephanie. I return home, amid the darkness of the still-continuing power failure. I see the driveway and road outside clogged with cars. What does this clustering mean—has an asteroid punctured the roof? Are the kitchen walls bleeding? And if so, exactly *where* is the Channel Six NewsTeam? To the side of the house I see Betty, my grandparents' mobile home, parked, oblivious, content, and rude, like a bullying woman in a restaurant who harangues the waitresses, eats like a pig, and is tolerated only because technically she is doing nothing illegal.

Once inside, the cars are explained. Grandma and Grandpa are holding a KittyWhip® sales conference in the living room—now a tableau of candle-lit squalor, with bodies sprayed across the carpet and floppy hippie couches. The audience is arranged in a semicircle around the emcee and Thronemaster, Grandpa, whose chair is made out of sticks taken from beaver dams (those ever-inventive hippies!). In front of him stands a small indigo velvet podium upon which rests the entire line of products in the KittyWhip® Kat Food System®.

Stephanie is among the bodies, as are Daisy, Murray, Skye, Mei-Lin, Pony, Davidson, Mrs. Dufresne, Eddie (he's back), Joann, and maybe twenty others, their rapt eyeballs replaced by the dollar sign$ of cartoon lore.

Kittykat and her pal, Rice—a cross-eyed Siamese eunuch from next door—are slithering about Grandpa's throne in hot expectation of treats to come. Where are the tethered goats? Where is the opium? This scene is so depressing. Squalor is so retro. I guess that's what the lack of electricity is—Instant Dark Ages—simply pull the plug. Give me metal, protein capsules, and radium *any* day of the week. Our inventions are what keep us out of the mud.

I go into the kitchen and Jasmine follows me. I ask her gruffly what Dan was calling about just as I was heading to the mall this morning.

"Shhh. Later," she says. "I wanted to tell you, Mom and Dad lost the house, so they're going to be living in Betty for the next few months. Be nice to them, okay? Come on in and watch the show. Hey. Are you okay?"

"I'm fine."

"No you're not." She narrows her eyes. "Anna-Louise found out, didn't she?"

"Yeah."

"Oh, sweetie. We'll talk about it after the meeting." She rubs my shoulder. "Have a cookie, okay? Chocolate, not carob, today. Am I lapsing into decadence, or what?"

"How'd your date with Mr. Software go?"

"From hell."

She returns to the living room just as Jim Jarvis and his wife, Lorraine, are being applauded and are walking up to the podium for a sample squeeze of the KittyPump®. This act is their ritual indoctrination into the seamless, hypnotic, and self-referential world of home pet-food parties. Whatever happened to work?

35

Jim Jarvis is the quintessential Lancaster citizen of the New Order. Prior to the collapse of the Plants (and Jim's accompanying career obsolescence), Jim—a terse, driven ice-yuppie—and his yuppess, Lorraine, lived in a monster house on the outskirts of town with maybe one window and with the biggest satellite dish in Benton County, nay, Washington State, plopped onto their roof like a wind-blown cocktail umbrella. Now they live in an RV parked off Route 666.

Jim *was* a pitchblende broker and spent his career roaming the globe—Gabon, Saskatchewan, Namibia, Queensland—in pursuit of this exotic ore. Now he and Lorraine peddle KittyWhip®.

Jim used to be a friend of Dan's, too, back when Jim was in the market for the developed properties Dan sold. Now they're both poor and probably don't talk to each other. Surprise, surprise.

At Dan and Jasmine's parties, Jim talked about the temperature of his wine cellar to us teenagers. I saw Jim as a guy who probably had cool loner fantasies when he was a passenger on planes, refusing to speak to his seat mates, nodding in silent agreement with newsmagazine think pieces, and being mannishly curt with flight attendants.

But Jim and Lorraine's lives are different now. Not so much because of poverty but because of an event that happened to them in Africa late last spring.

They had been on a weekend jaunt to visit an enormous lake, a lake so big it stretched to the horizon, its surface entirely covered in pink lilies and elephant-ear lily pads. On one of these jumbo lily pads Lorraine had placed their five-month old baby, Kirsty, to pose for what Jim and Lorraine thought would be a "cute" video. Within seconds, while the Sony whirred and Lorraine stood beaming in an outfit no doubt purchased from the gift shop of an art gallery, a large scaly brown fish jumped up from beneath a lily pad. It glommed onto Kirsty's chubby little arm and dragged her down into the swamp mud—a world where eyeless monsters eat tubers, shed skins, and reflect our darkest nightmares—a muffled world where dead babies cry together.

It happened in maybe three seconds, tops. On VHS, too. And now Jim and Lorraine are broken people, brain damaged, like a Floridian coral reef smashed by a wayward freighter, a reef that will never regenerate itself.

"Ty, you think the evil duo placed Kirsty on the pad ON PURPOSE? (nudge-nudge implied)," asked Daisy in her Copenhagen letter.

"It's hardly the sort of murder you can stage," I wrote back in my last postcard. "And besides, it wasn't like Kirsty was defective merchandise, or something. You know yuppies. Lorraine told Mom Kirsty had a talent for stringed instruments when Kirsty was only three months old. So I guess they had emotion invested in her. Not just money. People *will* surprise you."

Jim and Lorraine are quiet, nervous folk now, and like most quiet nervous folk, silently monitor your behavior to see if you're nervous, too, counting the chew marks on the ends of your pencils, inwardly tabulating your cocktail consumption, and pointing out to you in mock goodheartedness a twitch you maybe never knew you had. It's almost enough to make me wish Jim were his old insensitive self again. But no.

"You have to press down on the KittyPump like you're making a sundae for movie stars!" commands Grandpa to a quivering Jim, who meekly replies, "Yessir," baring his teeth with no smile in his eyes.

This is not ambition. This is desperation.

36

Stephanie, extracting herself from the enthralled mob, follows me back into the candle-lit kitchen. "What's wrong?" she asks. "*Ça va?*"

"Anna-Louise and I broke up." Stephanie's face is expressionless, diplomatic. "Or rather, she left me."

Silence. To fill this silence, I give her details—about the postcard from Kiwi, *("Where* is *that card?")* the recent stress, my flopping out at school. . . . From the kitchen, through the living room window we see a taxi drop off Monique. She darts in the front door while I'm telling a sympathetic Stephanie of my woes.

"We made love in a satellite dish!" she hollers from the hallway. "It was so warm—the dish—there is a focus of light." All heads in the living room, like a flock of fish changing direction, swivel toward Monique, headed kitchenward.

Feeling like a prude, I say, "*Shhh . . .*" I mean, I'm all

for self-expression, but keep your expression to yourself, please. Monique and her libertine sexual mores, while not exactly sluttish, have a kind of unclean tinge, like a pack of white sugar that has burst and is overflowing onto a supermarket aisle.

Stephanie, though, can't hear enough details, and makes assuaging noises to me, postponing tales of my breakup, until her tabloid needs are sated. The two rocket into a French-language rehash of Monique's sexual num-nums, and once the worst is over, switch to English, whereupon I, too, am privy to tales of the mighty millionaire, Kirk. Also present are Daisy and Murray, using the excuse that it's their house so as to catch the dirt. KittyWhip® has palled in a big way.

"Kirk has a flock of horses," tells Monique. "And he has a wife on a . . . a . . . *life-support* system. And he has a high-tech apartment. He has . . ."

"But what is he *like?*" I ask.

"Like?"

"What kind of person is he?"

"*Mysterieux. Très mysterieux.* I think he works for the CIA and maybe he was in Vietnam. He makes me think he is a, how you say, POW."

Jasmine enters the kitchen and shushes us.

"Monique snagged a millionaire," I say.

"In *Lan*caster?"

I see Kiwi's postcard over by the fridge and go to read it, tuning out Monique's hushed sexploit chat. Kiwi wrote:

Hi Mate,

Spring down here.
New Zealand's much smaller than when I left. School is a blot. Would much rather be drinking your "cock-tails" on S's roof instead of gazing at sheep with in-

creasing fondness. (Joke!) Ah, oui, Paris. Feels like a million miles away, and just next door. Not a peep out of Monique since I left, but then she's not the type of tart to write, is she? Next time you gush on paper to Steph, pass the word on to Her Highness to remind M. I bloody well exist. Teases, all of them.

Keep it in there. Skiing next July?

Kiwi.

On the fridge is a new drawing by Mark of a geisha girl with fangs carrying a martini. The drawing bears the caption:

the Geesha girl walks all tilted because her obi belt weighs 500 pounds because she has hidden Uranium! in her belt.

"You should make love in a satellite dish, Mrs. Johnson," I hear Monique extoll as I look up from the card. "It is a tonic, and you will receive a suntan, too."

"No doubt," blushes Jasmine.

Daisy's princess porta-phone burps into life underneath a stack of pizza flyers. "That will be for me," says, Monique, shuffling through the litter. "I gave Kirk your phone number so he could reach me here now. He went out to shop for a helicopter."

"My phone's over here, Monique," says Daisy, lifting the receiver up. "I'll answer it." Daisy shifts into a cartoon French accent: "Zees eez zee Monique rayzeedence. Who eez calling. Kirk? Hayllo, Kirk." Daisy makes wink-wink and does a bump-and-grind at Monique, but then her face empties. "Dan? Is that *you*, Dan?" Daisy is saucer-eyed. A sensation. "It's Dan! Calling for Monique—Dan is Kirk!"

Shrieks.

Monique tries to salvage what scraps of dignity she can. Grabbing the receiver, she huffs: "You are a liar." She strikes a pose of righteousness, her hand on her hip: "I will not speak to you. Good-bye."

"Hey," shouts Grandpa, "quiet in there."

Jasmine, her face happy, a rare event since I returned from Europe, yanks the phone from Monique and says, "Hi Dan. You'd better watch the kinky stuff or your insurance rates will skyrocket."

"Insurance rates?" asks Stephanie. I try to explain to her how premiums cost a fortune if you have an accident or keep high-risk items like swimming-pool diving boards on your property, but I quit bothering after a few sentences. Could the case be that Stephanie has no sense of humor?

While I explain to Stephanie the intricacies of actuarial humor, an unusual scene unfolds before me. Jasmine, leaning bumward on the kitchen counter, has her face in her hands, breathing in deeply of exhaled carbon dioxide after her bout of laughter. Monique, meanwhile, another notch carved into her makeup compact, has her hands on her hips and is making a show of tut-tutting Dan's treachery. It is at this point that the two establish eye contact, and my focus on Stephanie's questioning dissolves as I watch my mother begin to cry and Monique reach out to my mother to hold her in her young arms.

In the living room behind them, Grandpa flambées a bowl of KittyWhip®. The flames dance on the surface like little drunk blue ghosts.

37

Alert the Channel Six NewsTeam: much has happened recently.

Harmony, Stephanie, and I are riding the stationary bikes at the MetalBody gym.

"I exercise to make my body more sinewy," says Harmony, out of his Olde Englishe mode this afternoon and more into his sci-fi mode. "Less appetizing to aliens for when they invade."

"Explain, please, Harm."

"It's only logical. Which cows do you want to eat the most? Those Kobe cows from Japan, right? Those cows that never exercise and have beer massages. Tender and juicy and delicious. I mean, who eats racehorses?"

"I don't think you have to worry about being eaten by aliens, Harm."

"And just why *not*?"

"Because you're too old, already—you're twenty. Teen-agers would taste *way* better. More tender—less gristle."

"No way."

"Way."

"He is right," says Stephanie, wiping sweat from her forehead and halfheartedly flipping a page of a sweat-destroyed copy of *Vogue* magazine. "By the time you are twenty, you are full of smoke and drugs and *orr*-mones and you would not taste delicious."

"I think places like bar mitzvahs and sweet-sixteen par-ties have more to worry about UFO invasions than your computer lab, Harm."

"You think so? What a relief. *Finally*, a genuine advan-tage to aging."

Stephanie and I increase the tension meters on our bikes, but Harmony doesn't. He's just recovering from a cold and has to build up his strength gradually. "It's like you have all of these dead viruses lodged inside your muscles," he says, "like dirt in an unclean sponge, and the sponge re-quires several squeezes to remove all the dirt."

Gag.

It's early afternoon, the best time to hit the gym because the after-work crowd has yet to invade, and so only the unemployed, the semiemployed, and the marginally em-ployed people are here—people like bouncers, cocktail waitresses, and talkers on the phone-sex lines. Like all gymgoers, their eyes are riveted to the walls of mirrors and their flesh and their Lycra skins of coy, calculated skimpiness. Funny, but mass unemployment hasn't upped the number of afternoon gymgoers here in Lancaster, and those jobseekers *really* ought to be here since working out would give them a sense of empowerment that would help their job searches. Any career manual will tell you *that*.

"The jobless are probably all too proud and loafing at home, inhaling lite beer and trash TV," says Harmony.

"Life of shame," says I.

This past week—what a week—endorphins, adrenaline, testosterone . . . a real hormone cocktail.

First of all, Monique and the rental car are gone. She returned to Paris via New Zealand on her triangular round-the-world airfare after it was revealed that even amid her sexual explorations here in the New World she was, in fact, homesick. The humiliating Kirk episode de-stabilized her, and when she returned to the Old Decoy bed & breakfast, she discovered that her lonesome mother in France had Federal Expressed her an envelope full of scabs from her dying pet cat, Minuit.

"Four days in the New World," snorted Daisy. "What a trooper."

"And to think that all she saw of the New World was Lancaster and the surrounding bioregion," said Murray. "How surreal."

Stephanie is not unhappy with life's current turn of events. Life can now become more Stephanie-o-centric: *The Stephanie Show, starring . . . Stephanie!*

She has moved into the Modernarium, and my room is now strewn with jewels and perfume and undergarments. I like this feminine sloth. I want to fight crime with her all the time now. I want to sleep with her in broad daylight. Also, there is no longer any pretence of attending school these days—and nobody is mentioning my truancy, so I guess Jasmine told the family to be hush. What a life.

Brendan, the pride of Lancaster, saunters by in a Speedo and a white tank top so skimpy it might as well be a bra. Brendan has advanced to the National Bodybuilding

Championships, drug-free, in Phoenix next month and has provided Lancaster's citizenry with an ember of civic hope. Stephanie inhales. "Too bad Monique departed so soon."

"He looks a bit like Bert Rockney, doesn't he?" I ask Harmony, who nods in agreement.

"Essentially. But Brendan doesn't have 'roid-body."

Bert Rockney, as previously mentioned, is my favorite action-adventure death-toy movie star, renowned practitioner of the ancient Mongolian art of Chang-Ting. His muscles are solid tungsten rippled with gelignite—muscles he needs to fight the never-ending stream of ex-best friends and corrupt government goons who senselessly murder his wife, children, and parents from one movie to the next. What a star.

"Have you looked at those old male stars from, like, the 1940s and 1950s when they remove their shirts?" asks Harmony. "Jeez, they have *tits*. I mean, *they* were supposed to be death machines? Steroids sure have made going to the movies more fun."

"Agreed," I say. "But now people know what a steroided body looks like so 'roid-bodies aren't as cool any more. 'Roid-bodies are like the visual equivalent of a steak that's been overtenderized—that you can cut with a fork."

Brendan grunts and screams and raises about four billion pounds of barbells over his head, and his face turns maroon and bubbly, like cheap beef jerky, and the sound is so deafening, so absolutely rude, that all conversation in the gym stops while people pretend not to notice as Brendan so publicly suicides.

"Cat scabs?" asks Harmony? "Ick."

"Cat scabs are documents, too," I say. "Just like piss and shit are documents. Of sorts. Everything is a document."

"Minuit is such a cute kitten," sighs Stephanie. "But she is not long for the world. *Loo-kee*-mia. Soon Monique will have to place Minuit into her little basket, then into the river Seine."

Pause. (Respect for the dead.)

"Monique should have relaxed a bit," I say. "The Dan episode was funny, but people love you for making that kind of mistake. Besides—in the States you're allowed to redo history—erase your tapes and start over again; make a first impression twice."

"Monique knows only the European way," Stephanie replies. "I like your American way bett-*air*. Monique should have said 'I want to start over' and all you American people would *enjoy* allowing Monique to start over. Yours is a modern freedom."

The word *history* triggers Harmony into telling us his theory as to why so many people are going to the gym these days. "People need to be perfect in *every* way so their souls won't have to reincarnate again. So many people are at the end of their cycles now. That's why Earth is so overpopulated. It's obvious. People are fed up with having to relive history. They want to end it."

"You people know so little about history," sniffs Stephanie. "Such a tragedy."

Replies Harmony, "The only tragedy I can think of would be if Hollywood made a movie set back in history and the set was propped incorrectly—like Pilgrims on the Mayflower eating kiwi fruits or burritos."

Stephanie, appalled, dismounts from the bike, reclaims the sense of balance in her tottering legs, then bounces off to the change room to de-Spandex.

"Testy testy," says Harmony. "What a downer."

"Europeans spend their years in school being beaten like animals," I say. "They suffer so much in the process of learning that their knowledge feels absolute. They won't tolerate being challenged."

"Speaking of history, I've got hot gossip. You know that old guy who lives above Anna-Louise?"

"The Man with 100 Pets and No TV?"

"Right—the man without a PIN number. Turns out Lancaster is named after him."

"*Him?*"

"Well, his family. He's a Lancaster. His family invented the town. My mom told me."

I wonder if Anna-Louise knows this. Unfortunately it's a bit late to tell her. "He keeps about thirty dogs and cats upstairs. And birds and fish. I saw them all last week."

"Weird guy. He looks like his idea of a hot holiday is renting a metal detector and combing Pebble Beach for lost wedding rings."

"I suspect he's far beyond the concept of holidays."

"You should tell your mom about him. She's selling KittyWhip now, right?"

A hot tip! "Harmony, you're a born middle manager."

"Thanks."

KittyWhip® rages onward.

From the Modernarium's window I see Lancasteroids of all aspects popping in and out of Betty parked outside, all day long, like the druggie kids in hot pursuit of methadone. As these would-be sales reps—lips foaming at the thought of work-free income—exit Betty, their faces are far sprightlier than when they entered, with tufts of promotional brochures and cardboard boxes bearing KittyPumps® tucked under their arms. Jim and Lorraine Jarvis seem positively revitalized, as does Eddie Woodman.

Jasmine herself has converted the dining-room table into her sales nexus. Between her half-time at the Plants and her preoccupation with KittyWhip®, she has maybe not had all of the time to pry into my life she might otherwise have, and this is fine. But Dan keeps telephoning now, and Jasmine talks on the phone with him behind closed doors, and this is not fine. Something's up.

Stephanie emerges from the change room and comes to sit beside me on a stationary bike. "Off the bike and change your clothes," she says. "Let us go to your Toxic Waste Dump. I have an idea."

38

The Dump is fairly kicking. I see a fleet of Jeeps, pickups, and 4W-Ds bearing major Halogen light-show action, plus Skye's Wagoonmobile (her mother's rusted AMC Matador sloppily painted with daisies, peace signs, and pine trees and the license plate LIVED B4) and Harmony's Celica PRV, beating us here from the gym (the *P*rincess *R*escuing *V*ehicle, license plate: YE GEEKE).

"So I guess Harmony's pursuing Skye after all," I tell Stephanie. "Otherwise in the middle of a sunny day like this he'd have returned home to hack military launch access codes in his dungeon—his basement."

"Love is so beautiful," sighs Stephanie.

Inside the Dump, I see Harmony and Skye squatting under a booth tabletop, felt-penning onto its chewing-gummed and bephlegmed wood underbelly.

"We've all guessed which year panda bears will become extinct," explains Pony, headed to the pay phone up front to phone in for his answering machine messages. "When we come back for a reunion in twenty-five years, we'll see who won. I guessed 2011."

"I guessed 2013," says Gaïa, standing up from the table.

"2007," shouts Harmony's voice from underneath.

Stephanie and I walk past a cluster of video games, and the heat from our bodies activates their "beg cycle"—triggering mouth-watering, fun-choked displays of on-screen pyrotechnics: exploding blondes, Porsches having sex with each other; UFOs shooting beams of money, all followed at the end by a plucky don't-do-drugs video. One new machine I've never seen before, called Infection, looks utterly hot, and its beg cycle showcases an asteroid's populace fending off scourges of killer bees, kudzu vines, tourists, and lawyers.

"How intense!" I shout. "Stephanie. I must have quarters. Do you have quarters?"

"Not *now*, Tyler. Later." We sit down.

"God, I wish they'd install urinals in the ladies room," says Gaïa, as we arrive at the table. "At chest height. So when you did the *one-two-three purge* you wouldn't always mess the knees of your panty hose on the bathroom floor."

Stephanie's gaze is riveted.

"Hi Steph. And don't look at me like I'm a freak or something. It's not like I purge professionally," Gaïa confesses. "Today was only some red-flavored Jell-O and half an onion bagel. Catch me around Thanksgiving. I'll be, like, a walking landfill. Come on. I'm going to the bathroom now. I'll give details."

Stephanie eagerly rockets off to Planet Purge, the ladies' bathroom, to swap bulimia tales with Gaïa, leaving the rest of us at the table in a cone of silence.

"Sir Pony met his social worker today," announces Harmony. "'Tis it not glamorous?"

Pony has already returned from the phone; no messages on his machine.

"But Pony," I say, confused. "You're *rich*. What are you doing with a social worker?"

"Mom obtained some sort of official classification declaring our family emotionally dysfunctional. So now we all have to be interviewed. I can obtain free counseling until I'm twenty-one. And Mom gets free retraining in computers. She's learning DOS. About time."

Skatepunks thrash and clomp across the restaurant, dancing on their boards—cute but like Rottweiler puppies: dreadfulness is knitted into their genes.

"Inventing a new dance is like inventing a new way to have sex," says Skye, to which Harmony blushes. The two shoot each other *we're-involved* glances. Skye will benefit from dating guys other than realtors and Harmony will benefit from dating, *period*. I worry about him reading bad pornography misspelled by fifteen-year olds over his computer bulletin boards.

"I quit my job at the electronic plantation today," Skye then reveals, "down at the telemarketing hell."

"She's going through coworker-deprivation syndrome. I'm helping her work her way through the crisis point."

From Mink I order a twisty, tomatoey car crash of fries for myself plus a club soda for Stephanie.

"How's life without Anna-Louise?" asks Skye.

"Have you seen her?" I ask. "She won't answer her phone and I left about fifty messages for her so fair's fair. The situation wouldn't have turned out the way it did if she hadn't overreacted."

"Nobody's accusing anyone of anything, Ty," says Harmony. "Chill."

"I think you still miss her," says Skye, to which I tell her to butt out.

"When is la French babe leaving town?" asks Pony.

"Next week," I reply.

"Wilt thou be missing her?" asks Harmony.

I consider the question. I can't answer and so I mumble I don't know and make lines of *faux* cocaine from NutraSweet on the Arborite tabletop. I wonder how much time will be required to repair the damage I've done with Anna-Louise, or if the damage is to be repaired at all. As of next week I'll have no relationship, no school, no job, and no career prospects. French-fry computer, here I come.

"Did you see Heather-Jo on *Designer Squadron* last night?" asks Skye, changing the subject to Heather-Jo Lockheed, our favorite TV star. Heather-Jo bounces from one series to the next, always offering a pleasing blend of spunkiness, a loathing of crime, great hair, plus a firm, aerobicized body. In *Designer Squadron*, Heather-Jo's latest series, she portrays a fashion designer by day/crime fighter by night. "Heather-Jo's the greatest," says Skye. "She never runs out of outfits." We continue to discuss Heather-Jo's career as Gaïa and Stephanie return to the table. Since nobody feels comfortable with Stephanie, there is an uncomfortable pause.

"So . . ." meows Skye, wanting to shit-disturb, "What are your and Tyler's plans for the next while, Stephanie?"

"We are going to California," Stephanie replies, taking me aback while reaching for one of my recently arrived bloody fries. "Tyler is going to develop his skills and become a fashion photographer and I am going to study acting."

Silence.

"Is this *true*, Tyler?" asks Skye.

I nod, not quite believing I'm nodding. As I grow older, the act of imagining my life as a rock video becomes harder, but moments like this sure make up for the loss.

And Skye can barely control herself from running to the telephone to call Anna-Louise.

"When are you leaving?" asks Gaïa.

"Next week," says Stephanie nonchalantly.

"That is unbelievably cool," says Pony. "What'll you do when you meet Heather-Jo on the beach in Malibu?"

"Ask her to write her name in the sand, then roll in the words," I add.

I make eye contact with Stephanie and her eyes say, *"Oh come on—as if you didn't know we were going to California."*

"You'll become stars," says Skye, with a charitable lack of malice.

"Yes," I reply, "we'll become stars."

"You consider the idea. Okay?" says Stephanie while we drive home.

"But how would we live?"

"There is always work for *yong* people like you and me."

"But what about . . . *I don't know.*"

"Is there something keeping you in Lancaster, Tyler?"

"Well, no."

"And will you ever become famous or rich in Lancaster?"

"Not exactly."

"Then you have nothing to lose. Just *think* about the idea."

What is Dan's car doing in our driveway?

39

Life is maybe like deep-sea fishing. We wake up in the morning, we cast our nets into the waters, and, if we are lucky, at day's end we will have netted one—maybe two —small fish. Occasionally we will net a seahorse and sometimes a shark—or a life preserver or an iceberg, or a monster. And in our dreams at night we assess our Catch of the Day—the treasures of this long, slow process of accumulation—and we eat the flesh of our fish, casting away their bones and weaving the memories of their once-glinting skins into our souls.

Yes, Dan is in the kitchen, seated between a jovial, boozy-looking Grandma and Grandpa. Jasmine is standing over the sink. I can see them as I peer through the steamy window from outside, my basketball shoes crushing the frosted dead marigolds underneath as though they were breakfast cereal.

Dan is sipping from a bottle of DesignatedDriver™ non-alcoholic beer and feasting from an array of nutritional crack placed before him: Cheezie Nuggies, nitrite-soaked ham rollmops, and Nacho Nodules. My stomach feels like a deflated balloon.

"Dan's there," I inform Stephanie back in the Comfortmobile.

"Then take me to the Old Decoy. I am not staying here."

"Come on, Steph—"

"No."

At the Old Decoy, Stephanie exits the car. "Bring me my things, Tyler. I will be in my old *rooo*m watching HBO. Ciao."

Such a mess.

I enter the kitchen after depositing Stephanie at the Old Decoy and I feel a burst of warped psychic energy as Grandpa announces without irony, "Hey Tyler, your pop's back!"

Jasmine turns away from me, unable to look me in the eyes, thereafter becoming RoboWife, replenishing Dan's snack tray and futzing about the sink area, picking out the dead black ants she ground into her dress earlier on in the day. I wish Jasmine would look at me without the glazed, hearty expression she's using, but she won't. I suspect my efforts to have her look at me otherwise will fail, like trying to feed birds once the sun has set.

"I'm off the bottle now, Tyler," says Dan, "and I want you and me to become friends again." (Again?) "I want you to put the past behind us and start as a family."

Is he serious? Grandma and Grandpa sit waiting for me to agree, but I won't. The only reply is a mist of Jasmine's New Age tinkles rolling in from the living-room stereo. Dan farts. He picks up a hyacinth and waves it around to mask the smell and Grandma and Grandpa think he's just a laugh riot.

"So Jaz," says Dan, now on a comedy roll. "What do you call your new hairstyle—Day Pass?" More yucks from Grandma and Grandpa. I'm beginning to feel like a microwaved egg that will explode if anybody so much as breathes onto the surface. Sitting beside Dan in the kitchen is unleashing a flood of memories from when I was younger—trying but never being able to predict what would catalyze Dan into a rage after his fifth scotch and three bites of dinner. I'm remembering how Daisy and Mark and I simply stopped offering opinions or showing traces of emotion, refusing to sell triggers to complete his weapons-buildup scheme. And I'm remembering how it was we came to be emotionless robots when around him.

The topic changes to the economy of Lancaster. "Maybe you should just lower your expectations, Tyler," Dan says, as Grandpa nods in approval. Right. Don't they understand that asking me to lower my expectations is like asking me to change the color of my eyes?

I excuse myself and leave to pack Stephanie's things. Mark is in the hallway holding a microwave milkshake he had wanted to nuke but won't because he is afraid of going into the kitchen with Dan there. I carry Mark upstairs and he squirms and giggles and yells the words *confess! confess!* at me, then watches while I pack.

"Can I come with you to deliver the stuff to Stephanie's hotel?"

"You'd best not, Mark."

"She's not staying in your room any longer?"

"Maybe. Maybe not."

"Because of Dan moving back in?"

"I think so."

"Can I stay with her?"

"You, Daisy, and me should *all* go stay with her."

"Will you ever see Anna-Louise again? I liked her."

"Hand me that sweater."

Mark tells me the government is digging up a freight train it once buried beside the plants, a train buried back in the 1940s that was so toxic it couldn't be cleansed. And now the army is going to exhume this freight train because it wasn't buried deeply enough. The army is going to weld it up into small bits, and drop it into the deepest hole ever dug, and bury it forever. I wish the army luck.

"Oh, sweetness," Jasmine sighed to me last week while sorting through the Johnson family's destroyed cutlery collection: knives black from hot-knifing; forks black from microwaving; spoons kinked from Daisy's flirtation with the paranormal and her efforts at psychic spoon bending, "it's so much easier to live someone else's life than your own."

"I don't understand, Jasmine. How can you live someone else's life?" My question broke her out of her reverie.

"Of *course*. What am I saying?" She took a pair of scissors from the cutlery drawer and trimmed Kittykat's tray of SoberPuss® noneuphoric grazing grass. "I'm giving you bad tapes. Of course, you can only lead your *own* life, Tyler."

"Of course."

But now I wonder if Jasmine was telegraphing me a clue. Sending her *self* a clue about tonight's bombshell. Jasmine, *why* did you readmit Dan into your life? Toss the bum out. What tools do you need to remove him? I tell you what: I give you all of my strength—I seal it inside a little green envelope and mail it to you with hope and peace and much much love. Take all you need and take it quickly.

HAMPICK PLANET

40

In periods of rapid personal change, we pass through life as though we are spellcast. We speak in sentences that end before finishing. We sleep heavily because we need to ask so many questions as we dream alone. We bump into others and feel bashful at recognizing souls so similar to ourselves.

At the Old Decoy, Stephanie and I speak as though we are both spellcast—hexed—breaking and reigniting the spell as we go along.

"I think now is a good time to decide if you will go to California, Tyler."

"Now?"

"Yes, now."

"But now is so soon."

"Life is soon."

"But . . ."

"What can we say, Tyler? Call me tomorrow—after you have had sleep and after you have had dreams."

"I can't stay with you tonight?"

"No."

"You are a dog."

"You are not a dog."

"Bark."

"Drive away in your car."

Daisy and Mark and I are sleeping in my room tonight —sleeping on the floor inside a lasagna of sleeping bags and blankets—under the moonlight while faint acid-sweet tendrils of skunk stink crawl in through the window. Dan is in Jasmine's room.

It is well past midnight now, and Daisy and Mark thrash about in shallow sleep, occasionally reaching for me and for each other as we dream together. Out the window I see an unnatural brightness underneath the overcast clouds that have swept in from the Pacific earlier this evening. The brightness underneath these clouds is moony and pearlescent and warm—alive and inviting—as though the earth on the other side of the mountains is phosphorescent with light.

As though there is a city on the other side.

PART

III

PART
THREE

41

Flight.

A seagull glides beside me while I stand by the ferry's deck railing. The gull cruises at the ferry's speed and appears motionless—it just hovers there—like a good idea.

The ship's captain announces that we have just crossed an invisible line—a border—into Canada. Stephanie and I peer into the boat's wake, dumbly, expecting to see a dotted line. We are aboard a ferry headed from Port Angeles, Washington, toward Vancouver Island. My past lies behind me like a bonfire of anchors and I am freed from the trappings of identity. I want *more* invisible lines to cross: time zones; the 49th parallel; the Equator; the Continental Divide. I remember reading of an F-16 fighter jet with a computer-software glitch that made it flip upside down when crossing the Equator; I want to know the software secrets encoded deep within *my* cells. I watch Stephanie's Hermès scarf rustle in the wind and I feel unpredictable and shockingly new.

Stephanie and I spent last night in a cheap motel back in Port Angeles, but I was too excited to sleep. I was still giddy from having packed and slipped out of Lancaster early in the morning. And I was excited because of my plan to visit my birthplace—the old commune house in the Gulf Islands of British Columbia—and to afterward visit my biological father, Neil, in northern California as we drive to Los Angeles to begin new lives.

Life feels full of magic surprises.

In Canada the coins are gold and bear a picture of a loon. Stephanie uses these gold coins to buy milk chocolates and bottled water and a country & western tape from a roadside store. Later, above our heads on the miniferry ride to an island called Galiano—my birthplace—bald eagles hang out in the updrafts like preteens massed in a video arcade. A swan lands beside the ferry. A pulse of Canada geese patrols the waters in the distance. So many birds! And the water smells of salt and nutrition and the color green.

Upon arrival on Galiano Island we rumble down a series of stony roads, past ditches choking with greenery, past tumbledown old signage, until we come to the path I remember, an almost unfindable path, and I park the car.

Stephanie grabs my hand and I lead her through fronds of blackberry and salmonberry that reach out and stroke her cheeks like beggars' fingers. We cross a bog of skunk cabbage and pass under a dark, dry, muffled canopy of hemlock. We emerge into a small glade lit by a shaft of sunlight where there stands a dwarfish stone pillar of what was once a chimney. It is surrounded by a small mossy rectangle of fireweed, liverworts, huckleberry, ferns, and magic psilocybin mushrooms. There are almost no other traces of human habitation having once been here. All metals have rusted, all wood has rotted. The garden is overgrown and is twice my height with saplings.

"This is where you were born?" asks Stephanie.

I nod my reply.

Stephanie smiles and says to me, "This is a good place to enter the world."

I agree with her—it is a fine fine place. I touch a branch of hemlock to my forehead. I crown myself the king of trees.

42

Another day.

We thumb our noses at the steaming busloads of people we blithely pass along the Coast Highway headed south, down toward Oregon. The Comfortmobile's stereo booms scorching technotunes by Scottish teenagers filled with bad teeth and the need to sing.

On the left we see a freight train with antlers nailed to its engine pulling sausage-linked railcars loaded with oxygen tanks and Hondas with skins like melting cherry popsicles. Stenciled on the sides of other cars are other labels: MOLTEN SULFUR, LIQUID CORN SYRUP, and AQUEOUS HYDRAZINE. Stephanie and I comprise our own list of the chemicals needed in order to be a truly modern person: "Tetracycline."

"Steroids."

"Freon."

"Aspartame."

"Peroxide."

"Silicon."

"MTV."

Stephanie shoots a cap gun into the roof of her mouth. To our right a spectacular ocean vista emerges. I yank the car over and announce, "We now bring you a thirty-second beauty break," but Stephanie wants to stay in the car to untangle a cassette. She's pouting because she asked me to marry her and I said no way—it'd be years before I married her or any other woman.

I run to inspect this view from the cliff—the Pacific vista—the end of the world—and am thrilled at how unlike Europe the view is, Europe's overhistoried countrysides dusted with charcoal and laced with unmoving gullies of pureed smoker's lung.

And while standing on the cliff, my instinct is to scan pretty scenery—but not for too long. I feel the need to turn around to ensure I'm not about to be pushed over. I do this, but of course, when I check, all I see is Stephanie in the car making "can-we-go-now?" hand gestures.

Our diets stink: turkey jerky, carbon dioxide fizz candies, and diner food. For lunch we eat diner chicken with no skin. "Jesus," I say, "senior citizens don't want to eat chicken skin so *nobody* eats chicken skin. Grandma and Grandpa rule the world. And tell me—*where*, exactly is all the unused chicken skin going?"

We mull the question over a second, then conclude simultaneously: *"KittyWhip!"*

On a beach we find clams. Unidentifiable violet berries grow in the scrub beside the beach. How strange to find food just *sitting* there—unregulated, unhusbanded—inefficient. We look at these items and experience severe difficulty relating to them. "Not the least bit modern," we pronounce.

Down below, delightful, giddy flockettes of sandpipers and teeny seabirds like Christmas-tree ornaments, egg-shaped and canapé-sized, scamper into the sandy wash of a receding wave, pecking for nourishing little nothings left by the sea. "Oh look," I shout, "how complete!"

Later in a farmer's co-op we inhale the sweet malty feed-store smell. Seed racks and harsh eddies of pesticide vapor remind us that in spite of the blenderized state of our lives, the growing of food continues as ever.

When I ditched Lancaster, I snuck out quietly, at about six in the morning. Daisy and Mark were still groggy on the floor, but they knew what I was doing while I stuffed my most important clothes and shampoos into my suitcase.

"California—oh. Are you going to phone?" asked Daisy.

"I'll call in one month," I said, "after I'm settled. I'll call on your princess phone."

"What do we tell Mom?"

"I'm gone."

"You have an address?"

"Care of American Express if she has to. Tell her I don't want to talk to her now."

"Can I have your room?" asked Mark.

"God, the body's not even cold. Okay, you guys can borrow my stuff as much as you want, but I'll be needing it eventually."

The sun is in the other side of the sky at dinnertime when, in a fit of dietary guilt, Stephanie and I skulk into a yuppie delicatessen just over the Oregon border.

A clerk my age laser scans our small piece of smoked

salmon. He crabs about the classic rock music pumped in on the Muzak system. "Just when you think you've tossed the last handful of dirt onto the graves of those old rock stars, *kablooey!* Their coffins explode and they're back with *yet another* album."

"Tyler—" Stephanie semiwhispers. "Look—isn't that a famous person?"

Antennas up: "Where?"

"By the baguettes. With the famous-looking hair."

Stephanie's right: famous hair.

The clerk looks up: "Oh, Lee Simpson—he's in every day. The Hazelford Clinic is just up the street."

"Hazelford Clinic is just up the street? No way."

"Way. Just past the road construction."

"What is Hazelford?" Stephanie asks.

"Only the most famous detox clinic in the world," says the clerk with pride. "That's all."

I react: "Let's go exploring."

Smoked salmon in tow, we roar up Arbutus Boulevard in the Comfortmobile, up past the roadwork site, on to the low, matte-black stealth architecture concealing, no doubt, dozens of my favorite stars tethered to pegs in a basement, loinclothed and filthy and screaming for opium. Stephanie mans the car and I ready my camera. "Maybe we'll see Heather-Jo Lockheed," I say. "She's always in and out of clinics. You know what would be the best?"

"What?"

"To see Heather-Jo run screaming from the clinic building, red-eyed and naked under a blue Chinese robe, throwing herself onto the hood of the Comfortmobile, her tits wobbling and covered in car dust, begging pitifully for drugs and a ride to freedom. Now *that's* a star. '*Heather-Jo*,' I'd say, '*You just stop being so darned famous, and Heather-Jo—don't you worry, we'll find you a star famous enough for you to make it with. Just* don't *take those pills. Not yet."*

Unfortunately, we don't see Heather-Jo or any other stars. A trio of aviator-glassed goons at the security gate prevent us from even approaching the facilities. So I guess Hazelford *is* a good sanctuary for the famous. "Well I know the institute *I'll* be visiting when it's my turn to detox."

"You would be so lucky."

"No guests like Dan at a place like Hazelford."

"Make your reservation now."

The Heather-Jo incident, or the lack thereof, has made Stephanie more curious about TV here. We're holed up for the night in the motelliest motel going, Mel's Anchor View, of Astoria, Oregon, and we want to steal everything in our room: phoned-in artwork (little metal rectangles welded together), faded madras curtains with little 1962 gold threads, and side tables shaped like pee piddled onto linoleum. We're waiting for Heather-Jo's latest network hit, *Designer Squadron*, to start, and we're trolling the thirty-seven available cable stations for sizzling bits. Life is rich.

"This is wonderful," says Stephanie.

"TV is here for ten thousand years," I say. "It will never ever leave."

That night before we go to sleep we eat bread from the yuppie delicatessen. It smells faintly of roses. We drink water from the motel's taps. It tastes like melted snow.

43

Halloween night and we're prisoners of the The Lariat Motor Lodge, Mount Shasta, California—Jasmine's hometown. The Comfortmobile is having a CAT scan and Thorazine injections at a local garage. My poor baby is sick—coughed, then passed out at a Chevron station off Interstate 5 just hours ago.

To stretch our legs, Stephanie and I, wrapped in sweaters, walk through cozy suburbs and watch small children trick-or-treat. We survey midget punks and ballerinas and bag ladies and Supermen while Roman candles explode in the unlikeliest places at the unlikeliest times, triggering eruptions in the trees—I mistake the flight of frightened birds for shooting stars. On the ground among dried brown fall leaves I find a traffic-safety capsule of glow-in-the-dark Martian green guck, which we toss back and forth while we walk.

"Look behind you," says Stephanie, and I drop the light. "What a sophisticated costume."

Behind us is a small boy in black jeans, a black turtle-neck, and a little white fright wig. With him is a little girl in a similar white fright wig and a little black dress, and the two are holding hands, walking down the middle of a quiet street, their sacks half filled with candy, their minds hungry with the prospect of more candy to come.

"It's Andy and Edie," I whisper, happy to see Andy Warhol and Edie Sedgwick, happy at last, the way they are in heaven.

It really *is* as though children live in a dream.

Last Halloween back in Lancaster I made Anna-Louise play "planets" with me. We had been sitting at the Toxic Waste Dump eating lunch and reading our paper place mats. Anna-Louise had a "Mixed Drinks of America" place mat *("Tyler, five bucks if you can tell me what's in a Rob Roy")*. My place mat was "The Planets," complete with dizzying columns of fun numbers.

So afterward, out on Route 666, I bought a pumpkin from a farmer's stand, plus a few pea pods. I then drove the two of us out to an open field toward the Plants, and, after figuring a few calculations on my wristwatch calculator, placed the pumpkin down on the ground and told Anna-Louise to wait beside it. I then walked a healthy shout's-length away, where I then opened a pea pod and placed one lone pea on the dry dirt before me.

"You're the sun," I yelled to Anna-Louise, "and I'm Earth. The pumpkins and peas are the relative sizes of the two bodies. And the distance between us is the relative distance."

"This game is so *male*," Anna-Louise shouted back. "What happens next?"

"I don't know. Shine. Go supernova. Be a black hole."

Anna-Louise picked up her pumpkin, carried it against

her chest, and huffed like a locomotive over to where I stood with my little green pea sitting on the dry gray dirt. She then threw the pumpkin down on the pea, squishing the pea and crushing the pumpkin.

"Tyler," she said to me, scraping seeds from within the shell, putting them into her down-vest pockets for later roasting and planting, "name me *one* other possible way this game could have ended. Just *one*."

Yes, I am thinking about Anna-Louise.

I shake Stephanie.

"Tyler, why are you hitting me? I was sleeping."

"I wanted to make sure you weren't undead. It's only nine o'clock."

"It's been a long day. I want to sleep."

"I was only out of the room five minutes getting a pop. How can you go to sleep so fast? What will I do?"

"You are pathetic. Write a letter. Use the pretty *pay*-per provided by the ho-*tell*. Don't watch TV. I don't want noise. Leave me al-*ooone*." She bops me with her pillow. I leave the room.

The old man at the front desk asks me, when I ask for more paper, whether I'd enjoy using the Lariat Motor Lodge's business facility.

"Business facility?"

"Personal computer with dot-matrix printer. Fax machine. Photocopier. Have to lure in those yuppies. It's a slow night. It'd be nice to have someone else here in the office."

I say, "Well, if you don't mind—yes, I *do* have an important letter I've been thinking of writing."

"I'll fetch you the work chair," he says, grabbing a caster-wheeled office chair, pointing sagely to a pad on the chair's back: "lumbar support."

The PC is a beauty: a Macintosh with Microsoft Word, extended keypad, and ergonomically correct mouse. I dive into my letter and the sound of the night clerk's aging Zenith TV crackles behind me, hot and spitting, with squeaks like bubbling creosote and spits like timber on fire. Like the sound of a burning bridge.

44

Dear Frank E. Miller,

First, I would like to inform you of how much I enjoyed your best-selling autobiography, *Life at the Top*, which I have read three times. I highlighted your best sayings with a DayGlo yellow felt pen and also loaned *Life at the Top* to my friends (we are all twenty years old) who were equally inspired by your words. You are our role model!

Well, to business, Mr. Miller: I have an idea for Bechtol that could net good profit for your company. I will be brief.

To wit: I think our country is having a shortage of historical objects—there are not enough old things for people to own. As well, we have too many landfills, plus an ever-looming fuel shortage. So I therefore say, Mr. Miller, *"Why not combine these three factors with our country's love of theme parks and come out a winner?"*

I suggest, Mr. Miller, that Bechtol develop a nationwide chain of theme parks called *HistoryWorld*™ in which visitors (wearing respirators and outfits furnished by Bechtol's military division) dig through landfill sites abandoned decades ago (and purchased by Bechtol for next to nothing) in search of historical objects like pop bottles, old telephones, and furniture. The deeper visitors dig, the further visitors travel back in time, and hence the more they would pay.

HistoryWorld™'s motto: INSTANT HISTORY.

At night visitors would then stay in Bechtol's *HistoryWorld*™ on-site hotels featuring *HistoryWorld*™ museum franchises showcasing the history of history (*"Oh honey, look—a stratum of phone books—another year has gone by." Kiss kiss.*)

But these ideas are only the beginning of the *HistoryWorld*™ profit potential. Consider:

—As widows from London, England, in WW II will testify, antiques make fine fuel. Landfills are bursting with fuel: newspapers and wood in particular. *HistoryWorld*™ visitors would not only be excavating for exciting historical artifacts, but *helping contribute to alternative fuel sources, too.* Bechtol could easily sell the fuel recovered from landfills, perhaps even diversifying into a new chrono-fuel division. Being first, Bechtol would instantly become the industry leader. What an opportunity!

—*TimeSift*™ rubble-sifting machines would be needed to separate and calibrate the myriad dolls' heads, mayonnaise jars, soil, ski boots, and construction debris that clog all landfills. These *TimeSift*™ devices could be manufactured, of course, by Bechtol's currently underutilized military-hardware divisions and could be sold both domestically and abroad. Profit, ahoy!

—Underemployed people could be hired to help sort sifted debris into various types of recyclability, the results of which could be resold for (you guessed it) *profit*. Summer jobs for young people, and maybe the homeless, too!

—*TimeMagnets*™ could be developed by the electro-cryonic division of Bechtol to separate ferro-magnetic debris such as unrusted cans of lima beans, bedposts, and filing cabinets from all other clutter. This rescued metal could then be profitably recycled.

Of course, Mr. Miller, *HistoryWorld*™ will require a cartoon mascot. Might I recommend a seagull? Perhaps "Samuel the Seagull" or a similar character. Samuel can wear a little cartoon respirator. He could be good friends with Beth the Backhoe, too. But this is jumping the gun. The most important step now is to begin organizing *HistoryWorld*™. If executed correctly, *HistoryWorld*™ could utilize all of Bechtol's diverse corporate divisions *and* be a profit bonanza that helps the planet, too.

Mr. Miller, I would be happy to assist in the development of *HistoryWorld*™. Plus, as I live not far away from Seattle, I could be available for consultation almost immediately. *HistoryWorld*™ is an idea whose time has come, and I would be proud to have involvement with both it and Bechtol, should the project ever come to fruition.

Yours with admiration and sincerity,
Tyler Johnson
Dip. H/MM

PS: I am twenty years old and am graduating in hotel/motel management at Lancaster Community College, Lancaster, Washington.

45

We are yet again prisoners of the Lariat Motor Lodge, Mount Shasta, California—the Comfortmobile won't be discharged from the clinic until 5:30. Stephanie and I are allowed to keep our motel room until 5:00 and we are both sensationally bored—so bored we feel stoned, like we've drunk a bottle of cough syrup each. Travel restlessness fills us; we want to *move*.

Stephanie's juggling lace hankies and firing her cap gun at the ceiling. Lunch kills 3,600 seconds. I post last night's letter to Frank E. Miller in Seattle, addressed to "Biff" Miller, his college nickname, thus boosting the letter's chances of being read by Frank E. Miller himself.

On the way back from the post office, I stop at a Bank of America ATM and withdraw from my rapidly disappearing savings. I then convert my withdrawal into a wad of low-denomination bills. I feel like a crack dealer. I have an idea.

YOUR INABILITY TO ACHIEVE SOLITUDE MAKES YOU
SETTLE FOR SUBSTANDARD RELATIONSHIPS

YOU DON'T BELIEVE MAGIC IS POSSIBLE
IN LIVES LIVED WITHIN TRADITIONAL BOUNDARIES

I am writing a list of tragic character flaws on my dollar bills with a felt pen. I am thinking of the people in my universe and distilling for each of these people the *one* flaw in their character that will lead to their downfall—the flaw that will be their undoing.

Jasmine, Anna-Louise, Daisy, Mark, Dan, Stephanie, Monique, Kiwi, Harmony, Skye, Gaïa, Mei-Lin, Davidson, Pony, Grandma and Grandpa, Eddie Woodman, Jim and Lorraine Jarvis—everybody's here. Even me. And more.

What I write are not sins; I write *tragedies*. And I am writing these tragedies in a manner that the recipients can easily absorb. And I won't say whose flaw is whose. I continue. In no particular order:

YOU DISGUISE YOUR LAZINESS AS PRIDE

YOU ARE PARALYZED BY THE FACT
THAT CRUELTY IS OFTEN AMUSING

YOU PRETEND TO BE MORE ECCENTRIC
THAN YOU ACTUALLY ARE BECAUSE YOU
WORRY YOU ARE AN INTERCHANGEABLE COG

YOU MISTAKE MOTION FOR GROWTH
AND ARE LURED INTO VEXING SITUATIONS

YOU DEFEND OTHER PEOPLE'S IDEAS
AT THE EXPENSE OF YOUR OWN

YOU STILL DON'T KNOW WHAT YOU DO WELL

YOU ARE UNABLE TO VISUALIZE
YOURSELF IN A FUTURE

YOUR INABILITY TO SUSTAIN SEXUAL INTEREST
IN JUST ONE OTHER PERSON DRAINS YOUR
LIFE OF THE POSSIBILITY OF INTIMACY

YOUR OWN ABILITY TO RATIONALIZE YOUR BAD DEEDS
MAKES YOU BELIEVE THE ENTIRE UNIVERSE
IS AS AMORAL AS YOURSELF

YOU WILLFULLY IGNORE THE SMALL, GENTLE
OBSERVATIONS IN LIFE WHICH YOU KNOW
ARE THE MOST IMPORTANT

Stephanie is mutilating cash, too, garnishing my mottoes with messy red lipstick kisses as we bring into the foreground the secret language of money—biting the invisible hand that feeds us.

YOUR FEAR OF CHANGE IS TOO
CLEARLY VISIBLE IN YOUR EYES

YOU ARE WASTING YOUR YOUTH,
YOUR TIME, AND YOUR MONEY
BECAUSE YOU WON'T ACKNOWLEDGE
YOUR SHORTCOMINGS

SHAMPOO PLANET

YOUR REFUSAL TO ACKNOWLEDGE
THE DARK SIDE OF HUMANITY
MAKES YOU PREY TO THAT DARK SIDE

YOU WORRY THAT IF YOU LOWER YOUR GUARD,
EVEN FOR ONE SECOND,
YOUR WHOLE WORLD WILL
DISINTEGRATE INTO CHAOS

YOU WAIT FOR FATE TO BRING ABOUT
THE CHANGES IN LIFE WHICH YOU
SHOULD BE BRINGING ABOUT YOURSELF

YOU ARE DAZED BY THE EASE
WITH WHICH OBLITERATION CAN BE OBTAINED

YOU FEEL YOU HAVE MORE MEMORIES
THAN YOU HAVE ENERGY
TO PROCESS THOSE MEMORIES

YOU ARE UNABLE TO DIFFERENTIATE BETWEEN FACADE
AND SUBSTANCE

Hours later we pay the Comfortmobile's hospital bill with some of our "tragic cash." The mechanic, after reading his money, can't herd us out of his garage fast enough.

Stephanie and I are eager to flee Mount Shasta. Our plan is to drive at warp speed down Interstate 5, then branch over Route 299 onto Highway 101 toward Humboldt County and my dad's house. We could have spent the night in Mount Shasta, but we felt the unfightable urge to move.

Hopefully tonight we'll drive through Trinity and Siskiyou Counties before we OD on driving and need to crash in a cheap motel.

Our drive into the night is chatless and tunage-free. The scenery is flat, dry, and Lancasterish. Stephanie falls asleep beside me and I think about the family and friends I've left behind me back home. I pull into a Circle-K grocery to buy a nostalgic bag of Cheezie Nuggies and a ginger ale, feeling a twinge of pride in belonging to a society that can maintain a beacon of light and technology like this Circle-K out in the middle of nowhere. Convenience stores: the economic engine of the New Order.

The store inside is a spacious warehouse of potato chips, chocolate bars, pop, and car magazines—and little else. Dwindling numbers of species outside; dwindling selection of products inside. It's the new balance of Nature.

The store is also lit to the point of painfulness by a ceiling loaded with more fluorescent bulbs than a landing mothership. Shielding my headachey eyes, I make my consumer choices, then head to the counter, where the clerk is wearing sunglasses. I pay the clerk with a five-dollar bill on which I have felt-penned the words:

I AM AFRAID OF THE DARK AGES.

46

Have you ever researched your family tree? Have you ever tried to meet an unknown relative merely because you shared blood? Telephoned a stranger out of the blue? Knocked on the door of this stranger's house because you knew shared chromosomes pulsed behind it?

Maybe you have and maybe you were pleasantly surprised. But then, maybe you regretted doing so. Maybe you realized some folks are best left a name and a date on a piece of yellowing three-ring notepaper in the back of a kitchen drawer, your sister's hot date's phone number scribbled in one corner (MURRAY IS A GOD: 684-1975) and a half-finished game of hangman doodled on the other corner (H__ATH__RJ__L__CKH___D).

Maybe you saw these strangers and you said to yourself, "You are not me"—but you were wrong. They *are* you; you are them. You are all one forest.

My biological father, Neil, lives in a cedar-shingled Hobbit-type house trimmed with purple, deep inside the redwoods. On the thatched roof above the Plexiglas light bubble and long-dead solar panels is a rainbow wind sock; a sky-blue 1940s truck muralled with latex paint clouds is parked out front amid a patch of lupins, Shasta daisies, Scotch broom, and California poppies. Stephanie and I have had to unlock two gates and pass three DO NOT ENTER signs to access this house, aided by an iffy map sketched by Jasmine years ago which had the two gate keys taped to the bottom. What a treasure hunt.

For today's big surprise meeting I'm wearing a shirt and tie. A decade has passed since I've seen Neil, so I want to look mature. I am expecting much insight into why I am the way I am as a result of this trip, and my knees go limp upon seeing the house.

Neil's children, maybe ten of them, blond with pale blue wolf eyes, are strapping each other with frizzes of redwood bark as Stephanie and I drive up. Two girls hold Barbie dolls with third eyes painted on their foreheads. All of these children fall silent when they see the Comfortmobile, then fall to the ground, like in a 1950s nuclear alert.

"Jesus."

"*Sacré bleu.*"

The kids start wailing and screaming, crawling to the side of the house. Two women in white prairie dresses run onto the porch, each wiping her hands off on an apron. One of the women shrieks inside, and Neil, white-bearded like God, clad only in bib overalls and cowboy boots, runs down the house's porch aiming a 12-gauge shotgun as Stephanie and I stop our walk toward the house, frozen— petrified.

"What do you want?" he barks.

"Neil?"

"What of it?"

"I'm Tyler."

Neil knits his brows, cocks his head, then says, "I don't know any Tyler. Tyler—oh—*Tyler*. Tyler?" He lowers his gun, whistles an all clear. He lumbers down the steps to hug me, his snowy beard clinging to my crispy gelled hair as to Velcro. The past minute of fear is erased. "And this —" he says, turning to Stephanie—"Is . . . uh . . . *Daisy*." He goes to hug her and Stephanie flinches.

"No, Neil. This is Stephanie. A good friend. Daisy is in Lancaster."

Neil hugs her, regardless.

The children are swarming about us, touching my tie and reaching for Stephanie's hoop earrings. In their faces I see snatches of my own face—I didn't realize I had so many half-siblings, and I experience an odd pleasure while meeting them—like eating a pear you know was harvested from a twig grafted onto an apple tree. The kids are wearing T-shirts with molecules printed on them: LSD, chocolate, testosterone, valium, THC, and other mood-altering chemicals.

"Come inside," Neil says. "Have lunch. Be with us. Let us gather."

"Pa sells these shirts at festivals," one of the kids offers. Her shirt is filthy.

"My decoy business," Neil says, then whispers into my ear: "*The Feds*."

"Does MTV have a molecule?" I ask.

"What's MTV?" Neil replies. "I don't like designer drugs."

The scariest aspect of the kitchen is that there are no boxes or cans or other tokens of this nation's mighty food-distribution system—no recognizable brand names. No processed foods. No microwaves. No electricity. Nothing. Jars are filled with bits of plants and grains that I don't recognize, even with Jasmine's training. Crystals are nudged into all corners of the ceilings. Incense reek permeates all porous surfaces. Knickknacks are smooth and carved from redwood: hippie accessories to Eden. This kitchen makes the kitchen in Lancaster seem like the Space Shuttle.

And these two women, Laurel and Jolene—spacey-eyed and barefooted—don't talk. Nada. They *do* smile a lot, but their smiles are creepy hippie smiles, like the smiles friendly folk give you in a small town when your car breaks down and they feed you and feed you and you think it's great, only to discover in the end you're going to be their Thanksgiving dinner. Nonetheless, Laurel and Jolene have fixed a no-doubt nutritious lunch, a flavorless legume casserole.

During the meal, as we sit around a large redwood dinner table, Neil is wholly uncurious about my visit. He doesn't ask me even one question. Not even, say, *"How long are you here?"* or, *"Why are you here?"* He is also bleary-eyed. Stoned. I think the women are tripping, too. The kids aren't high, though. They're bestial, alternating between being mean as a sack of cats, or as dull as a sack full of sacks. Boy, they need discipline.

"Jasmine is in good spirits," I offer. Neil nods, saying this is great, but Laurel and Jolene don't respond to a mention of their once-rival. When this lunch isn't scary, it's boring. I give a few sundry details about life in Lancaster.

Stephanie keeps squinting, trying to see hints of my face under Neil's beard. "Oh lady, you've got to stop looking like that," Neil says. "I'm freaking out."

"Zut! My apologies," says Stephanie.

I give up on conversation with these deadheads, and talk to Stephanie as though only the two of us are present. This strategy seems to work well, relieving the elders of taxing thought processes. "Jasmine met Neil at a Rainbow festival in Redwood City. Neil was a guide."

"A guide?"

"He guided people through acid trips. Sweated it out with them in bathtubs. Talked them down. He and Jasmine lived in the middle of a total scene: bikers, speed freaks, suicides—casualties lying all over the place. Neil guided Jasmine through a bad dose of microdot. They lived for a while in the woods outside of Mount Shasta, then moved to the new commune in B.C. together."

"Freaks." Neil chuckles trollishly to himself.

"Jasmine says that because of both acid and Neil, she's well aware of the infinitely rich possibilities of life. She says acid opened doors she never knew existed. But she also said that once she began to fear acid, she could never drop it again."

"The Fear," Neil says with authority, then brusquely adds: "Coyote, take Norman his lunch."

"Yes, Pa," says one of my half-brothers—Coyote, I suppose—grabbing a plate of casserole and heading out a rear door.

"Who's Norman?"

"Jasmine not told you?"

"No."

"Norman is your godfather."

"Wild!" This is just the sort of exciting fun fact I was hoping to find by visiting Neil. "Really?" Imagine—being able to meet the human specifically chosen to provide me with religious instruction.

"But Norman's kind of out of things. He's not much to talk to," Neil adds.

Silence. I know what *this* means. "Casualty?" I ask.

Neil, Laurel, and Jolene nod.

47

After lunch Neil shepherds me into a tepee sweat lodge in an alder grove behind the house. Stephanie, daggers in her eyes, has been delegated by Neil to stay behind in the kitchen to help clean up. "We have male energies and lore to exchange."

As Neil and I walk out back, naked except for yellowed, frayed guest towels wrapped round our waists—towels stolen two decades back from the Fairmont Hotel in San Francisco—I see Stephanie's face through an oval kitchen window, her hands washing dishes in the sink. She's angry as a buzzing hornet at having been abandoned in the 13th century.

The children swarm about us, their directionless motions and fluttering long white hair mimicking the imbecilic liquid world of fish under the sea. In their hands are strings of plastic and clay beads, which they trade with each other like strands of genetic material. These children are not allowed to enter the sweat lodge with us.

Smoke streams out a hole in the roof. Inside the air is chewy and salty and hot. The gel in my hair is an odor magnet and I'm going to emerge from this experience smelling like lox. Redwood planks burn my thighs while Neil lights a joint and offers me a toke. "No thanks. I have to drive."

He arches his eyes in surprise. "Young people have no memories. You're unable to mourn the past."

"Huh?" These hippies.

We sit and get mellow while Neil smokes his "Dr. Jay."

"Did Jasmine tell you the story of Norman and the bicycle?" Neil asks.

"Never."

"After Norman flipped out in Santa Cruz we had to babysit him. We smuggled him up to British Columbia with us, up to Galiano Island."

"I was just up there. Up at Galiano."

Neil ponders this. "Yeah? See anything?"

"Zero. No traces left of the commune. Except a pile of chimney stones—and there are condominiums half a mile away."

"The disappearing act. Is the blackberry path still there?"

"Barely."

Neil tokes the joint, holds his breath, then blurts out a cloud of muck. "The path used to be more like a road—it's where Jasmine was riding when the bicycle story happened. She was pregnant. With you. She was riding to the general store to phone Vancouver. Norman was running the other way screaming at an invisible attacker—the Pope or a bank regulator from the Channel Islands. I think he was yelling about deutschemarks—and he plowed smack into Jasmine. The two went flying."

Another long, windy toke. My hair feels like it's dissolving. "They were both lying on the ground, stunned, collecting their breaths—staring into each other's eyes like they'd just made love. Then Norman reached over and placed his hand on Jasmine's stomach—*you*—smiled, trembled, then calmly walked away. He stopped being chased by bankers after the crash. He stopped being paranoid—even though he was still a casualty in other ways. But because of the transformation—the loss of paranoia—Jasmine thinks of you as being blessed. Special. She ever told you she thinks you have healing power?"

"No."

Neil finishes off what's left of the joint. "She does. She still sends Norman birthday presents. And pictures of you. That's how I recognized you." One final toke. "You're a photographer?"

"I'm hoping to be a professional. We're moving to Los Angeles right now."

"Snap a picture of Norman for Jasmine. We haven't had cameras here in years."

"Does Norman talk? Does . . ." But Neil stops responding. He's fried. Meanwhile, the steam heat becomes too much for me. I sit for a few minutes with my catatonic biological father, then leave the sweat lodge and scurry back to the house, air freezing on my sweaty bare skin. Stephanie is standing out by the garden. Seeing me she pleads, "When can we *leave?* I want to *leave.*"

"Hang on. I have to wash the smoke out of my hair. Is there a shower here, or do they just wait for rain? And I have to take a picture, too."

"Please, be sna-*pee.*"

Around the front of the house, the children are clustered around the Comfortmobile's rear driver-side tire, hooting and hollering like skatebrats at the Ridgecrest Mall.

"What's up, Coyote?" I ask Coyote—the only demi-sibling I'm able to identify. Coyote points his thumb at a skinny man, dressed in rags with a hillbilly beard, sitting cross-legged beside the car, licking his reflection in the black paint.

"Meet Norman," says Coyote.

Get me out of here.

An hour later, at the Hitching Post Cafe in Ukiah, California, I am recovering from my father's house.

The cafe's shellacked Elvis burl clocks, its pie racks full of gooey, chemical-based lemon pies, and its edelweiss still lifes painted onto saw blades seem positively life-affirming after this morning's descent into madness.

We can't eat enough chemicals: "*Caffeine—caffeine—caffeine*," I chant to the waitress.

"NutraSweet!" adds Stephanie.

"Edible oil products!"

"White sugar!"

"Now!"

Stephanie and I spent the first three miles back on the open road screaming like banshees—like we'd just escaped being roasted alive—giddy with a sense of escape. It was enough simply to rinse my hair, change clothes, and peel out through the gates.

Now we just want to see the future. Any future.

48

Another day: San Francisco and wooden houses painted the color of children's thoughts. Stephanie and I are lost in rolling fog, sniffing the asbestos tinge of the Comfortmobile's taxed brake pads.

The fog disappears and so does our breath: "Check the view, Stephanie—talk about glamour—a real futurescape: Bank of America—Intel—TransAmerica—and across the bay, nuclear aircraft carriers in Oakland—all of this, *plus* the earthquake faults threatening to cum at any moment. What a city—it's so *modern*."

Later we break for a cappuccino near Cyclotron Road by the Lawrence nuclear facility on a street of freaks on the liberal nipple of Berkeley. Stephanie phones France— Monique's kitten, Minuit, is still on the verge of death.

Next stop: a pilgrimage to Apple headquarters in Cupertino, then into the Silicon Valley: Los Altos, Sunnyvale,

Palo Alto—twelve lanes of traffic zooming past eucalyptus trees on fire. Hot hot *hot*.

Traversing the Bay Bridge, sun glimmers on fragments of abandoned earthquake-ravaged freeway held up to the sky by uncollapsed poles—like the sculpture garden at the Ridgecrest Mall. "Stephanie, all I need is air in the spare."

The traffic jams abruptly. Lolling here in this glorious West makes me think of photos of those dead factory towns in other parts of the world—those zones of long-dead, rusting technologies like ball-bearing and naphthalene factories—tetraethyl lead, PVC, and carbon black—powered by bituminous coal and ideas that aren't working anymore—cities so big and so dead as to have their own complete cosmologies of the afterworld. I feel sorry for these places. Examples? I envision screaming housewife mummies in pearls dog-paddling in the molten coke lakes of the anti-Pittsburgh. I picture eyeless ghost engineers huddled above the blueprints of iron machines that will eat the sky in slow motion. I imagine skeleton passengers on a BOAC prop flight that will never land, their bones clad in smart wool suits, lifting cocktails to grinning skull faces, rattling and chanting with rage at their eternal damnation, gleefully clacking their fibulas together and toasting the black-and-white industrial landscapes below—the anti-Bremen, the anti-Portsmouth, the anti-Hamilton, the anti-Yokohama, and the anti-Gdansk—the plane puncturing the fluffy clouds of smokestacks—billowing gray tufts of dioxides and burning time.

Now, contrast these visions with the shiny turquoise buildings of the West: blue-jeaned employees playing with hackeysacks during lunch hour; employee babies learning Japanese in corporate crèches, freeways brimming with the success stories of the New Order—software, jets, and submarines; white bond paper, vaccines, and slasher movies. With relief, I have found the antidote to my father's house.

"Stephanie," I say, "we are going to become rich in Los Angeles."

"I hope so, Tyler. Life is rich."

"You read my mind."

The Silicon Valley is a necklace of futuretowns. What is a futuretown? I shall explain.

Futuretowns are located on the outskirts of the city you live in, just far enough away to be out of reach of angry, torch-carrying mobs that might roam in from the downtown core.

You're not supposed to notice futuretowns—they're technically invisible: low flat buildings that look like they've just popped out of a laser printer; fetishistic landscaping; new-cars-only in the employee lots; small backlit Plexiglas totems out front quietly brandishing the strangely any-language names of the company housed inside: Cray. Hoechst. Dow. Unilever. Rand. Pfizer. Sandoz. Ciba-Geigy. NEC. Futuretowns are the same in Europe as they are in California. I figure they're the same the planet over. Futuretowns are like their own country superimposed onto other countries.

Stephanie and I drive through these futuretowns of the Silicon Valley with tunage cranked to eleven.

"What should we play next?" I ask.

"British industrial noise!" Stephanie wisely decides. We scavenge the tapes from the backseat, which has degenerated into a jambalaya of bicycle shorts, cassettes, maps, and turkey-jerky wrappers.

We then return our gaze to the mirror-boxed futuretowns circling us—the hard drives of our culture, where the human tribe is making flesh its deepest needs and fears:

teaching machines to think; accelerating the pace of obsolescence; designing new animals to replace the animals we've erased; value adding; reconstructing the future.

We don't set our TV shows in futuretowns, and we don't sing songs about them. We don't discuss futuretowns in conversations and we don't even have a real word for them. Industrial parks? I think not. A contradiction in terms.

Futuretowns aren't places—they're documents. They are the foundries of our deepest desires as a species. To doubt them is to doubt *all*.

We stop for gas in Santa Clara. Stephanie goes to a Pacific Bell booth to phone France again. Alone in the car I see the digital numbers on the gas pump race forward like time; only 2,549 shopping days left until the year 2000. I felt-pen more words onto a stack of one-dollar bills:

LET'S JUST HOPE WE ACCIDENTALLY BUILD GOD.

49

For breakfast this morning, in Kern County, California, we ordered orange juice in an extremely Marge roadside diner. There was a fry grill framed with Polaroids of overweight people, a stainless-steel basket filled with eggs, peanut-butter sandwiches on the menu, and huge portions—truly terrific plate coverage. Outside, beyond the roaring 18-wheelers loaded with crisp produce, were planted orange trees as far as the eye could see—the orange-tree capital of Earth. Yet when our orange juice arrived, it was the frozen reconstituted type.

"Orange juice from Flor-*ee*-da," noticed a perplexed Stephanie.

"Look at the orange juice this way, Stephanie—say you want to Fed-Ex an important letter to an office upstairs in the same building. That letter still has to be flown to Memphis first. Florida juice here in Kern County is a similar distribution quirk."

"Isn't this wasteful? Of *faw*-ssil fuels and *ay*-nergy?"

"No. Consider this morning's *'citrus moment'* a tribute to this nation's mighty distribution system. Modern cooks ask modern questions about shelf life and the ability of a product to withstand trucking. Not *freshness*."

"*Zut*. My mistake."

The final day of our drive; tonight we will arrive in Los Angeles. Our conversation revolves around the mechanics of living in Los Angeles: rents, job-seeking, and locating stars.

We drive through Tehachapi. "*To hatch a pea*," our waitress, Kerry, tells us in this pretty prison town where at lunch we witness overdressed visitors nursing diner coffees while waiting for their turn to visit loved ones. For lunch we eat hamburgers that taste like they fell off a truck—an entire meal that owes more to the Teamsters, Du Pont, and chemical engineering than it does to, say, earth, soil, or the great chefs of Europe.

We detour past Edwards Air Force Base, then through Palmdale, the Air Force suburb, with suburbia-type houses plopped in a desert like that of Mars. Then an hour later we pass through the mountains, down into San Bernardino, into the Los Angeles Basin, and join Interstate 10 into the city.

Yes, remarkable events have begun happening in my life; I am living in remarkable times. Chugging in front of the Comfortmobile is a truck hauling a wagonload of pearl onions grown down in the direction of Indio. This truck is propane-fueled, and we drive inside its warm, sticky sweet slipstream as though swimming in a gin gimlet, all the way into Los Angeles.

Road trips are like fast-forwarding through life, zapping out the boring bits, fulfilling my (according to Anna-Louise last Christmas during a long bout of zapper-intense TV-channel trolling) male need for magic. But as I inhale today's warm onioney gentleness, I remember the advice of Jasmine—never the best of drivers—given to me at the age of sixteen: "Do as I say, Tyler, and not as I do. If you're driving along in a car that is too comfortable and too quiet for too long, you can space out—overrelax and forget you're actually responsible for driving. And when this happens, you're much more likely to crash. Be my boy, Tyler. Do me proud. Be vigilant. Hang on to yourself."

I put on my sunglasses and before me lies a big new city.

50

All the purchases in my shopping cart today are either pink or purple: ham, grape Jell-O, raspberry cookies, bacon slices, licorice whips, and kidney beans. I have to wonder what these color choices say about my mental state these past few weeks.

Stephanie is across town auditioning for a TV infomercial today while I traipse about the Alpha-Beta here in West Hollywood. Should she land the part, she'll be standing with a phalanx of other Stephanie units, forming the bikinied backdrop behind a fading TV star currently hawking real-estate get-rich-quick seminars pitched nightly on the junky syndicated TV stations around 12:30 A.M.

"My big break, Tyler. This show will be *ree*-peated each night for weeks and weeks. Such exposure."

Stephanie car-phoned from her agent's Infiniti stuck in

a gridlock near Hawthorne, "mere sniping distance away from the Mattel toy factory," I informed her. In return I was told not to wait up tonight, that she had another audition to attend after that. "A genuine *fee*-lm. A slasher *moo*-vie. Mine will not be a speaking part, but I will be able to scream."

"Good wuck."

"Excusez-moi?"

"I said good luck."

"You sounded different. Oh—I must go. Jasper has another call arriving. Jasper says your dislike of torture is bourgeois. Ciao."

"Ciao." Call terminated.

Jasper is Stephanie's agent. Well, sort of an agent, since none of his clients have green cards or union tickets. Symbiosis.

Jasper is from London and has pale skin that looks and sweats like a plastic-wrapped Thanksgiving turkey thawing on the kitchen counter. Jasper avoids all fellow Brits —I suspect because he doctors his accent and doesn't want to be caught. He's, like, *"Pip pip—tennis anyone?"* and, *"Roger"* all the time. It's a bit much. Jaspers are *every*where in L.A., and, though I dare not mention the thought aloud, Stephanies are everywhere, too. But Jasper and Stephanie merely view their commonness as a challenge—like a lottery draw with an exorbitant prize—the more ridiculous the chance of winning, the more frenzied the ticket buying. I had never noticed this competitive streak in Stephanie before.

I pay for the groceries and lug them to the Comfortmobile. After combating traffic with KROQ cranked to eleven on the Comfortmobile's FM dial, I arrive at our apartment with my bags of food—a comfortingly normal act—keys in the lock, juggling the bags—which makes me feel settled for what is the first time since I blew Lancaster a month ago. And I realize as I dump the bags on the counter that life has been too speedy of late; there has been no time to establish any daily rhythm of life. No time to feel, "*Ah, this is my pace.*" So I calmly feel my pace for the first time. I smell the pilot light on the stove, hear the hum of the fridge and the rattle of the hallway fan. Now that I feel settled in, I can call Daisy up in Lancaster. The promised month has passed. Seems like a year.

Over in the corner I see my camera, which I have yet to even take out of its case, having been steered away from fashion photography and bullied into a rent-paying McJob by Stephanie. The job? I man the hellish bubbling wing computer at WingWorld, a franchise that vends those parts of the chicken that remain after the white meat has been used in nuggets and the scary bits have been ground into KittyWhip®.

I am saved from utter job-despair hell, however, by the possibility of a job bussing tables at the Hard Rock Cafe, the acme of franchise-food-chain glamour, sometime later this month. Jesus, who works with me at WingWorld, has a friend who has a friend who has a friend who has a sister who checks coats at the Hard Rock.

California is great.

I go change into my work uniform.

We're not spending much time together in our West Hollywood microapartment, Stephanie and me. Neither of us, for example, cooks. Stephanie may be great at bottling vinegars, but her food flair is limited. Mine is nonexistent. Her one attempt at a seafood stir-fry was so riddled with broken shell fragments as to be life-threatening—like the little bits of broken IV needle they discovered in the

X-rayed corpse of Howard Hughes. Our freezer is technically foodless, filled only with ice-cream sandwiches, which I like to eat after sweating over the frying wings and oil all day, and with dozens of frozen spoons, which Stephanie places over her eyes to reduce swelling before she bounds off to her never-ending parade of spurious auditions.

We located this cool little apartment on our first day in L.A. through a local weekly newspaper. It's on the ground floor of a peacoat-blue stucco building designed in the 1920s to resemble a misproportioned Barcelona hacienda. The overall effect is an architectural style christened "Drug Lord" by Jasper. Ours is one of six bachelor units surrounded by loquat trees, bayonet aloes, and helicopter noise from the LAPD drug squad invariably hovering overhead.

Our landlord is Mr. Moore, a scary old guy. He used to be a film extra in the 1940s and 1950s and his face has been lifted so many times his eyebrows are now technically on the top of his head, long since electrolysized off, with only two little matte nubbly patches remaining visible on his skull dome when the light catches them a certain way. On our back stoop, Mr. Moore, fed up with winos and drug deals, has graciously spray-painted:

NO DRUGS
NO PISS

Living in the suite next door to us is Lawrence, a male model who spends entire days buffing his convertible Rabbit with a seemingly inexhaustible stack of FUCK EXXON T-shirts left behind by a previous tenant. Lawrence and Mr. Moore are always at odds over the water bills. "You'd think Mr. Scenery in number six thinks water is free, that it comes out of a tap or something," snorted Mr. Moore between puffs of one of those long, thin, brown cigarettes smoked only by old people. He was in visiting a week after we'd moved in. "Hey—I like what ya done to your place," he said when he saw our decorating. "Snazzy. Class."

To our semifurnished apartment we added only a few items, such as an abandoned bench seat from a Chrysler K-car found in the back alley, plus a stack of unpaid bills we use as drinks coasters. On the walls are tacked full-color tabletop-sized ripped fragments of billboards we found stashed behind a smoke tree off Normandie Avenue. There are three pieces: a man and woman's weightlifting torsos, a Porsche, and big torn letters spelling the semi-words CAINE ABUSE HOTLI. These fragments are so cool, why doesn't anybody sell them retail? They redeem our otherwise squalid suite. I must remind Stephanie to remind me to write a letter to the "Idea File" column of *Young Entrepreneur* magazine.

Nonetheless, hip as our pad may be, I certainly miss the creature comforts of the Modernarium I left behind in Lancaster. Maybe once I become more established I can fly north, rent a U-Haul, then drive south with my reclaimed beloved consumer durables. But at my current rate of savings, such a move might not occur for the next, say, two hundred years.

On the way to WingWorld I place my phone call to Daisy from the Pacific Bell booth at the corner using Harmony's "emergency only" AT&T calling card number. What a pal. I can't afford a phone; life is so expensive. Why wasn't I taught this fact in school?

While I wait for Daisy's princess phone to ring in Lancaster—snug within its nest of pizza flyers and vegetarian cookbooks—I scan the garage-sale action in the front yard across the street. This is the home of the ghostly Heroin Family: junkies, pale white and solemn, standing like demon clerks over stolen motel ashtrays priced at $10. Jesus, how depressing. Free Prozac with each purchase.

A click.

"Hello?"

51

"Daisy, it's Tyler."

"You're back from the dead!"

Squeals of delight segue into a medley of greetings amid crackly reception—Daisy's sprawled on her bedroom floor using the cheapo extension. I envision her braceleted hands idly picking pieces of glitter and toenail clippings from the jute scalp of her Love-Me Pink shag carpet. "Oh, Tyler—you sound fab. Sorry, my brain is, like, Channel One today. I'm on a lemon juice, cayenne pepper, and maple syrup fast. It's day four. Where *are* you— Hollywood?"

I feel my immediate circumstances—my road trip— my apartment—Stephanie—my present world tumbling away from me upon hearing a voice from Lancaster, as though none of the past month had ever happened. Leaning against the sun-baked aluminum phone booth shell, the metal like a hot iron searing my lower back muscles, I feel as though I'm falling into a hole, shrinking into the receiver—like a quasar collapsing into itself—warping into Planet Home. "I'm in West Hollywood."

Shrieks: "*Are* you? I mean, Tyler, I was only kidding. Are you a star yet? Have you seen any stars?"

"Hollywood's not like you think," I say, scrutinizing the Heroin Family as they now share a dripping nectarine in slow motion, contemplating the profits to be reaped from selling the magazines they've swiped from the waiting rooms of La Brea Avenue muffler dealerships. "Actually, I live here now. Stephanie and I have an apartment. Are you smoking, Daisy? I hear little inhales."

"Grandma's cigarettes. The brown ones."

"During a *fast*? That's smart. Mmm . . . a butt. Real tasty. Daisy, how often have I told you smoking is for poor people? Squash it out."

"Oh, piss off, have you seen any *stars*?"

"We saw Bert Rockney's stand-in parking a car outside an AA meeting on Wilshire Boulevard."

"That's the most glamorous news I've ever heard."

"Daisy, how *is* everyone?" The sound of Daisy's voice is creating in me the same sensation of breathlessness and hope I feel when I hear that a small gentle swampland creature, previously believed to be extinct, is discovered to be alive and thriving. I feel faint with homesickness.

"Everybody's fine. Mom. Mark. Mom's raging at her women's meeting. Mark's on the road KittyWhip-ing with Grandma and Grandpa. They make him wear a little kat kostume. He looks so sweet. He does a little dance."

"Murray?"

"Unemployed still. Tyler, *you* have ambition. How can Murray land a good job? You have to help him."

"Murray? Seeking employment?" I'm taken aback—like the time I learned after umpteen years that Harmony knows how to play the flute.

"Well, we're toying with the idea. I mean, we have to support each other. We want to get married."

"Daisy, are you pregnant?"

"No. We just want to get married."

"Does Murray have any skills?"

"He has great dreads."

"Well *that's* food on the table."

"Wait, Tyler, you don't understand. In the month you've been gone, his dreads have *billowed*—achieved major volume action. They are just so majorly intense. He should be famous, Tyler. Hey, and where are *you* working? What are you doing? Are you one of TV's hot hunks yet?"

"You might say I'm in the oil business. It's complex—hard to explain."

"If I know you, Tyler, you'll be marketing vp by next week. Are you coming back to Lancaster? Say yes. We've been keeping the Modernarium as a shrine to you. You're never here any more. First Europe and now L.A. I miss you. How's the French Babe?"

"She's okay."

"Just *okay?*"

"Yeah. She's auditioning twelve times day. She's never home. She's auditioning right now for a role in *Death Hotel Part VII*."

"She's going to be in a *Death Hotel* sequel? Man, you're fixed for life."

"I guess."

"How *are* things between you and her?"

She notices a patch of hesitation. "Tyler, you're pausing. Something's wrong. I know you. What? Spill." I hear Daisy scrunch her cigarette and make that final exhale. "You know, Tyler, Mom and me were ticked off at you for not giving us your love-life details, but we still have lots of room left in our hearts for forgiveness."

I'd rather not depress Daisy and tell her my relationship with Stephanie is like a dying baby that hasn't been given a name yet, so nobody's sure the baby is real to begin with, so I say, "She's gaining weight."

"Anna-Louise will love to hear *that*. She misses you. Did you hear me say that, Tyler? I bumped into her at the Eightplex. Murray and me went to see *Too Young to Drive*. (A hot movie, by the way. Run, don't walk.) But Anna-Louise would sooner die than admit you're on her mind —and forgiveness is more than you deserve."

"If Anna-Louise won't talk about me, how do you know she misses me?"

"Because you were conspicuously unmentioned. And because she's power dieting now. She's the one who turned me on to The Purge. If she'd forgotten you, she'd be up at the salad bar digging in for seconds."

"Daisy, don't guilt me. Not now. I feel bad enough already."

"Do you?"

"Yes."

"Dan's gone."

"What?"

"He's gone. He was only in the house less than a week, then Mom gave him the boot. She's obtaining a court injunction to keep him away."

"That's wild—that's unreal. Why?"

"He drank."

"Oh."

"The usual 'just one beer after a hard day's work' routine—became abusive when challenged. He was in the back yard burning leaves so Mom locked him out then and there. He started hollering she was a dyke and throwing yard furniture at the doors. Mrs. Dufresne called the cops.

So now he's back in the James Bond palace in Onion Canyon."

"Unbelievable."

"So why are you in California? Come home."

We exchange more news, silly and sad. Skye is suffering from a chronic shortage of outfits. She and Harmony are still dating. Eddie's in the hospital with pneumonia. The weather is clear and cold. I give her my address.

"Daisy, what did Jasmine say when she found out I'd left?"

"She hippied out. She said you were making a voyage and your departure was understandable, nay healthy. But the week Dan was here was madness. Mom was a robot. Your leaving town was smart. I think your leaving gave her impetus to boot Dan out faster than she would have otherwise. So Mark and I owe you one."

"Hey, you still owe me from the time last summer when you made Vietnamese soup on the hottest day of the year."

"Let it heal, Tyler. Hey, what's your new phone number?"

"We don't have a phone." A junkie from the Heroin Family approaches the booth, rubbing a quarter in his fingers, no doubt to respond to local joke ads for a rock band stapled to telephone poles saying: *Make Big $$$ Reselling Your Leftover Prescriptions!*

"No phone? Are you communists or something? Everyone has phones. No one *doesn't* have a phone. How can you function? That's like not having lungs."

"We'll have a phone soon."

"Where are you calling from? A booth in Havana?"

"From the corner. On Harmony's AT&T number. And somebody needs the phone now. We should wrap up the call."

"But what happens next? Are you staying in Hollywood? What about your durables—your minifridge? What about *us*? We miss you."

"I'll call soon. I need to straighten some things out in my head. Give me, like, two weeks. I'll know better then. Tell Jasmine life's cool."

"You're Mom's favorite, Tyler. You know that."

"I miss you, Daisy. And Mark and Mom and everybody. This trip's different than my trip to Europe. I don't feel complete any more. Even though I'm not alone."

"Rage on, my darling brother."

Our call ends and the Heroin man takes the receiver from me, careful not to step on my shadow.

52

Repairmen fixing pipes in Lawrence's apartment next door found old bones plastered into the wall—femurs, clavicles, spines. . . . Just what species of bones, authorities don't know yet. So Stephanie and I are using what has developed into an LAPD exhumation as a creepy excuse to hightail out of the building and over to Venice Beach, where we'll spend a whole day together for the first time in weeks. Stephanie promised not to do auditions or plot with Jasper or other members of his "stable," LaShanna, Tanya, and Korri.

Venice Beach: proof of the biological impossibility of imagining a person being simultaneously good-looking and poor. Denim hot pants; black socks; angry swarms of café racers; anabolic maxed-out candy-flake muscle-car technology; kicky Mustangs; DeathStar 4×4s; beatific Santa Barbara Jesus teens with velcro neon money belts;

VW microbus vans with LED ZEP and ZOSO latexed onto the sides; Golf convertibles tempera-painted with the words: SHANNON LINDA DENISE DIDI and PATTY; fiberglass air dams; Kevlar pectorals; rollerblade skates the color of polio-vaccine sugar cubes. Decades worth of weight training, tetracycline, orthodontia, MTV, and NutraSweet paying off in one grand, glorious spray. A Porsche 911 the color of a swimming pool skulks by and the driver inside smiles with platinum teeth at Stephanie and me and says, "Dial 911, baby."

"These people are all so modern!" I exclaim to a totally uninterested Stephanie, draped in black to keep the sun's X rays from her skin, which is almost opalescent from UV blockers. She's simply not entering the spirit of the beach.

I, however, am entering the regional spirit, but I do wonder whether all of today's youth, while spectacular, is wasted, like fireworks in the middle of the day. Then again, the scene is so sexy—so sexy I'd like to explode and shower these hot cars and hot bodies with my scalding interior guck—like a deep-sea creature that explodes when lifted into the reduced pressures of the shallows. I run my fingers through my hair, swept backward today, with a lotion, not a gel, for a relaxed natural, rained-on look.

"Tyler, I want to sit in the shade," says Stephanie, who then squeaks a French curse when blasted by an AK-47 squirt gun. "Why are they shooting me? I am a stranger. It is so *ee-ra*-tating."

"Take spritzing as a compliment. If the kids think you're cute, they spray you with their Kalashnikovs. At the end of the day the big status symbol is to be moist."

I stand with the tourists in the shade behind a Mexican-food stand. Stephanie returns from a nearby bathroom from which I had heard a ruckus.

"What was the noise about?" I ask.

"Four girls caught their friend splashing her shirt with water. I think the friend must have been feeling cute."

Behind her black glasses, Stephanie then begins to sulk in a world of her own, and wherever her world is, I am no longer allowed. I dig into my fanny pack, then continue with my now-compulsive habit of felt-penning on money:

IMAGINE
YOURSELF
BEFRIENDING
A MONSTER

YOU ARE NEVER FAR
FROM
THE SOUND OF
AN ENGINE

GROW
A
TAIL

WE'RE ALL
THEME PARKS

TECHNOLOGY
FAVORS
HORRIBLE PEOPLE

I have had joy in helping Stephanie share in the exuberance and abandon of the New World, but in the process, I have witnessed a flaw emerge, like a silent genetic disease knitted into her DNA, which has now inevitably unraveled at this later date. The flaw is simple: because Stephanie was not born here, she can never *understand* here.

"People in California meet people they have not seen for two years," she says while driving home from Venice, "and they say to each other, *'So who are you now? What is your new ray-ligion? What new style of clothes are you wearing these days? What kind of diet are you eating? Who is your wife? What sort of house are you in now? What different city? What new ideas do you believe?'* If you are not a completely new person, your friends will be disappointed."

"So?" I ask.

"Do you not see anything wrong with this constant change?"

"Should there be? I think it's great I'm allowed to reinvent myself each week." I then notice that a block we are driving through has three toy stores featuring stuffed animals in the windows and point this out to Stephanie. "There must be a cancer clinic nearby," I add.

"Why is that?"

Anna-Louise would have understood, I think. I miss talking like a telethon.

We pull into the apartment complex just as the News-at-Six van pulls away. The cops are gone. Mr. Moore, in an ascot and smoking jacket, having made his first film appearance in decades, races giddily out to the car and informs us the bones in the plaster were those of dogs and cats, dating back from the silent-picture days when the apartment was built.

"They even found dog collars. Solves a case on the books for half a century, when half the pets in Bel Air just disappeared. Nobody ever knew where. Just imagine—I have a historical-type building now." Mr. Moore drifts away, muttering more to himself than to Stephanie and me how maybe he can obtain a historical plaque from city hall.

The two of us creep slowly into our apartment, hyperconscious of the frozen meows and barks now embedded into our walls, no longer able to innocently feel sheltered within these rooms. Stephanie then darts into the bathroom to rinse off the UV blocker. After this preen she heads to the phone booth at the corner to call LaShanna and Jasper. Returning, she informs me she will be taking me out for dinner this evening.

"What a nice surprise," I say.

"Yes," she replies. "A real treat."

"Where?"

"Morton's."

"Morton's? Did you audition for God, or something?"

"A friend of Jasper's made a reservation for me."

The next few hours are spent preparing for dinner's dress code: preen intensive—Industry. Hair will be lightly moussed in the manner of Cory Bestwick, star of Daisy's favorite new teen motion-picture sizzler, *Too Young to Drive*. Garments: simple blazer with Italian tie—very Century City. Footwear? Bally clones.

Stephanie also, in a never-before-seen burst of domestic pride, neatly packs up her clothing and doodads, which have up until now been strewn about the microapartment like bird poops. I imagine she's finally feeling settled in.

When we leave the apartment hours later, Stephanie keeps me waiting in the car out on the street while she rushes in to ensure the apartment is properly locked. I am glad to see she appears to be bonding with our space. So maybe things aren't what they seem.

53

Through the crisp linen, paintings, angled mirrors, and *fleurs* of Morton's, we maneuver to our table like hunted fish in the sea—spadefish and amberjacks, being shot with the argon laser who-are-you? stares of the Industry. Great hair here. We are seated at eight o'clock sharp at a table we're not quite sure is Siberia—"crypto-Siberia," I call it. Stephanie (for once) was definite about being punctual.

I mention to Stephanie that rich people can always send in spies to monitor poor people, but the poor will never be able to send in spies to monitor the rich. "So the rich will always win," I say, and an older woman with her platinum-coin-colored hair in a bun at the table beside me hears my statement and winks my way. She returns to her cluster of friends and enemies, all sipping little white drinks—a cluster of lazy monkeys sipping milk from the teats underneath docile roadside cows in New Delhi.

Wine is offered. "Dan always said if they keep the wine

bottle on its side, then mentally double the price." Stephanie nods condescendingly and orders a Montrachet-something. Those French. I just about faint when I discover how much the wine costs. "Can you afford this? We could have had a phone for three months for that bottle."

"I can afford it."

"Do you have news to tell me?"

A pause. "Yes. But later."

"I bet I know what it is."

"You probably *do* know. You just don't know it."

"Coy coy coy."

Over my shoulder, Stephanie stares at the woman who winked at me. Stephanie's staring is obvious and I point this out. "She resembles my *maw*-ther. Don't you think?"

I've only seen Stephanie's mother in photos. "Somewhat."

The wine is uncorked. Stephanie mumbles appreciatively, offers a nice little smile, then sighs. "My *maw*-ther was never in love, you know."

"No?"

"No." She raises her elbows on the table and cups her chin. "My *faw*-ther, Alphonse, was not the grand passion of her life. He knows this; she knows this. But they manage anyway." She sips wine from her glass. I sense how fully Stephanie fits into this restaurant's world of candles and gems and silver, with darkness outside the windows and purchased comfort and warmth available only inside. Stephanie has just tonight erupted in my mind into a world more physically luxuriant than any world I might ever offer. I am beginning to understand where she disappears when she spaces out.

"My mother has been comfortable," Stephanie goes on, "but she will never have a grand passion and she knows this and she is now maybe wondering if the comfort and

safety of staying with my *faw*-ther was worth that loss."
Another sip. "And now I think she is like a cheetah in the
zoo, which has lived a comfortable life but has never run
fast, the way nature had intended her to. Okay, the cheetah
is alive, but, *so what?*"

Stephanie is not looking at me now. She is buffing her
nail polish with her fingertips, a nervous gesture of hers.
"But this is silly, no? You would be amazed at how many
people have never fallen in love before. Who says life is to
be easy?"

"That's what *I* say whenever Harmony goes goo-goo over
the Dark Ages with his Olde Englishe schtick. I remind
him life is essentially the Vikings slashing your family to
ribbons, then setting fire to your crops."

"Nature is not democratic, no."

Thus inspired, a few minutes later, while Stephanie
ducks into the bathroom for a protracted preen-a-thon, I
felt-pen onto a five-dollar bill (attracting not a few nosey
peeks from nearby diners) the words:

ONLY

DEMOCRACY

SAVES US FROM

THE RAVAGE

OF

BEING ANIMALS

Stephanie returns and for a few minutes the mood is
slightly more cheerful. "I liked your friends in Lancaster,"
she says. "Your Harmony. Your Skye. Your Gaïa. Your
Anna-Louise." Stephanie has never actually spoken Anna-
Louise's name before. I am pleased to hear her do so.

"I'm glad you like them. They're a good crew. They could
be a bit more ambitious, but . . ."

"Tyler," cuts in Stephanie. "About this ambition—" She finishes her wine. "You asked me in France and I never answered you. You asked me what makes French '*teens*'" (Stephanie makes quotation marks with her fingers) "so unambitious. They are not unambitious, Tyler, but I must tell *yooo*, I am tired of your ambition talk. I ask *yooo*, which is more fair: to promise your children the moon and then give your children nothing—or promise only a little—be realistic—so when your children become civil servants or drive a truck they are not unhappy? I think your ambition is *crooo*-el. Pour me more wine, *s'il vous plaît.*"

We order dinner and eat in relative silence. I'm eating shrimp; Stephanie's eating lamb. I am on the lookout for stars but see none, and Stephanie is monitoring her watch the way she has been all evening.

"Why are you pushing your shrimp to the side of the plate?" Stephanie asks, looking at my plate.

"I'm stockpiling them as my reward for eating the rest of the dinner. Like a 32K memory cache on a hard drive."

A small sneer. "You know what is the most middle class trait of all, Tyler? The ability to postpone plea-*zhure.*"

I drop my fork. "Stephanie, why don't you take your strange class hatred and phobias and lug them back to your cramped, futureless little country? We don't want them here." She continues eating, as though I had not spoken. "Sorry," I add limply.

My appetite is shot. If one person in a relationship is feeling bad vibes, guaranteed the other person is feeling bad vibes, too. "It's just that all of your history in Europe is so seductive. All of your costumes and buildings and old music and perfect little tins of cookies. History tricks you into not valuing what you have now. History's dead, but right now is *alive*. History is jealous of right now—jealous of that life."

"I see, Tyler."

The rest of the meal is glacial. Dessert arrives, a little baba-on-fire cake, lit with a discreet flourish by the waiter who then disappears. We both stare at the icy blueness of the flame and I feel so lonely my stomach feels numb. Maybe Stephanie feels this way, too.

It is within this sad silence that Stephanie surprises me. While diners at the tables nearby watch, Stephanie pats her hand onto the rum baba's flames, her fingers and *faux* diamond bracelet touching the little blue tongues, extinguishing them in the process. Stephanie looks up at me with her eyes unguarded in a manner I never knew they could be. "Sure, Tyler," she says, her hand unflinching and covered in sticky sweetness and alcohol and carbon, "there are flames, but what's underneath—the cake—isn't *really* on fire." She looks down at her burnt hand. "*Is it?*"

No.

54

In our daily newspapers here on Earth we chronicle transitions: births, deaths, marriages, advancements and demotions. But I think there exists another Earth parallel to our own—an Earth that publishes a parallel newspaper highlighting the invisible transitions that occur in our day-to-day lives, transitions small and delicate; lovely and forever. To wit:

Fun Fact: 4,560,110 Earthlings fell in love today; 4,560,007 fell out of love.

Color Photo Caption: Paulo Maria Bispò, a beet farmer from Olivarria, Argentina, found a gold meteorite lying in his field while plowing yesterday afternoon. Mr. Bispò, father of three, will have the meteorite made into two gold front teeth replacing his current applewood dentures so his smile will be "like the sun from which this heavenly stone was born."

Black-and-White Photo Caption: Local children warmed their hands while the desert sky above Carson City, Nevada, USA, was black today with the smoke of hundreds of burning roulette wheels declared rigged by the Nevada State Gaming Commission. Meteorologists say the smoke will not affect global weather patterns.

Fun Fact: 3,089,240 women realized yesterday they are trapped in loveless marriages; 3,002,783 men.

Color Photo: In Pretoria, South Africa, the slopes of the city are a mass of lovely lavender jacaranda blooms; in Turukhansk, Siberia, the peat of the Siberian carbon sink—the planet's largest biomass—is browning with much dignity and is preparing to sleep for its one billionth winter.

Sporting News: 11 percent of motorists in the city of Tokyo, Japan, location of a major international sporting event this week, voluntarily stopped driving their cars so that competing athletes might breathe clean air. Tonight, one voluntary nondriver, Reiko Fukusawa, 24, an office worker from the Saitama Prefecture outside of Tokyo—a woman who considers herself to be overweight—will go to sleep and she will dream of athletes and their bodies and in her dream she will fly and tumble and she will be reunited with a part of her self she had thought she had lost many years ago, back when she was young.

* * *

Sidebar with Pie Chart: 2,499,055 people were unable to sleep last night, waiting for medical tests to come back; 130,224 with good reason.

Feature Photo with Ministory: Astronauts on board the Space Shuttle conducting tests in orbit today released into their capsule's atmosphere a small blue bird, Kippy, hatched in outer space. Scientists captured on film Kippy's first confused weightless zigzags in the air. With no genetic memory of weightlessness to guide Kippy, he and his recently matured little wings essentially had to reinvent the whole process of flight from scratch in the free fall of orbit.

"We gave Kippy a seed bell for his bravery," said flight captain Don Montgomery. "He was brave. Kippy didn't have to fly, but he flew. Myself and the rest of the flight crew are very very proud."

55

Loss.

Stephanie left me—a week ago, after the dinner at Morton's. Throughout the meal I had been repeatedly asking her what her big surprise was; she wouldn't tell. Later, as we stood by the French doors up front, Stephanie disconcertingly made no effort to put on her jacket, and when I asked why, she began visibly screwing her features up for some form of confession. At this point a man approached her from one of the restaurant's other rooms—a sullen and blatantly monied coke-lord type with an ape neck, a slicked-back hairdo, and an almost visible fog of cologne. This guy materialized and stood behind Stephanie, placing his hands on her shoulders in an intimate fashion.

Stephanie seemed annoyed; I gathered this guy wasn't to have arrived until I was gone. "Um. Tyler," she said, "meet Firooz."

Firooz and I barely acknowledged each other's presence,

our retina-to-retina contact was a mere brush as Firooz's mouth began flirting with Stephanie's neck. My own re-action was unexpected, like getting seasick during an earthquake. My ears burned. My brain rewound. Truth and reality became murky—a fax of a fax of a fax of a fax of a photograph.

It was fast. Another man, a goon of Firooz's, I guess, with a gun holster visible under his jacket, held open the doors and asked if I was leaving. Stephanie handed me a slip of paper with a phone number written on it and whispered, "Sor-*ree*, Tyler. We had fun. It's over. Firooz's friends have moved my things for me tonight while we ate. Good-bye."

This was termination; bargaining was not an option. I was de-relationshipped.

"Stephanie . . ." *Kaboom*. A deft thug fist contracted on my neck—LAPD-endorsed pain-compliance techniques—and I saw the glint of gun as the door shut; in my peripheral vision was the spectacle of rich people eating their dinner. In my ears was an angry silence and the voices of curious carhops possibly wondering if I was low enough on the food chain to mock out loud.

Moments later I was out on the street, gracing the side-walk of Santa Monica Boulevard, feeling like one of those houses where the family has mysteriously disappeared for-ever with their meal still on the dinner table. Too fast. Too fast. In the same way that leaves look greener at sun-set, my perception of light became acute—my pink skin was pinker; white Toyotas were whiter; my black shoes blacker. Flowers were gorgeous. A wave of grand lucidity washed over me, and the world seemed the way it does just moments before the onset of a fever—the moment just before perception collapses like an imploding building and one becomes very very sick.

56

I am strolling down Hollywood Boulevard. Yes, strolling. I sold the Comfortmobile last night to pay for everyday expenses. That car was a bubble containing the happiest years of my life and I was silent as I watched its new owner drive away last week, a UCLA student named Bernie who called my little baby car-car 'Becky' while I winced. Afterward I stomped inside the apartment and fumed; I am feeling hard to reach these days. What has happened to the fine sense of independence that was once mine?

I've been living by myself here in West Hollywood, here in the microapartment. I'm determined to make a go of independence. But independence is harder than I thought. And so expensive.

I feel different these days, too, having never been totally

alone by myself. In Europe there was Kiwi or at least the prospect of a transient Eurofriend. Here in L.A. there is nobody to talk with—what people I do meet are freaks and I'm hesitant to start conversations. I don't want to become a magnet for psychopaths.

What do I do? I try and keep to my regimen: I make sure I am well dressed at all times; I ensure my hair is always properly groomed—once hair goes, all else follows—I can't allow myself to have a bad hair day; I make sure the micro-apartment is kept in order. Also, I have discovered talk-radio shows on the AM band. I have discovered an "All Conspiracy" station that comes in from the Valley. I have yet to actually phone in.

I have chores. This morning before walking to the Bou-levard, I was using some of my money from the sale of the Comfortmobile to shop for a white-noise machine. I'm hav-ing trouble sleeping because I'm so worried about being poor. My bedroom is so echoey. Small sounds suddenly bother me. Clinks and clanks and thumps. You know you're poor when you can hear other people's noises through your walls. Last week in my quest for sleep and dreams I traded my billboard fragments to Lawrence for Valiums.

"Dishwater strength," Lawrence said, handing me a brown plastic vial as we looted the pharmacopia of his bathroom cabinet. Half the bottles had no labels.

"How come no labels?" I asked.

"Contents are too shameful. Here—we'll start you out on Valium. You can work your way up. I don't want you having a reaction and putting feds on my tail."

"What are *these?*" I asked, picking up a small clear bot-tle, evidently prized, meriting its own shelf.

"Zopiclone. You can't buy that with just billboard pieces. Unavailable in the U.S. You'll need the scoreboard from Dodger Stadium to buy those. Knock you out yet give you a natural REM cycle. Brain caviar."

There is a reason I am walking down Hollywood Boulevard today. I quit my job at WingWorld yesterday. I decided I will not burn wings every day merely to give myself enough sustenance to be able to continue working at WingWorld to make enough sustenance to continue working at WingWorld to . . . The loop of evil. Who invented these McJobs, anyway? They're work, but they're not a living. The undead working at unlabor.

But WingWorld is my past, now. This afternoon here on the Boulevard I am experimenting with a seriously scorching entrepreneurial idea I flashed onto last week—the idea that gave me the confidence to quit. I figure, even if I have to live inside a rolled-up carpet in the alley behind the house of the Heroin Family, I would rather be a loser on my own terms than spend one more nanosecond behind goopy vats of Cajun Crocodile, Barbecue Blitz, and Mister Mustard sauce listening to Jesus lie (as truth turns out) about mythical nightclub jobs.

The first step of my entrepreneurial idea entails picking up a few supplies—hence my current mission on the Boulevard, a lovely place, a puree of franchise environments and out-and-out sleaze—Hamburger Hamlet, Taco Bell, and The Big Fucky. The sidewalk is encrusted with crushed hamburgers, IV needles, and lost maps—Disneyland with lesions. I see the confused faces of German tourists, their expressions not yet having turned to disappointment. Adding to the surrealistic tone are an overabundance of Christmas displays, no doubt ordered over the phone from 1-800 MELTING CLOCK.

I saunter past Graumann's, like most all businesses on the strip a simulated version of its own history—a new structure pretending to be an old structure. As Lawrence said last week, "None of those old guys who designed these buildings remembered to put in nooks for the T-shirt shop."

On Fairfax I ultimately find what I'm looking for—the raw materials for my entrepreneurial venture—a jumbo pad of tracing paper plus a box of 64 wax crayons in a graphic-design supply shop. I make my purchase and leave, keeping my receipts. I'm a business now.

Just as I leave the store, there is a small earthquake— not much, but enough to activate every car alarm in the Los Angeles Basin. From Wilshire Boulevard to Compton, the city is on fire with noise. I sit on the steps in the heat of the sun and listen as one by one these car alarms extinguish themselves until once more only the muted roar of the city is audible, and the city, bathed in sunlight, once again resumes dreaming its collective dream.

Cars roll down the city's roads, plants grow from its soil, wealth is generated in its rooms, hope is created and lost and recreated in the minds and souls of its inhabitants, and the city continues its dream and searches for those ideas that will make it strong.

57

I am a star making stars of the stars. I am making wax-crayon rubbings of the brass celebrity stars inlaid on the sidewalks of Hollywood Boulevard. These stars take thirty seconds to rub and I can do them in any color. My overhead is low—I don't need a booth. I simply stake out Elvis and Marilyn and supply and demand are simultaneously met as eager flocks of tourists shell out cash. Supplies? All I need are rubber bands to scroll the booty.

I am kneeling on the ground to find my new wealth. I am reminded of parades when I was young, back in Lancaster, back in parades when beautiful women dressed in papier-mâché nuclear reactor costumes threw candies to a youthful me, scrambling happily on the sidewalk, down on my knees, like now, gathering up life's rich bounty.

Days later, on my white T-shirt I have felt-penned:

StarStars™
$5.00

"Hey mister," asks an old lady with maroon hair, "do you know where Lucy's star is?"

Everybody just assumes I'm a freak because I'm doing what I'm doing, even though I'm dressed innocuously in jeans and a T-shirt. A Seeing Eye dog licks my face. The air is revolting; I sneeze and grey nodules of guck pop out my nose like the little gray mice that crawled in and out of the water pipes in the Paris *métro*.

I have become a magnet for street freaks, and the Boulevard's rich wealth of street life gravitates toward me—not so much to include me in their lives as to provide a geographic anchor for their own lives, to prevent themselves from feeling like unsold Christmas trees littering city streets on the morning of December 26. Occasionally street freaks ask me the time or if I want an Orange Crush or if I want a take a toke of whatever they're smoking, their faces wrenched, like they've just had a handful of diet pills and a piece of bad news. They are undemanding. They are the only community I have now. Their hair is big; their heaven is The Whisky a Go-Go; their music is speed-thrash-metal. Every so often I give them a star rubbing of a James Dean or a Liz Taylor and they're happy, providing me with entertaining snippets of dialogue for the next few hours, in between Japanese and Germans and Ohioans purchasing memories of Lucy and Marlon Brando, e.g.:

"So, like, this morning Danny drips bacon fat in his lap and then this afternoon he's up in the Benedict Canyon making a deal and these Dobermans jump him and rip up his thighs."

"I'm telling you, man, it all stems from Tolkien."

58

Success! Yet another afternoon I return home with cash loaded in my pockets, (*Young Entrepreneur*'s Monthly Profile: "Tyler Johnson—Rubbed Out in Hollywood"). In my mail slot are two letters awaiting my arrival. One is from Jasmine and one is from Daisy. In my exuberant mood, I tear Jasmine's letter open first. Here is what it says:

December 5

Dear Tyler,

I think we are all given veils when we are born which prevent us from seeing our mothers as they were when they were young . . . young and full of gin and dancing in the arms of a man who is not our father. I know *I* have trouble seeing a youthful version of my own mother because of my own veil, and I think I see you with a veil now which prevents you from seeing *me* clearly.

Where to begin? Small details first: Mark is at
school this afternoon. Daisy and Murray are out (I kid
you not) job hunting. Their hair looks just dreadful,
Tyler, and I don't know how I can get them to do
something about it. I sound eighty years old saying
this. I'd best stop.

I am alone here in the kitchen. Sun is streaming in,
I am sipping "my tea" (chamomile today). You can
well imagine the scene . . . and the room is unmoving
save for an overweight Kittykat sleeping on top of the
fridge, dozing away her KittyWhip®. (She is eating
far too much these days. Your grandfather keeps sam-
pling new product lines on our furry family member.
Oh—Kittykat just looked at me—I guess that means
she wants to say hello. "Meow." [That was too cute.
I'm losing it, Tyler.])

Anyway, in this peacefulness here in the kitchen I
am reminded of a repeating dream I have (I know,
you hate hearing other people's dreams, but sorry,
pumpkin, here goes). I see myself in this unknown
house, and I am walking around, snooping into rooms,
confident and unafraid because I know I am the only
person in this house. I walk into a room—I see a hair-
brush, a bottle of perfume, and a small framed picture
of a boat. Then I realize that I am back in time and
this is my mother's room and I am now her. I did not
expect to grow old, Tyler.

I can't wait any longer. I'll get to the point: *no*,
Tyler, I'm not angry at you for not phoning or writing
or communicating for these weeks you have been
away doing God-knows-what and *scaring the daylights
out of me*. And in some ways I deserve this silent treatment. I might have had more time to listen to your
life situation instead of being so wrapped up in my

own life just before you left. *But the same could be said for you, too, my little puppy.* Care works both ways.

Tyler, you think you know me, but you don't. I don't mean this as a challenge or a put-down. No one really knows anybody, I think. But you're trying to make me be something in your own mind which I just am not. Honey, I love you so much, but don't judge me, okay? What I did with Dan is dumb, but it was *my* dumbness, not yours. In a way I'm saying, *butt out*, but in a way I'm also saying, *I have enough faith in you to let you go your own way. Don't be too preoccupied with the actions of others.* I mean what I say only with kindness and love. Don't grouch out yet.

But in rereading this, I see I'm not being clear enough.

Okay . . . I remember telling you maybe two months ago, Tyler, how there will come a time when you will discover a thing called loneliness. You wouldn't listen then (and what young person ever has?) but I suspect that now, down in Los Angeles, you have discovered such a thing. My guess is not some magic divination on my part but, rather, a deduction. Stephanie telephoned two nights ago from Lake Tahoe asking for a brooch she'd forgotten here in Lancaster. I was, to say the least, surprised you weren't with her. She left you, eh?

She turned out to be one mercenary little cookie, didn't she? (Slap your hand, Jaz, honey, I'll best be quiet here, as I do not know your true feelings for Steph. Wise word of advice here, my son: never comment negatively about a recently departed loved one to the dumpee [meow, meow, meow]).

Sorry. I'm angry because I think Stephanie used you merely to prevent herself from being bored while she maneuvered her way into a green card here. There, I've said it. If you think I've been nasty, forgive me . . . but respect my honesty. I didn't like her one bit.

But *are* you lonely down there, Tyler? Remember: *the time you feel lonely is the time you most need to be by yourself.* Life's cruelest irony. The point I was trying to get at through all of this is, until you've been lonely yourself, please try to diplomatically avoid speaking about the lives of those who have been. Like me.

Oh, Tyler, just look at me . . . Is it my fault I'm not married? Am I going to spend my golden years in a spinster's Soviet doing 4:00 A.M. bread-baking duty?

There are so many gestures in life we cannot undo. Lost opportunities. I just accept this now. I have no regrets and I'll just have to accept my boo-boos and move on with life. I don't want to end up a "crusty old broad," as you so zestfully describe poor Mrs. Dufresne, who, by the way, has freshly repainted her Disney lawn statuary this week. Looks smashing.

The door's knocking. Must run.

TEN MINUTES LATER: An order for KittyWhip®! You would be proud of me. That was Mrs. Dufresne, speak of the devil, ordering a KittyPump, so we must remember not to mock her lawn ornaments in the future as she is now a valued customer. See, Tyler, I can learn this stuff, too. I'm not too pooped out an old hipstress.

Speaking of KittyWhip®, my little entrepreneur, I took your advice and made a cold call this morning to Mr. Lancaster, the man you call The Man with 100 Pets and No TV. He is a charmer! And you know what? He really *does* have 100 pets! His apartment was like a zoo, and he has converted what used to be the dining room into a lovely shallow carp pond. So pretty. We had a beer together (I think Mr. Lancaster, [his first name is Albert] is, as you might say, "a cocktail enthusiast," but then again maybe he's just lonely. Wonderful as Albert's little animals may be—his plentiful doggies and kitties and birdies—humans are the only creatures one can talk to, and apparently Albert doesn't talk to people much—or vice versa.)

He is a sweet man. He gave me a kitten when I left—little Norman—Kittykat's new foster brother, currently wetting the throw rugs and undergoing a spell of Tough Love until he improves his litter-box aptitude. You'll like Norman. Kittykat doesn't. That's why she's up on the fridge. They'll bond eventually.

After visiting Albert, I then (you're a big boy, you can handle this) knocked on the door of Anna-Louise, who answered breathless from aerobicizing. You kids! Anyway, Tyler, I told Anna-Louise about the Lake Tahoe call (weight of guilt now off my shoulders) and we had tea and it was *she* who suggested I write you immediately. I myself was reluctant as I thought you needed more time to figure life out for yourself. She maybe thought I was irresponsible in not trying to contact you sooner, but who am I to be a posse, having run off with Neil when I was seventeen (my poor mother!). The need to flee must run in the family. Better handcuff Daisy to the radiator.

So I guess Anna-Louise is still concerned about you. She knows you better than you think. Enough said. Now there goes the phone! Hang on.

ONE HOUR-ish LATER: That was a woman asking when the last time the chimney was cleaned. Bloody telemarketers (pardon my language [is Skye still doing that?]). Then I went out to bring in the garden furniture for the season. Then Norman did his duty in the litter box and needed a kibble reinforcement. All these distractions.

My mood has changed now. And the sun has gone behind the clouds. I'm in this mood I feel occasionally . . . this mood where there's a very good friend nearby who I should be phoning. *If only* I could reach that friend and talk, then everything would be just fine. The dilemma is, of course, I just don't know *who* that friend is. But in my heart I know my mood is merely me feeling disconnected from my true inner self.

Listen to me, Tyler—prattling on like an earth mother. God, I've been dialing my inner phone so long now, if the other end answered, I'd probably blank out and forget who I'd called. Do you ever feel this way?

Argggh. There are so many secrets locked inside all of us. So much darkness. Maybe you have begun to notice this. From the address you gave Daisy over the phone, I see you are in West Hollywood. If I remember from the old days of the VW microbus, West Hollywood was pretty, but not exactly the moral Dingly Dell. Maybe you have started to notice the unsunny side of human nature more closely now you live there.

Ah. My own youth . . . Tyler, I'd like to think "my trip around the block" these past few years has not been entirely for naught. So at this point, I think I will offer you a perception of my own which might save *you* some time.

What I will tell you, son of sons, is this: shortly, if not already, you will begin noticing the blackness inside us all. You will develop black secrets and commit black actions. You will be shocked at the insensitivities and transgressions you are capable of, yet you will be unable to stop them. And by the time you are thirty, your friends will all have black secrets, too, but it will be years before you learn exactly *what* their black secrets are. Life at that point will become like throwing a Frisbee in a graveyard; much of the pleasure of your dealings with your friends will stem from the contrast between your sparkling youth and the ink you now know lies at your feet.

Later, as you get to be my age, you will see your friends begin to die, to lose their memories, to see their skins turn wrinkled and sick. You will see the effects of dark secrets making themselves known—via their minds and bodies and via the stories your friends—yes, Harmony, Gaïa, Mei-lin, Davidson, and the rest—will begin telling you at three-thirty in the morning as you put iodine on their bruises, arrange for tetanus shots, dial 911, and listen to them cry. The only payback for all of this—for the conversion of their once-young hearts into tar—will be that you will love your friends more, even though they have made you see the universe as an emptier and scarier place—and they will love you more, too. Zero balance (a get-cracking term from the KittyWhip® manual).

Our achievements may make us interesting, Tyler, but our darkness makes us lovable. You will have dark secrets, Tyler, and I will still love you. Dan has his dark secrets (well, they're not really secret with him, are they?) and I still love him in my own way. And yes, Tyler, I have my own dark secrets. And I hope you'll love *me* still. Beauty and sadness are woven together; even Frankenstein gets lonely. So Tyler, you'll just have to forgive Dan. If you do, you'll beat me to it, but forgiveness is what we have no choice but to work toward, or else we are just animals. Dark animals. And *that* is too much to bear. God likes you less for staying home and doing nothing than he does for you going out and maybe getting into a little trouble. Risk the trouble of forgiving Dan. Then forget about him.

Enough, enough. The last thing you need is your hippie mother being heavy on you. You are my son, Tyler, and I hope I've guided you well. Our home wasn't like on TV but you know you are always loved here and that there is nothing you can do which will make me not love you. Do what you will, but after doing it, come home. Soon. We miss you, we love you, and maybe Norman will be able to tell you why it is Kittykat pounds her paws on your roof.

Too cute again. Just an old hippie. Stand in light, O product of my heart.

Your mother,

Jasmine

59

Next is Daisy's letter, which contains yet *another* forwarded letter folded inside—a letter forwarded to me from (no!) Bechtol in Seattle.

December 4

Dear loveless BROTHER. This letter arrived for you yesterday. Isn't Bechtol the company headed by that guy you won't shaddup about . . . Frank Mailer, or something? No doubt some glitzy job offer. If your job turns out to be management, see if you can scrape up work for Murray. Alas, MY BELOVED remains a job-seeker. He could have had a job loading the salad bar at Daley's Rib House, but he would have had to wear a HAIR NET. How degrading.

Needless to say, there is MUCH HOT GOSSIP here, but I'm not telling you one drop of it. This is a sleazy ploy on my part to get you to COME HOME. Or to at least PHONE again. Or write. Why the silence?

Hug and kiss.

Daisy.

PS: Souvenirs enclosed: 1) set of depressing dead Walkman earphones 2) Pleasingly colored leaf found in backyard 3) Kernels of popcorn from the Eightplex, workplace of . . . ANNA-LOUISE

The Bechtol Group   Nov. 12
Seattle, Washington

Dear Mr. Johnson,
   Mr. Frank Miller read your letter dated October 31 with great pleasure. He has requested me to ask you to make an appointment to visit us here in Seattle at your earliest convenience. Please phone to arrange an appointment for whenever this suits your schedule. Mr. Miller and I both look forward to the opportunity of meeting you.

Sincerely,

Donald B. Kepke
Director
Employee Recruitment
Bechtol

60

I phone Bechtol from Lawrence's apartment so as to preclude the unflattering traffic noises surrounding "my office"—the booth at the corner. Mr. Donald Kepke of Bechtol's employee recruitment division up in Area Code 206, Seattle, takes my phone call without hesitation—a good omen.

"Mr. Miller will be inspecting a car factory in Tennessee on Friday," says Mr. Kepke. "Might you be able to visit us Thursday? Thursday would make Mr. Miller's life easier."

"Of course, Mr. Kepke," I say, flattered by his concern, "I'll simply switch my return flight plans." (Yuk yuk. What—I'm going to tell Frank I ride buses?) We dicker politely over small details.

"Very well, Mr. Johnson. We'll look forward to meeting you Thursday at ten A.M."

No hint about why Bechtol wants to meet me. They just

want "to talk." Obviously they must be interested in *HistoryWorld*™. Hmmm.

In my head I complete a micromanagement review of the phone call. The takeaway? I think phoning from California made a good, businesslike impression. Also, because my letter from Bechtol was forwarded to me so late, by default I won the upper hand in the detached coolness department.

I look out the window at the Heroin Family and their never-ending sidewalk sale. "Do you know, Lawrence," I say, hanging up the receiver, "I've been in L.A., what, five weeks now? And in that five weeks, not *one* of my dreams have been set in L.A. Do your dreams happen in L.A.? Where do *you* dream at night?"

"I don't dream."

"Depressing, Lawrence. *Every*body dreams."

"Not true!" Lawrence is sorting and color coding his museum of Polo shirts. "I think most people dream in the houses they grew up in. Even if people move to New York or the ocean bottom or some place cool, their dreams are always located wherever they grew up. The house you lived in when you were young is, like, your hard drive for life."

"So why don't you have dreams?"

"Army brat. We moved too often when I was young. I don't know where my house is."

Next day.

Before I split L.A. this afternoon I need to make souvenirs for the gang at home. I have moseyed off to Vine Avenue, location of more celebrity stars and a relatively freak-free environment. Behind me stands the pancake-stack Capitol Records building, round and totally 1960s the-future-is-now architecture. At my feet lies the star of John Lennon. From my fanny pack I remove a selection of crayon color nubs remaining from yesterday's magic commerce: plum, wild strawberry, tangerine, lemon, forest, and sky. I then rub away, sweeping broad rainbow strokes across the paper rectangle, tracing Lennon's star below.

My arms are tired; I'm low energy. I couldn't sleep last night, what with all the news and transition in my life. Funny—there is nobody in this city with whom to share my entrepreneurial success. There is nobody I know here in Los Angeles with whom I have more than a few hallucinatory unhappy weeks of memory, and even those few people with whom I have fragments of memory were out last night—Lawrence on a look-see for an Esprit catalog, and Mr. Moore at his AA meeting. So I talked to my radio.

I rub. I hear a 911 siren fire up below me, down in the churlish dioxide lagoon of Hollywood Boulevard, down in the tinsely gridlock. There amid the stalled cars, I see what appears to be Stephanie—maybe it is or isn't—a Stephanie clone or replicant—in a red Ferrari—or maybe it's some other green-card scrambler.

Well.

Stephanie did what she had to do. Sure, she says ambition sucks, but then just *who* was the person being ambitious? How long ago did *she* begin planning her voyage to where she is now? How does *her* mind work? I just don't know. At best, her thoughts to me are like a film projected onto a black wall—the images are clear, but there is never true whiteness. Did she have a Ferrari ride down the boulevard in mind when she took me home that first night in Paris, the night she almost traded me in for a carton of Marlboros? How can I ever know? I must admire her long-term planning, though. Maybe there is a valuable management principle there itching to be learned. Convert lemons to lemonade, boy.

I breathe and stop, placing a finished rainbow tracing

onto a small pile. A man asks if he can buy one of my rubbings, so I say sure—it'll pay for cab fare back to the microapartment so I can pick up my luggage.

Pocketing the man's cash, I absentmindedly lower my hand onto Lennon's star, heated all morning, its brass like a stove element from having baked in the sun. I sear my palm and the flare of pain is like a spike.

I lift this hand to the sky, idiotically waving it in the wind. Strangers in passing cars wave back. I then race my scorched palm up to my tongue, close my eyes, lick my wound and kneel under the noon sun. In my ears I hear a noise, and this noise is the sound of the color of the sun.

61

Next day.

Pepper has been added to the footsteps of Bechtol's employees this morning. The skies over Seattle have been ripped and torn since 9:00 A.M. by the invisible fists of practicing military, jets which build an invisible ceiling of tribal safety over the city as they shriek back and forth between here and Tacoma. Bechtol employees have been entering the carbon-black revolving doors of the Bechtol Tower only to dash back out again onto the piazza where I have been sitting and watching for almost an hour, too late to witness the jets, which are faster than sound.

As ten o'clock approaches, I enter the elevator up to the 73rd floor where I surreptitiously preen in the tasteful brown-toned mirrors. But I guess I'm too obvious because a woman exiting on the 54th floor says, "Wait," smiles, and tucks in my rep tie properly under the back collar. "Good luck!" she says, then waves. I love strangers.

Doors open. Bechtol's offices are full of suntans and laser

printers and razzle-dazzle—and the employees look fabulous—killer eggheads who no doubt had chocolate cake and martinis for breakfast. I notice the dead brown bits on the leaves of the plants in the lobby have been carefully trimmed away—always a telltale sign of a thriving firm.

When I tell the receptionist I'm here for my appointment, I'm told Mr. Donald Kepke will be out in one moment. Would I please be seated? Expecting to dig in for the long haul, I stare blankly at the morning newspaper, but I absorb nothing, I'm so excited about meeting Frank E. Miller.

Mr. Kepke arrives at 10:00 sharp, a precisely and powerfully dressed man in a navy blue suit. "Didn't keep you waiting long, I hope?" He says.

"No. Not at all."

"Donald Kepke."

"Tyler Johnson."

I look at Mr. Kepke's shoes and I've never seen shoes tied the way his are. Oh God, rich people probably have a way to tie their shoes I'll never know about.

We shake hands. He is, no doubt sizing me up. Wave of panic—maybe I should have done crispy hair today—but my own hair dryer died and the hotel didn't have one. "Come on back, Mr. Johnson," he says. "Let's meet Frank."

This is rapid.

We stroll through a maze of office: low-eyestrain gray-and-emerald paint and carpet; plush sound baffles; glass walls surrounding miniconference rooms; a digital chart monitoring Bechtol's New York Stock Exchange performance; unplugged computers dreaming of pie charts; ample aisle space for smooth traffic flow; multiple keypad and voiceprint identification barriers. The office is all too much for me. I feel like I'm eating one of those medieval dinners—"Pig-in-a-Sheep"—in which the chef places a pigeon inside a chicken inside a goat inside a pig inside a sheep inside a cow, all turning on a spit.

We round a corner, then *voilà!* (swoon), there's Frank E. Miller sitting behind a dark wood desk, just like the photo on the flap of his book. He's talking about polar-bear rugs, of all subjects, into his headset phone. He motions for us to sit and gestures toward a coffee pot. To his right is a brass telescope. To his left is a map of the world. Behind him is the dormant volcano of Mount Rainier.

Mr. Kepke pours me a coffee. Frank bellows a "goodbye" into his headset (a headset not unlike the french-fry computer headset I wore at WingWorld), then beams over at the two of us. He appears to be in a fine mood. "Johnson," he says, motioning me his way, "how do you feel about the future?"

What an opener.

"Well, sir," I stutter, "I think in order to be happy—in order to deal with the future in a correct and positive manner—one shouldn't go around thinking life isn't as good as it used to be. Life must be *better* now than it ever was before, and life is only going to become better and better in the future."

"Exactly. Exactly. Fellow of mine moaning on the phone because the Eskimos aren't curing their bear rugs with urine any more. Some new way. Never liked the pee cure, myself. Bravo for the Eskimos."

Frank stands up and we shake hands. "You're the one who wrote the landfill letter. Great stuff. Great stuff."

"Thank you, sir."

Mr. Kepke adds, "Your letter has become an in-house classic here at Bechtol. I hope you don't mind, but the letter has been copied and faxed a few times. You are a local celebrity on the 73rd floor."

"I think you should work here for us, Johnson," Frank E. Miller butts in. "Can't offer you a big stint, but you'll advance quick enough. We need idea people. We need people with dreams. Can't have new products without ideas, and you can't have ideas without dreams. Donald will fix you up. Donald, find Tyler a job here. Wait—I *did* ask you how you felt about a job at Bechtol?"

"I would like to work for Bechtol very much, Mr. Miller."

"Frank. Frank."

"*Frank.*"

"If you'll come with me, Mr. Johnson, we can arrange a position for you now."

"This is quick, Johnson," says Frank. "But do a good job and we'll meet again soon."

"Yes sir."

"Frank."

"Yes, *Frank.*"

"Do me proud, Johnson—proud."

We shake hands once more, then Frank reactivates his headset and Donald Kepke steers me away, dazzled, while I mentally replay my nanochat with Frank inside my head. I am steered over to Mr. Kepke's side of the building. I am steered over into his office overlooking the ocean.

An hour later I am in the bus headed back to Lancaster. Stephanie was right about one thing: *life is soon.* Two weeks from now I will move to Seattle to join the hospitality-quality-control division of Bechtol's Pacific Northwest Region. I'll have a company car, medical/dental, training seminars, and productivity bonuses. If I can be tops in my region I'll be eligible for a trip to Cabo San Lucas, Mexico. If only.

The bus changes gears. We top the Cascades and begin our long slow descent into the fertile dry plains of central

Washington, through vineyards and roaming cattle and big skies and memory.

Somewhere past Yakima the old woman sitting across the aisle from me falls asleep and her dentures fall into her lap then onto the floor. I pick them up and put them in her hands, pulling her fingers across them so that they won't slip out again. I then return to my seat and something happens to me—something inside me is exhausted and worn out and stops spinning and I break down and cry.

I cry because the future has once again found its sparkle and has grown a million times larger. And I cry because I am ashamed of how badly I have treated the people I love—of how badly I behaved during my own personal Dark Ages—back before I had a future and someone who cared for me from above. It is like today the sky opened up and only now am I allowed to enter.

62

Tell me."

"Tell you what?"

"Tell me the first thing you ever noticed about me. Why were you attracted to *me* of all other girls. I want to know. What was the initial attraction, Tyler?"

"Honestly?"

"Honestly. You're not even on probation, yet. So give honesty now or never."

This phone call is my first effort in my campaign to have Anna-Louise change her mind about me and allow me back into her life. We've agreed to *maybe* meet for lunch—a big start. I don't even know what the new superthin Anna-Louise looks like now. I'm having trouble envisioning her in her apartment. Daisy tells me she wears her hair in an Alice band. "A child of poetry and bones, dear brother of mine."

As I speak I am on Daisy's cordless phone. I'm in my *old*

room now—it's no longer just simply my "room." I'm sitting on top of my minifridge, which Jasmine, Daisy, and Mark stocked like a hotel minibar for my return—just the way I like it: mixed beers and sodas, Toblerone chocolate prisms, tinned cashews, macadamia nuts, scotch, and beef jerky. Nothing depressing and real-life like vegetables. "We bought name brands!" Mark proudly announced as I opened the door in a wash of fondness. "All of them safe and heavily advertised."

"Tell me, Tyler," says Anna-Louise on the other end of the line.

Back to the phone call. Back to her request to tell her why I chose her over others. "Fair enough," I say. "I have made a vow with myself to tell the truth as best I can to the people who matter to me. Did you ever collect stamps?"

"Huh? No. What do stamps have to do with anything?"

"Everything. This is important, Anna-Louise. This is the truth."

"I'm listening."

"Okay then, *stamps*. There are maybe a hundred of these tiny countries around the planet which earn, like eighty-seven percent of their gross national product selling postage stamps to preteens of the industrialized nations. No gimmick is too extreme in order to snare the teen market—stamps with holographic cartoon characters on laserized gold foils which sing when rubbed. Stamps with one-eight-hundred numbers. Any gimmick at all.

"So I, of course, collected stamps and neatly mounted them in my album, building equity while learning geography and fun facts like which countries export feldspar and barley. But part of the fun of collecting stamps was traveling places in my head. I considered my collection an inventory of all the places I'd like to visit but would probably never have the chance to—places too far away, too expensive—whatever—places I'd only ever visit with my stamp album.

"There was this one country, some unfortunate Arab emirate with no oil, which put out a series of stamps with perfume. I bought them from the H.E. Harris Stamp company of Boston for sixty-nine cents. And the perfume from these stamps promptly permeated my entire album, giving it a previously missing olfactory element—a smell all its own, like the way a salmon's river has its own unique smell; the way your own house has its own smell.

"And so the *point* of this story is that when I first met you at the photocopy machine, sure, we talked like a telethon and everything, but the perfume you were wearing then—that perfume was the smell of my stamp album, the smell of countries I always wanted to visit but never thought I'd be able to. It was like you had the world inside you."

Silence on her end. "Anna-Louise?"

"I'm here." She breathes. "What did you dream about last night?"

"That's easy. I dreamed it rained for weeks and weeks and there was a flood and a lake formed on your front lawn. And one morning a swan landed in your lake."

"Swans are prayers, Tyler."

"Are they?"

"Yes. And tell me—what are you worrying about these days?" She is sounding like a child asking for drinks of water because she wants to delay going to bed.

I think. "I worry my body is aging too quickly. My eyebrow hairs are becoming thick and wiry, like the hairs that are growing out of my nose now. Why aren't we warned about decay like this in school?"

"Are you still wearing your creepy cologne?"

"No. I'm trying a new one. I want to smell modern, like a copy of *Vanity Fair*. And my hair is loose, uncombed—kind of just happening all by itself. A first for me. I'm trying to change."

"Change how?"

I breathe in. "Make myself vulnerable. Admit I need someone else."

"Are you trying to manipulate me, Tyler?"

"Anna-Louise, I can't undo what I did. I made a mistake. Allow me to admit it. Cut some slack."

"You're going to have to give me time, Tyler. You were rotten to me. I don't know my opinion about you, Tyler. I only know how I feel. So I'm torn." Anna-Louise adopts her about-to-hang-up voice, "Okay, you're on probation. That's all. I don't know about lunch yet. Let me think."

"I leave for Seattle in twelve days. Just after Christmas."

"Don't pressure me, Tyler."

"We'll talk again?"

"You're on probation."

63

Mark and I are in the living room using toenail clippers to snip fabric pills from the black Orlon covers on Jasmine's bubble-shaped 1970s quadriphonic stereo speakers. Jasmine floats in occasionally from the kitchen to beam at us, silently pleased to have me back at home, not having alluded to my departure at all since she picked me up at the Greyhound station three days ago, choosing instead to enjoy my two weeks at home unblemished by the taint of recent history, enjoying my two weeks over Christmas before I move to Seattle and join the Bechtol team.

As Mark and I complete our task, he fills me in on a comic strip he is drawing for his school English class. "It's called *The Fleshlings*. It goes like this: all the animals in the world are upset. They're going undercover because they are trying to retrieve a secret treasure stolen from them long ago by the humans. They dress themselves inside human-being costumes and they call themselves the Fleshlings."

Mark shows me his drawings while I continue to snip away the pills. The Fleshlings he has drawn wear ridiculously bad costumes: little tails and wings sprout from beneath badly tailored suits; beaks poke out from sagging latex rubber nostrils; triangular ears point out from askew wigs on the heads; bathing beauties in bikinis have furry paws.

"But what happens is the animals, the Fleshlings, while looking for their treasure, can't help but fall into the human life. They just can't help themselves. The foxes start working in Wall Street. The dogs start hanging out in bars drinking cocktails and watching ESPN. Calm giraffes become airline pilots. The sheep do *any*thing.

"The human beings, meanwhile, start having to spend all of their time preventing the chaos resulting from all of these extra Fleshlings living in their midst. This means hiring more police, creating meal kitchens, training social workers and continually inventing exciting, action-packed TV-show pilots."

"So what happens next?"

"The humans learn about the Fleshlings in their midst and decide *they* now have to go undercover in order to learn more about what the animals are plotting. So the humans start disguising themselves inside animal costumes."

"And?" Snip snip.

"History repeats itself. Once inside the costumes, the humans, instead of becoming like animals, become even more human-like. They begin organizing the other animals into teams and political parties. They start building fences around bits of land and plant seeds and give all the animals names and organize twelve-step programs to help pull the little creatures out of their depths."

"How does it end?"

"In the end both the humans and the animals forget what they were looking for in the first place—why they're even in these costumes to begin with. But they continue wearing the costumes, regardless. At the very end only a small secret society of both humans and animals remember the search for the treasure which was stolen long ago."

"Great sequel potential, Mark."

"Thanks."

As we finish clipping the pills from the 1970s speakers, we brush them with my magic grooming brush and place them in the living room's corners, straddling Grandpa's KittyWhip® conference paraphernalia. I dust the speaker legs' surfaces with a damp towel and they look almost new.

"They look great now, don't they, Mark?"

"Yeah," he says, "but they'll still sound the same. TV is best."

Anna-Louise cancelled lunch today. A bad sign. Here I am, leaving for Seattle now in only one week and I have yet to even *see* the woman. Phone calls only obtain her answering machine. And as I box and wrap the contents of my bedroom, I wonder, is Anna-Louise monitoring her phone calls and deliberately not answering when she hears my voice? I can't even begin to guess. I'm hedging my bets, though. Yesterday afternoon when I knew she was at the community college I left a sack of Halloween candy on her doorstep. I also snuck around back where I had planted the crocus bulbs slated to spell LOVE ME come spring and I scrambled the word "ME" so now the bulbs will only spell out "LOVE." I think the "ME" part might be perceived as too egotistical. Can't be too careful.

Boxes, boxes, boxes. Packing isn't physically tiring but it *is* emotionally exhausting. It's getting to be late at night and my brain is worn out from having to make so many choices bang bang bang one after the other. And my skin is a mess from eating too much minibar food—most of it has to be eaten before my move. As for the Globe Farm, I know I'm keeping it. It is now in a packing box awaiting rebirth in my new home, tentatively slated to be an upper-floor suite in a Seattle house belonging to Harmony's aunt. It is a wooden granny-style house on a quiet street and outside my windows there will be rain and leaves and birds and I will drink coffee and breathe gentle air and watch clouds. A new life.

As well as packing, these past few days I've also been scanning want ads in the Seattle *Post Intelligencer*, looking for cars, planning *Comfortmobile II: The Eliminator*—CD player, car phone, minifridge, and deluxe coffee-cup trays. On the strength of my Bechtol position I'll easily be able to secure a car loan. Employment is great.

"Tyler—telephone." Jasmine hollers from downstairs.

"I'll take it in Daisy's room." Grandma and Grandpa have appropriated my own cordless phone for themselves. I'll have to liberate it from the bowels of Betty when they return tomorrow from their KittyWhip® franchising mission over to the towns of Pasco and Benton.

"Hello?"

"Tyler Johnson? Ray here—from the Cowboy Bar."

Ray? Cowboy Bar? "Yes?"

"Yeah. We used to work together at the Chevron station. Remember?"

"Right. Ray! Back in high school. Oh hi. How are you?" (How bizarre for Ray to phone.) "What's up?"

"Life's a bowl of chain saws if you ask me, Ty. But I think a girl of yours left a piece of jewelry here at the bar. At least that's what Ronnie says. You know Ronnie—Dan's friend."

"I know Ronnie."

"You might want to pick it up before Lillian grabs it with her beak and stuffs it into her nest. She's sort of a klepto. Anyway, it's a pin or something. It's in the cash register under the bills."

"Sure. Thanks, Ray." Pause. "I'll be out in half an hour or so."

"No probs, my man. Take her easy."

Stephanie's lost brooch. I might as well be a good Samaritan and pick it up.

"Off to the Cowboy Bar," I tell Jasmine who's down in the kitchen.

"You? The Cowboy Bar?"

"They found Stephanie's brooch."

"Oh, her."

"Yes, her. Might as well. I need a break from packing. You staying up?"

"No. I'm off to bed. The women's group is having a breakfast tomorrow. Mark's spending the night with Weirdo and Dougie. Daisy's away for the weekend with Murray. So it's only the two of us here."

"If you want, you can watch the *Creature Feature* with me on cable."

"I'll pass. I'm zonked as it is. You want the car?"

I give her a peck on the cheek and take the keys from the hook. "Good luck tomorrow."

"Have fun at the Cowboy Bar."

"Right."

64

When I arrive at the bar, Ronnie, Dan's "associate friend" from the real-estate era, claims not to remember my face at first. Then he meanders into recognition, forging the Dan connection: "I know you. You ate a hamburger in Dan's new Jaguar and he never forgave you because it never smelled like a new car ever again."

"That was me."

"Dan's quite a guy."

"He sure is."

Lillian, the manager with the key to the till containing Stephanie's brooch, is on a break, and I'm stuck waiting for her to finish.

"Hit me."

Ronnie implores me to wallop his heart of Kevlar—a vest made of bullet-proofing material. We're standing at the counter of the Cowboy Bar, out on Route 666, out past the house farms of Onion Canyon. Above us on the big-screen play uncensored bootleg tapes from the last war: charred black bodies extrude like vile pastry dough from torn-up Chevrolets; scraps of laundry hang from lines tethered to crashed fighter jets plastered with political slogans; decapitated spray-painted corpses hang from the bedroom walls of looted Hiltons.

I whop Ronnie's scrawny little chest on the heart, not hard because I know his body is bullet-proof. Nonetheless, his baseball cap falls off.

"Gotcha. Didn't feel a thing. Check out these materials." From an aluminum briefcase Ronnie shows me samples of the wonder materials used by the manufacturer of the protective gear he now represents. "It's all inside: Nomex, PLZT, Tyrolite, thermoplastics, polycarbonate resins . . ." Like gems, he offers me squares of materials that have never existed in our universe until recently—man's uniqueness made concrete.

I handle Ronnie's safety materials with extra reverence, as though I'm holding celebrity babies. The walls of the Cowboy Bar which surround me now seem ethereal and pointless in comparison to these materials here. The bar's walls seem like blocks of Styrofoam stapled together and coated with Outsulation, waiting for the first rain or wind to raze them—unable to protect me from the forces of badness like these materials in my hands.

"Word is," Ronnie says, "the Plants will be ordering big what with the new toxic cleanup legislation being passed. In the truck I have a whole line of anti-isotope gear. Want to see it?"

"Think I'll pass, Ronnie." My feet crunch on something small. I reach down and pick the irritant from the rubber of my basketball shoes—a punched-out tooth—which I then flick in disgust over into the corner, into the dust bunnies and all other swept-away lost teeth. I swig from my bottle of DesignatedDriver™ beer.

* * *

Strange how when I was in Europe I missed the Cowboy Bar atmosphere—its New World cow-rolling-on-a-spit sizzle—bars the size of malls; malls the size of kingdoms —the full-volume feeding-trough sexuality of the Cowboy Bar, and the country-and-western brutality that sometimes feels like freedom, sometimes feels like hell.

"You should come and visit me and Renée some time," Ronnie offers. "We're out on Onion Slopes. Not far from Dan's. Hot development. It's just not selling right now."

"Sure, Ronnie. Thanks." I've only been to Ronnie's place once, years ago, dropping off blueprints for Dan. Renée, Ronnie's wife, answered the door rubbing lanolin salve into raw spots on her shins and elbows. "Carpet burns," she said in response to my stare. While I waited for Dan to fetch some other documents, Renée sat opposite me on a couch and toyed with a blister on the corner of her mouth. To avoid staring at her again I instead absentmindedly toyed with yellow spots on the brown couch fabric. "Those are amyl-nitrate stains," I was then informed.

Ronnie is eating the latest bar-food craze: boiled fertilized hen's eggs. "They're great," he recommends. "They taste like eggs and chicken together."

"A taste sensation, no doubt."

On the big screen above, a minicam zooms in on a gelignite-bombed office once inhabited by rebels—lamb bones and table scraps are stuffed into sooty shot-out VDT screens; a bank of Cray supercomputers has been used for target practice.

"Dan was here earlier on," Ronnie tells me.

"Was he?" I reply, counting my blessings I missed him.

"Looks like he may have a job."

"Yeah?"

"Might be a free-lance frequent-flyer mileage-points broker. Like, if you have 210,000 miles on Delta, you can barter them for a trip to Thailand. Or wherever."

"Is that legal?"

"Does it matter?"

Ronnie eats another egg. "Dan wasn't making much sense, though. Shitfaced drunk. Wasn't saying many nice things about your mother, either." Ronnie's face becomes vaguely challenging. Like many drunk people, he knows he has revealed a small secret that can only lead to the telling of another bigger secret, and the relief at not having to conceal is so great, it becomes facially visible. I keep my cool. "Yeah. He said the sheriff was around today. With an injunction to keep him away from the house."

"Oh?"

"Didn't like that too much. Didn't like that much at all." Ronnie is enjoying watching my reaction. Myself, I enter the one-dimensional mode. "Says your mother's been a bit uppity recently. Trying to erase him. Said she's cut her hair short—like she's getting her kicks somewhere else these days."

"Oh?"

"Said she might be needing a lesson."

"Lesson?"

"Like she might be needing a souvenir. Like I say, he was drunk."

"Souvenir?"

"You ask him. Like I said, you just missed him. Left an hour ago. Might have even been headed over to see your mom then. Maybe not. He thought about it. But then" (snide tone), "he's got that injunction now, *doesn't he? He'd never want to violate the injunction.* Might get his hand slapped."

I run to the parking lot.

65

At the back of my mouth is the taste of iron and I can barely connect thoughts together while driving home. My breathing is loud and regular, as pronounced and easy to hear as when I am snorkeling underwater.

Lancaster is empty and cold. Our house, when I sweep into the driveway, has many lights burning, but the lights seem unable to generate warmth. Dan's car sits in the driveway.

I efficiently exit my vehicle and close the door behind me with a surprising sense of calm. Leaves covered in frost are mulched into the grass and crunch like broken glass under my shoes as I walk to the front door. I open the door.

Inside there is no TV on. The cats have vanished, and all the kitchen lights are burning. I hear the hum of the fridge while walking down the hall. I then head up the stairs when I hear a thump. The beads on Jasmine's bedroom door chatter; I pass through these beads and there is Dan. He is holding Jasmine's arm behind her back and is trying to cut her hair with a pair of black scissors.

"Just one lock," he says, not seeing me. "For my hope chest, okay, baby?" Jasmine is silent and struggling, her hair matted and sticking to her face. There is no indecision here. These muscles which I have been pointlessly working out at the gym for years have finally found their use. This use is to kill Dan.

"You . . ." I blurt, running to the bed, "get . . . away . . . from . . . my . . . *mother*." With a crack I grab his hair and yank his head backward, simultaneously gouging him in the spine with my knee, aiming to paralyze.

"Tyler—" Jasmine shrieks while pulling herself out from under Dan, who, still holding the scissors, tries to turn around. I grab his right hand and smash it into a water glass next to the bed, making blood spray like a lawn sprinkler, yet he still holds the scissors. Momentum then favors Dan's position and he rolls me over onto the floor on my back, knocking over a box of jewelry and cosmetics. Dan holds the scissors into the air, then plants them once, twice, into the side of my chest, into my lateral muscles.

"Dan what are you doing—don't," screams Jasmine, hunched over in her nightgown, her face purple and wrinkled, flaring and wet like a newborn baby's. Jasmine grabs the chair from her makeup table and tries to bash Dan but he deflects the chair away, causing him to lose his balance. I spin him onto the floor and the scissors clatter and splay across the room as they fall from his hands, like the scissors Anna-Louise and I left behind in that lungectomized British Columbia valley.

"Who do you think you *are?*" I sob, Dan pinned down, my fists rhythmically clobbering his rapidly pulping face like a cooper's hammer, his body twitching, his teeth gnashing and floating in a foam of red. "What gives you the right to *do . . . what . . . you . . . have . . . done?*"

After a certain point Dan stops fighting back, but I can no longer stop myself and I continue, wanting only to destroy him.

"Tyler," my mother says. "Stop." But I can't stop. I am now locked into this activity of breaking Dan's body. I am no longer fueled by clarity. I am fueled by eruptions of memory. Memory of the toxic locomotive engine buried out by the Plants that cannot simply remain buried but must be chopped to bits and cast into the center of the earth. And I am fueled by the awareness of all the badness in this world—badness I have tolerated because I had never chosen to see it for what it was. And I am fueled by my embarassment at my profoundly mistaken belief that simply living in freedom in itself guarantees the continuation of that freedom.

Dan's body emits a glurp of a sigh. My pounding slows. "Tyler, honey—you'd better stop," says Jasmine cautiously.

"Mom—" I cry, "I was so nice to him for so long and it never paid off."

"I know, honey, I know."

My arms slow to a stop. I feel feverish—hallucinogenic. "Mom, there are these flowers in the desert—" but I can't continue. Tomorrow, in another world, I will tell my mother about these flowers that grow in the Nevada desert, tricked into blooming by the false sun of nighttime nuclear explosions, in good faith reaching out for light, instead only pollinating the sterile sands, forfeiting the future of all flowers to follow.

"I know, honey, I know." Jasmine comes around from behind and holds me in her arms as I sit astride the now-silent Dan. She rests her head on my shoulder.

"You said you needed my help, Mom. I was supposed to be your arms and your eyes and your legs."

"I know I said that, honey, I know."

"I'm your immune system, Mom."

"I know, honey, I know."

66

There have been many changes as of late. For starters, Daisy and Murray were married this morning, out in a small town on the Pacific Ocean. Surprise! For wedding gifts they gave each other tattoos, flowers for their hair, and "cool worthless gifts." For their honeymoon they are going to chain themselves to trees on the Olympic Peninsula with a group of antilogging youths.

"Oh, Tyler," Daisy mooned to me on the phone this afternoon, "doesn't it sound dreamy? I really *am* the luckiest chick on earth."

Needless to say, we all wish the loving couple much luck and send them love and kisses. If I were a king I would shower them with real estate.

When the newlyweds return, they will *both* be working for YEAR-3000, a toxic-waste cleanup company commissioned by the government to detoxify the earth surrounding the Plants.

"You'd approve totally, Tyler," said Murray, "we receive medical/dental, we don't have to trim our dreads, *plus* we get free semidisposable white jumpsuits made out of this antirip material called Tyvek."

"It's so glamorous," chimed in Daisy, "we feel like Federal Express parcels."

Other hot news: Heather-Jo Lockheed and Bert Rockney are to be married. Yes, it's true. Next month. Already an entire skyscraper full of lawyers in Los Angeles is busy arranging the film and video rights to the ceremony, which should, no doubt, garner millions of acre-years' worth of TV viewership around the globe. A banking holiday could well be declared in some states; the *Star Enquirer* forecasts a spontaneous eclipse of the sun.

Other news: on a sad note, Eddie Woodman died two days ago of pneumonia at Benton County General. Says Grandpa, "A real shame. As fine a KittyWhip rep as there ever was." Joann and Debbie have yet to schedule the scattering of his ashes into the Columbia River as was his request, and I hope I will be in town when this occurs.

Speaking of Grandpa and Grandma, they managed to buy back their old house in the Onion Canyon—just in the nick of time, as the Feds swooped in and put an end to the KittyWhip® Corporation.

"But we're liquid!" Grandma chimed to my mother over *my* stolen cordless phone while dancing circles through her new/old house, its furniture now vanished, replaced with numberless boxes of tinned cat food. Old people will always win. The system is absolutely rigged in their favor.

Oh, yes—Skye and Harmony are living together. Theirs may not exactly be frolicking love like that found in soft-drink commercials, but, as Skye says, "At least there's nothing scary about Harmony and hopefully he doesn't see anything scary in me. We go way back, to pre-school.

We *know* each other. People I don't know just make me want to say *yikes!* I'll take history over mystery any day of the week.''

Strange to think of Skye becoming so old and lazy about meeting new people at her young age. People *will* surprise you.

Says Harmony: "The fair damsel knoweth many ways to microwave fair pizza.''

I wish I could say Anna-Louise and I chose, like Harmony and Skye, history over mystery—but then, maybe I *don't* wish this.

After the fight with Dan, word flew around Lancaster soon enough about my having been stabbed and about Dan's being placed on life support—the police cruisers; the dropped charges; the bandages—all of it. Whatever concerns Anna-Louise may have had about our nonfuture together were outweighed by her concern for me as a wounded physical organism. Hence her phone call to me earlier tonight—and hence my trip over here to her apartment hours later, after attending a wedding-celebration dinner at the River Garden earlier on, depositing Mark and Jasmine home on the way over in Jasmine's car (seat belt off—aggravates the stitches).

"You look wonderful,'' I told Anna-Louise when she opened her door, a spare, stripped-down, fuel-injected version of Anna-Louise, reduced and more efficient, like a new generation of microchips. Not a speck of fat, all swathed in Lycra.

"Thanks.'' (Platonic peck on the cheek.) "I didn't eat the Halloween candy you brought, by the way. But it was a nice thought.''

"Halloween candy smells nice, though, doesn't it.''

"It does. I wish it were a perfume.''

Just then the walls of her apartment creaked. "The walls have been doing stretchies all day. Adjusting themselves to winter, I imagine. Come on in, Tyler. Have some tea. Are you hungry?"

"We ate at the River Garden."

"So I'll make you a sandwich."

Shortly we sat down together and drank tea in the living room, now a changed place from the old days, full of exercise toys and progress charts. Outside, the sky was already black and the panes themselves were frosting up. We both felt glad to be inside, not out where the cold and a full moon were egging less fortunate souls on to madness and death. Above us creaked the floor between us and The Man with 100 Pets and—excuse me, *Albert Lancaster*—the floor between ourselves and Albert Lancaster. A small fire burned in Anna-Louise's fireplace. I was trying to connect in my mind this new, sleek, unpuppyish Anna-Louise with the version I'd known before.

And over the next few hours Anna-Louise and I had much to talk about, too—the fight, Daisy and Murray's wedding, Eddie, Grandma and Grandpa, Kittykat and Norman (still not bonded), as well as all of our friends. Plus I showed her the blue nylon trellis of stitches on "my godlike lats," wincing at the ticklish pain of adhesive-tape removal when she pulled back the gauze for a close look.

And it was all nice. But there was much left unspoken.

We didn't discuss Los Angeles. We didn't discuss the forest we once planned to build if we won the lottery. And we didn't talk like a telethon once the whole evening. And when it came time to go, I was sent away with a cheery good-bye, a "get-better-soon," and another peck on the cheek to bookend the evening's experience.

Once out on the sidewalk I had the distinct feeling that a point was being passed, a point after which, I might never again have the opportunity to say certain things to Anna-Louise with a certain level of intensity ever again. There was a sense of loss in this, but there was also relief—relief that something messy had been avoided, and, I am ashamed to say, the relief outweighed the sense of loss, and, you know—I think it was the same for Anna-Louise, too. So I guess I broke something valuable. Or traded it away.

Of course, when Jasmine's car didn't start it was very late out. After Anna-Louise let me back into the apartment, we quickly discovered that Lancaster's tow trucks were going to be occupied for the next three hours with Christmas-season woes. Ditto taxis.

Anna-Louise sighed. "Spend the night here, Tyler."

I looked at her.

"On the *floor*, Tyler. On the floor." She sat down on the stool in the alcove containing the phone between the kitchen and the living room and she scritched away flakes of frost from the inside of a window far away from a radiator. "Tyler, I didn't want candy, I wanted *you*. And you hurt my feelings. I'll survive, sure. And I forgive you, okay? But let's give it a rest. You've got a friend for life in me, Tyler, and you can tell me absolutely anything you want and you'll always be in my heart. But you're still on the floor. I'll go find some pillows and blankets."

67

And so I am on the floor.

And Anna-Louise is asleep on the bed above me, her slender now-adult face scrunched into a corduroy pillow. And she looks so young and so old, dreaming as she no doubt is of calculus and dead friends and trees and flowers and of her escape one day, like the escape I once made, to the big city—a place where many a man will have no trouble finding her just as lovable as I find her now.

Yes, I am on the floor. This is the New Order. And this is fine. I can't sleep, anyway, while I listen to Anna-Louise, a heavy sleeper, dream her dreams in her mind's place— a small room stuffed, no *choking* with flowers—dreaming flower dreams with all her flowers. "What," I whisper to the elbow sticking out from the mattress above my head, "are you dreaming of, Anna-Louise?"

Lying here on the floor, sipping a cola, looking at the ceiling, I make a tally in my head, I make a sum—credits and debits—a balance of accounts. What secrets have I traded these past months for other secrets? What sweetness for corruption? Light for darkness? Lies for truths? Curiosities satisfied in return for anxieties? Overall there appears to be a net loss. I feel there has yet to be one more major revelation coming my way, because I think there's some insight I've just plain missed. Or is this sense of overlooking simply what happens as one gets older? I finish my cola.

I lay my head down and now I feel drowsy. Maybe in a few months Anna-Louise will come to Seattle to live with me and she can sleep on *my* floor and we can share a place for a while, and make new friends, and have meals in good restaurants with these new friends and then we will drift apart and lose contact over the years—forget to write Christmas cards or phone. And then our memories will decay, like the heavier transuranium elements, and we will find ourselves divorced from other people and living in big houses with interlocking pavement stones, room deodorizers, and genuine ten-karat gold faucets. And then we will get even older and our memories will fail almost completely. But no matter what happens—no matter how wide the gulf between us becomes—we will each be the last people we forget in each other's memories. Because we were each the first to be there.

I am awakened, strangely, by warm water dribbling underneath my feet. I open my eyes and there is the cool clear light of the moon illuminating the floorscape. Above my head I hear a flutter, and while I am groggy, I see shapes moving in front of me. The geometry of the room is wrong, but it takes me a second to figure out exactly how. A spaniel puppy licks my face.

What was once a ceiling has become a bridge. The floor

above Anna-Louise and me has collapsed from the weight of the carp pond's water and has fallen into the bedroom below—become a gangplank for the many animals of Mr. Lancaster's menagerie.

The room comes into focus. Budgies and canaries are sweeping into the bedroom's air. Kittens prance and chase the carp which writhe and twitch and flop on the floor by my feet. The lovely mooch of a spaniel puppy licks the cola dribbles at the bottom of the glass at my side and shudders with pleasure as I scratch its head. Animals, one by one by one, are adorning all surfaces of the room, and more of them keep flowing downward into our lives, some pulled by gravity, some by curiosity, skittering down on the slightly springy springboard of the collapsed ceiling.

Anna-Louise's stereo system is completely wrecked, drenched in water and now home to a trio of pink birds. Not that this matters. All of the technology in the room is wrecked, but it seems beside the point.

Looking up above, I focus and see Albert Lancaster, his legs dangling from over the edge of the ceiling. Further behind these legs is his shadowy self. He's sipping a beer and looking at us and the changes in our world below him. I take the glass beside me, clean from the lick of the dog, and raise it up in a toast to Albert. "*Skaal,*" I say.

"*Mphhh* . . . What did you say, Tyler?" Anna-Louise mumbles on the bed up above me.

I stand up, and a tame blue bird lands on my shoulder and tries to nibble on my earlobe. I gently shake Anna-Louise fully awake. "Anna-Louise, wake up," I say. "Wake up—*the world is alive.*"